HIS RUNAWAY LADY

Joanna Johnson

MILLS & BOON

First Published in Great Britain 2020
by Mills & Boon, an imprint of HarperCollins*Publishers*
1 London Bridge Street, London, SE1 9GF

© 2020 Joanna Johnson

ISBN: 978-0-263-27697-8

MIX
Paper from
responsible sources
FSC C007454

FSC
www.fsc.org

This book is produced from independently certified FSC™ paper
to ensure responsible forest management.
For more information visit www.harpercollins.co.uk/green.

Printed and bound in Spain
by CPI, Barcelona

Thanks—as always—to the ones who make the tea,
listen to the doubts and say the nice things.
I love you all!

Chapter One

The moment Sophia Somerlock had been told the name of the man she was to marry was the same moment she knew, without hesitation, that she had no other choice.

She would have to run.

Huddled into one corner of the swaying coach, Sophia twitched aside the dingy velvet curtain obscuring a window and looked out, attempting to distract herself from the terror that circled in her stomach. There was nothing to see other than ghostly trees, barely lit by the moonlight struggling through the dense canopy above. Savernake Forest stretched out silently on either side of the rough road to Marlborough, only the rattle of the wheels and hollow clip of hooves breaking the heavy stillness of the summer night. Another glance showed the white shape of an owl disappearing into the darkness, leaving the reflection of Sophia's pale face to peer back at her in the glass.

Mother will be beside herself with rage when she realises I've gone. I can scarcely believe I found the nerve.

How many vases would Mother smash in her fury, now deprived of the usual target for her wrath? Sophia wondered with rising fear. Bearing the brunt of that foul temper was Sophia's only purpose in life, after all, aside from one day being sold into a lucrative marriage from which everybody would profit but herself. That was the sole reason Mother hadn't abandoned Sophia to a convent after the death of Papa as she deserved. She'd been told this almost daily ever since she was six years old, but now she had fled the future mapped out for her, the ungrateful little beast, and the passion of Mother's anger made Sophia's blood run cold at the mere thought. While Papa had lived Mother had hidden the worst of her cruelty from him, never in his hearing abusing the spirited little daughter she had never wanted and resented for claiming a share of his love, but since his passing Sophia hadn't known a single day without guilt and fear and that spirit had been well and truly crushed beneath the heel of Mother's boot.

Almost alone in the carriage, Sophia reached to tuck a stray sweep of bright copper hair back out of sight beneath the bonnet taken from her unsuspecting maid. The elderly gentleman seated opposite looked to be fast asleep, but she wouldn't risk him waking to catch sight of her distinctive flaming mane. Long, thick and refusing to hold a curl—much to Mother's annoyance, as though Sophia had grown such determinedly straight hair just to spite her—it was the only feature she had inherited from her real father, the final link between them Mother had never been able to sever. Lord Thruxton might insist she call him Father now, having become Mother's husband the day before Sophia's seventeenth birthday five years before, but nobody would ever replace the kind, handsome man she had loved and who had loved her in return until the fateful day her stupidity had cut him down. She would always be a Somerlock in her heart, no matter how many times she was introduced as Miss Sophia Thruxton. Papa's name would live on inside her for ever and there was no way she would ever become a Thruxton for real, neither by marriage nor by force.

Sophia squeezed her clammy hands together so tightly it hurt, the reflexive action of many years' standing, although nothing could drag her thoughts away from the great house she had left behind. Fenwick Manor had felt like a prison for all its splendour, caging Sophia within its walls and not a friendly face among those who lived there. Mother detested her, of course, and Lord Thruxton—*never 'Father'*—remained coldly indifferent to her presence, only becoming animated when dear Septimus came to call—his beloved nephew and heir, and the most terrifying future husband Sophia ever could have dreamed of.

It was the worst-kept secret in Wiltshire society that Jayne Thruxton had been declared insane after only two years of marriage, Sophia thought with a shudder as the coach ploughed on through the night, each hoofbeat carrying her further and further from the fate she had fled. Everyone pitied Septimus and his bad luck in acquiring a lunatic for a wife—although from the whispered conversations she had overheard between her mother and stepfather Sophia knew otherwise. Jayne had seemed as rational a creature as ever lived before she was tormented half to death by the malice and brutality of her handsome, charming husband, a facet of his personality concealed from her—and society at large—until it was too late. If she had voluntarily entered an asylum it could only have been for one of two reasons: either Septimus's treatment had addled her wits, or life in an institution had seemed a better prospect than remaining in her marriage. Neither motivation was one Sophia wished to experience for herself and the bleak truth had given her the courage to hide beneath the clothes of a servant and disappear into the night, a rash action that flew in the face of every instinct for her obedience. Quiet compliance was all she knew now, the strong will she'd once possessed hammered flat by years of torment—or so she had thought, before the prospect of a life even more miserable than her current existence forced the decision that even now clamped her chest in a vice of fear.

It's hardly surprising Mother chose a man like that for me after what I did to poor Papa, a fitting punishment for my actions. She has told me often enough I was the reason she became a widow sentenced to mourn the only man she would ever love for the rest of her miserable life—as if I needed proof she only married again for the title. If she couldn't be happy, why should I?

That had been the constant refrain of Sophia's wretched childhood, she now thought grimly. Papa had died when she was just six years old and since that moment Sophia had known herself to be a monster, an unwanted creature starved of the approval and tenderness she craved so badly and yet knew she didn't deserve. Grief and guilt so strong it almost drowned her was her inheritance, encouraged daily by Mother's cruel tongue, and she'd certainly never expected to marry for love when the time came for Mother to see some return on her grudging investment in her only child. There was nothing about Sophia that might rouse fond feelings in a man, after all—how could she ever believe otherwise, told as much repeatedly from the first moment she could begin to understand?

'I'll marry one day, won't I, Mother? To a man like Papa?'

'You'll marry, but not to a man like your father. He was kind and strong and handsome— now, tell me, would a man like that, who could have his choice of wife, want somebody as worthless and troublesome as you?'

'I suppose not.'

'You suppose correctly. My life with your father was perfect before you came and ruined everything with your wickedness, always getting between us and turning his attention from me. Why would any man look upon you with favour after learning of your sins?'

The elderly passenger twitched in his sleep as the coach rounded a bend and began to slow, the driver's low command to the horses breaking into Sophia's unhappy memories. A swift peep out of the window showed a couple of men waiting for the post carriage to draw near, the torch they stood beneath obscuring their faces in shadow, and Sophia felt her chest tighten with apprehension at the sight.

With each new passenger that boarded the coach the chance of her being seen by some acquaintance of the Thruxtons grew. All it would take was one dropped hint, one accidental glance, and her mother and stepfather would know which way she had fled. The midnight carriage had seemed such a safe bet—surely everybody she knew in the county would be abed by now—but evidently she wasn't the only one with travel in mind, sneaking from Fenwick Manor with breath held for fear of discovery. If she was seen now the risk she'd taken would have been in vain, and she would be left with no choice but to face the consequences. She could do nothing but sit, helpless and afraid, as the coach drew to a standstill and the murmur of voices filtered in from outside, the light from the torch growing brighter as the door opened and the two waiting men climbed inside.

The first was a stranger and Sophia felt some of the tension leave her limbs as he dropped into a seat. He looked at her with a quick flick of appraisal, taking in her heart-shaped face and slanted green eyes with an appreciation he never would have dared had she been dressed in her usual finery. In a servant's clothes she was evidently a fair prospect, however—Sophia might have spent a moment pondering the difference an expensive gown could make had the second passenger not made her mind stutter to a sudden halt.

Her stepfather's bookkeeper settled himself in the far corner of the cabin, nodding distractedly at each of his fellow travellers as he carefully arranged his belongings beneath the seat. The elderly gentleman opposite woke for just long enough to mutter a quiet greeting but Sophia's lips were frozen with dismay and nothing could have dragged a word from her suddenly dry mouth.

It was exactly what she had feared: somebody connected to her family sat mere inches away, currently fussing with his greatcoat but soon enough likely to take a better look at his travelling companions. He might know her—hadn't the man visited Fenwick Manor on more than one occasion? It could take him a second to fit together the pieces of the puzzle, but how long until he spoke her name and every eye in the coach turned to look at the woman fleeing from a marriage brokered by people who cared not three straws for her happiness?

The horses began to move and the carriage creaked forward, the bookkeeper now smoothing down the knees of his trousers. Finally satisfied everything was as it should be he glanced about the carriage again—at last noticing Sophia's stiff form seated next to the window and looking for all the world as though she wished she could burst through it.

She screwed her eyes closed, turning her head away to conceal her flushed cheeks and the tic of fear she felt working in the muscle of her jaw. If Lord Thruxton's man were to recognise her now all would be lost. He'd never believe she had permission to be riding post at past midnight, dressed as a maid of all things, and in his good intentions would no doubt return her to the one place she wanted nothing more than to never see again.

For one golden moment she thought perhaps her luck had held. The man didn't address her and when she dared open one eye she saw his gaze fixed on the floor—but then he leaned towards her and Sophia felt her lungs empty at his polite frown.

'Begging your pardon, ma'am… I wasn't sure at first, but now I think I must be right. Might you be—?'

She felt her mouth open in a grimace of horror, hardly hearing the rest of his enquiry.

He knows me. He knows me and he'll try to take me back.

The picture of Septimus's face swam before her, handsome as ever but with cruelty etched in every line, and her throat clenched at once. To be handed back to him made her feel faint with terror. Neither Mother nor her stepfather would be in the least concerned should Septimus decide to abuse his new wife. He would be allowed to treat Sophia however he chose and the sad fate of her predecessor was enough to convince her that his choice would be unbearable.

That poor woman will spend the rest of her life in an asylum and still she believed that a better path than to remain as his wife. Whatever Septimus did to drive her to such desperation is not something I wish to uncover for myself.

The bookkeeper still watched her with growing unease and Sophia took a deep breath in. She would have to do something if she wanted to slip free of his dangerous concern for her, and she would have to do it fast.

Sophia rose to her feet so quickly the man fell back in surprise, his eyes widening as she stood above him and hammered on the roof.

'Stop the coach! I wish to get out!'

The coach jerked roughly as the driver brought the horses up short, the other passengers jolting in their seats and reaching to steady themselves in alarm. The elderly gentleman called out but Sophia paid him no mind as she wrenched the door open and half fell down the step, snagging her cloak as she went but stopping for nobody.

Her feet hit the ground harder than she'd expected and for a second she stumbled, but she righted herself and without pausing for breath waded through the scrub that edged the pitted road and bolted between the first bank of waving trees.

'Miss Thruxton! Come back!'

The words echoed in the air behind her, slicing through the quiet of the night, although Sophia didn't stop to look back over her shoulder. All she could think was that she needed to run, and keep on running, until the light of the carriage's lanterns was swallowed by darkness and the voices were replaced by the soft rustle of leaves in the midnight breeze.

In every direction the forest stood about her like a labyrinth, the straight trees guarding her flight through the gloom so dense she could hardly see her hand in front of her face. Fleeing like a deer from hunters her breathing grew ragged as she blundered amid undergrowth and sharp branches that reached down to catch at her clothes, but still she kept up her blind charge, one foot in front of the other with no thought in mind but escape.

Sophia was falling before she had the chance to realise what was happening, her dress catching and the breath forced from her body by the ground hurtling up to meet her. Rolling in a tangle of long skirts down a steep slope, she came to a violent stop against a gnarled old tree—and felt her head spin with sudden agony as pain bloomed like a flower in her left leg.

She tried to sit up, but a grating sensation scattered stars in front of her eyes and she folded back again, chest heaving in mute despair at the hopeless predicament she found herself trapped in. Another attempt at moving was met with equal failure, all strength stolen from her shaking limbs by pain, shock and the effort of running faster and further than she ever had before.

How did this happen? How did my plan go so badly awry?

She licked dry lips, fighting the growing wave of fear that rose inside her. There was no way she could get up, let alone continue her aimless journey to a destination she didn't even know.

Lying alone in the forest with no hope of walking and too dark to find my way even if I could. Perhaps this is what I deserve for disobeying Mother and trying to cheat the destiny I was intended to have. Whatever made me think I deserved anything more, after what I did?

How long she lay for Sophia couldn't tell, her head swimming with pain and nausea swirling in her stomach. The leaf canopy that stirred above was thick and no moonlight slipped through to dapple the damp ground, only darkness and the whispers of the sleeping forest surrounding her as she closed her eyes and prayed for deliverance.

Something cold and wet pressing against her hand woke Sophia from her doze, feeble daylight casting a green haze over the forest floor. For a moment, the unexpected sensation almost succeeded in distracting her from the throbbing in her leg, before awareness set in once more to make her draw in a harsh breath.

A scruffy-looking dog gazed at her sympathetically, raising his nose from her hand and his ears twitching backwards at her wince. They moved again as a voice came from somewhere behind Sophia's resting place—a man's voice, cutting through the brush to set her heart pounding with sick apprehension.

'Lash? Where are you?'

The swish of boots through long grass grew closer and Sophia attempted to push herself up from her bed of fallen leaves, desperate despite the fresh lights that flickered before her eyes as she moved. She dug her fingers into the rough bark of the tree at her back, feeling every muscle shriek from lying all night on the hard earth and her injured leg wanting to buckle beneath her as she hauled herself upright.

As soon as she was on her feet she knew she'd made a mistake. A hot gush flowed to pool in her shoe and the crackle of pain that fluttered made her cry out before she could bite it back. By the sounds of it the stranger was still approaching, the dog at her side gently waving his tail as his master drew near, and although every instinct screamed at her to run Sophia could no more hobble away than she could have flown. The unpleasant, liquid warmth still tickled on her skin and, swaying slightly, she reached down to press her shaking hand against it—just as a man appeared around her tree.

He stopped abruptly, dark eyebrows cinching together as one quick look must have taken in her bedraggled clothes and breathing fast and erratic. She in turn had just enough time to note the concern on his face—*a handsome face, at that*, she thought with a glimmer of surprise—before she saw the blood that slicked her fingers, and her eyes closed again in a dead faint that sent her crumpling back to the ground.

Fell Barden regarded the figure sprawled across his boots for a moment in silence. At his side Lash looked down at her likewise and the two exchanged a glance Fell could have sworn the dog understood.

Didn't expect to find this while looking for kindling, did we?

A young woman falling at his feet wasn't something he could recall experiencing before—and certainly not such a pretty one, he saw with faint bemusement. She lay among the leaves with her bonnet half off, exposing a great swathe of fiery hair, and the bloodless colour of her face was more than countered by the scarlet stain spreading across the cream fabric of her skirts. Who she was and how she came to be unconscious in the forest he had no idea, only that she'd looked terrified to see him in the split second before she collapsed, eyes the colour of sea-glass stretched wide in fear and pain that immediately set alarm bells ringing. By the look of her she'd been out all night, muddied and bleeding in the dewy dawn with no obvious explanation of where she came from—or where she might be going.

The dog sniffed cautiously at the red splash on the stranger's torn gown and Fell ushered him away with the toe of his boot, crouching warily to look closer. It didn't take a doctor to see the woman had hurt her leg, one ankle twisted at an angle, but it was the jagged slash to her shin that made him suck a breath in between his teeth. Although congealing slightly the wound had evidently opened up again at her attempts to move and with practised speed Fell staunched the worst of the bleeding with his own knotted kerchief.

'No wonder she didn't run. That must have hurt like the devil.'

He frowned, the already-creased plane of his forehead crinkling further. She couldn't be left where she was, that was obvious, but what should he do with her? He could hardly take her back to his modest cottage with the forge, standing some distance apart from the other houses in Woodford Common behind a screen of trees. The woman would wake soon, no doubt, and be frightened half to death at finding herself alone with him, crippled by her injury and unable to escape...

But where else is there?

There was nobody in the village likely to help him, he thought with dark certainty as he rocked back on his heels, hoping for a flash of inspiration. Every community had its black sheep, the one only fit to live on the fringes and draw sideways looks from the rest—and Woodford Common had outdone itself, boasting a half-Roma bastard from who knew what English father. The villagers might tolerate him now for his skill with iron and anvil, but for all his thirty-one years Fell had known how far beneath them he was considered—until he himself had come to accept his lack of value and that he would never truly belong.

Ma had given birth to him in the forest like an animal, the village gossips were maliciously delighted to repeat time and again, a young Romani girl nobody had seen before, alone and unmarried and barely more than a child herself. It was nothing short of a miracle the parish rector had been visiting Woodford at the time and found her, later giving Ma a position in his household as a maid. *That* had drawn much protest among the busybodies of the community, but Rector Frost stood firm: let he without sin cast the first stone, he'd ruled, showing Fell's mother the Christian charity some of his congregation preferred to preach rather than to practise. Essea Barden and her baby boy had been allowed to stay, Ma grateful beyond measure to her rescuer, but guarding the secrets of where she had come from and the name of Fell's father with a determination nothing could touch.

Fell tapped his fingers on his stubbled chin, vaguely feeling the black bristles. If only the good rector was still alive, surely *he* would have cared for this mysterious woman, but he had passed away long ago and his replacement had shown little interest in the illegitimate son of a former servant. In truth, there wasn't anyone Fell trusted enough to ask for help and, with a sigh of resignation, he carefully gathered the unconscious shape into his arms.

'Looks like we'll be having a guest at breakfast today.'

The dog stirred his wiry tail as if in agreement as Fell straightened up, the bundle of woman he carried as still and passive as a doll. She weighed next to nothing, a mere scrap of a thing wrapped in a cheap cloak and her face, scattered with an Orion's belt of freckles, relaxed as though in the depths of sleep. Whether it was fear, pain or the sight of the blood on her fingers that had rendered her insensible he didn't know, but Fell's brows twitched briefly as a gleam of concern sparked swiftly into life.

What can she have been doing, out here all alone? The night's no safe place for a woman on her own—and especially not a woman like this.

She was an undeniable beauty, he'd seen at once with a flicker of interest, even if his more rational side had no desire to notice. With a bright copper mane and delicate features the stranger was a rare sight and no mistake, and Fell found himself uncomfortably pleased by the feeling of warmth his soft burden spilled across his chest as he walked, a sensation he hadn't felt since…

Give that a rest.

He shied away from the thought, the memories it dragged along with it nothing he wanted to revisit. Shunting the ghosts of the past back into the shadows where they belonged was second nature now, years of practice honing the skill until usually he could manage it with ease—but something about the shape of a woman in his arms again threatened to unleash the flood, snatches of images long repressed rising to break through the walls.

Charity's eyes were brown, not green, and instead of copper her hair was the colour of wheat.

The memory tried to close its hands around his throat, but he flung it away, square jaw hardening in determination. One woman was quite enough to contend with without echoes of the past clamouring for his attention, too. If the stranger he carried stirred something in him he hadn't felt in years, he'd pay it no mind, and certainly not while she lay unconscious against the rough front of his shirt. When she awoke she would doubtless be frightened and dazed, and nothing in his conduct should give her cause for additional alarm—even if the fine lines of her face tempted him to glance down more than once to take another look.

Lash padded ahead of his master and Fell followed with rising apprehension. This wasn't at all how the day had been *meant* to start. He'd wanted to gather some kindling and cook breakfast before stoking the fire in the forge, melting iron for the best horseshoes for miles. The villagers of Woodford Common might not truly accept him but they couldn't argue with the quality of his work—the one part of his existence about which Fell felt any measure of pride. Everything else about him was submerged in the doubt, uncertainty and feelings of inadequacy he'd had, despite Ma's best efforts, since he was a child.

It was bittersweet when she returned to visit now. Fell could never shake a pang of something close to jealousy when she would arrive with no notice, slipping down from her horse with a cry of delight at his emergence from the forge. Ma was so sure of who she was, *what* she was and where she belonged, a certainty that always seemed to slip through Fell's fingers when he tried to grasp hold of it. Neither fully Roma nor fully English, he wavered somewhere between the two worlds, never knowing where his true place lay or what identity he should adopt. Any talk about his father was skilfully dodged, but the question left a huge hole only shame and vague resentment of his mother's impenetrable secrecy could fill, her stubborn concealment of the truth fostering tension between them even now he was grown. The taint of bastardy followed Fell wherever he went, both his illegitimacy and his Roma blood securing his place among the lowest of Woodford's residents.

Not that I'm not used to it by now. I've had long enough to see how the world works.

His mystery guest had grown heavier by the time his cottage reared up out of the trees in front of him, watching his approach with friendly windows beneath a thick brow of thatch. Another snatched glimpse at her face showed her eyes still closed, amber lashes sweeping on to pale cheeks to free another glimmer of appreciation Fell set firmly aside. It wouldn't have mattered if she'd been a frail grandmother, or a tiny child, he would still have taken her in. The fact she fitted neither of those descriptions, but was instead the kind of young woman a more foolish man might lose his head for, made not a bit of difference.

A kick with one large boot was enough to dislodge the door and Fell stooped to enter the low building without hitting his head, crossing with only the barest hesitation to place the woman across his own bed. She lay without moving, only the steady rise and fall of her chest signalling she wasn't made of wax as Fell awkwardly removed her bonnet, his eye drawn to the patch of darkening blood drying stubbornly on her skirt.

That'll need tending before anything else.

He watched her for a moment before turning away. Hot water, cloth for bandages, rags to clean the wound… There were various things he'd require and none of them immediately to hand. With a sigh of resignation he raised an eyebrow at the dog sitting at his feet, who responded with a thump of that straggly tail.

'Perhaps there won't be time for breakfast after all.'

Chapter Two

A ceiling of rough boards stretched overhead as bit by bit Sophia's senses collected themselves and she opened her aching eyes, the pain in her leg flaring to greet her return to consciousness.

Absolutely nothing in the small room she found herself in was familiar. The simple wooden furniture and plain bed she lay on were entirely alien—as was everything except for the dog that curled next to her on the thin mattress, the same one that had found her in the forest.

With a start of alarm she tried to sit up.

If the dog was here...

'You're awake. I was starting to wonder if I should be worried.'

The voice from behind made her jump, a movement she regretted as her injured leg crackled and a gasp escaped parted lips. She

tried to look over her shoulder at the figure leaning against the doorframe, her heart slamming
into the bodice of her dress as if fired from a
cannon as he stepped into the room.

'No need for that. I'll not harm you.'

She watched with eyes wide in fright as the
tall, dark-haired man she *just* recalled seeing
before she'd slid to the ground moved slowly
to sit at the foot of the bed, careful not to touch
her. His movements were measured as if he
suspected—correctly, as it happened—she
might baulk and try to run, and his attempts to
avoid startling her slightly dimmed the bright-
est spark of her fear.

'Who are you, sir? Where am I?'

Now she could see him clearly Sophia felt
herself colour beneath his direct gaze, heat
simmering in her flushed cheeks. Her fleeting
impression in the forest had been correct: the
stranger was handsome indeed, olive-skinned
and firm-jawed with a width of shoulder she'd
certainly never seen on any idle gentleman. He
wore a shirt with the sleeves turned back over
brawny forearms and a blacksmith's leather
apron across his barrel chest, the hands that
rested on his knees huge and scarred and ingrained with what looked like soot. The overwhelming impression was of a solid wall of

male, sitting near enough that she could have brushed him with her stockinged foot—but it was his eyes that made her blink with surprise that veered sharply into wonder.

The left was dark and shrewd as a raven's, obsidian in his weathered face, while the right was the colour of warm honey and moss, the hazel and green mixing together like a landscape in miniature. They were eyes to lose hours in, their uncanny colours the background for a complex mix of curiosity and—unexpectedly, Sophia thought dazedly—concern that danced in their depths. There was a beauty in their strangeness and Sophia felt her blush intensify as she realised how much she wanted to stare, the face they were set in almost as intriguing in its striking appeal.

What are you thinking? The sensible voice inside her head heaved aside girlish sentiment to regard her with a frown. *You know nothing about this man. Plenty of dangerous individuals have comely faces—as Septimus should have taught you.*

The thought of the man from whom she'd fled made Sophia's face crumple in fresh fear, Mother's glare joining it to increase the horrors racing in her mind. It was impossible to tell what time it was, although the sunlight attempting to stream through thin curtains signalled a new July morning, and the possibility her flight had been discovered turned her blood to ice. Would they have begun hunting for her yet? Had the bookkeeper already visited Fenwick Manor, full of apologies for being unable to stop Miss Thruxton from disappearing into the warm night?

The man must have seen the terror in her face and misunderstood it, for when he next spoke his voice was low and steady and, despite the rush of anxiety in every vein, Sophia felt a glint of feminine appreciation for its deep, pleasing tone.

'No sirs here—only a blacksmith. My name's Fell and this is my cottage. I found you in Savernake Forest and brought you back here, to Woodford Common. Have you been to this village before?'

Sophia shook her head distractedly, too many worries chiming in her ears to make them ring. Woodford Common? Surely she'd heard the name, or perhaps seen it written on a signpost at the side of the road through the forest. It was close to Marlborough and perhaps a distance of twenty-five miles from Fenwick Manor.

'No. I've heard of it, but never visited.'

Fell nodded and she couldn't help a swift

glance risked in his direction, again glimpsing the dark shine of his hair complemented by skin far richer than she was used to seeing. The combination was alluring, a flit of interest Sophia shied away from in alarm. Any coy appreciation for her mysterious host would do nothing to unravel an already confusing situation, one that without careful management could all too easily get out of hand.

'Do you remember anything about where you came from, or where you might have been going?' He crossed his arms over his chest and regarded her narrowly, as though trying to read something in her glowing face. 'I can't imagine you came to be in the middle of the forest without good reason.'

Sophia hesitated, the truth stalling on her tongue. He'd rescued her from her initial predicament but that didn't mean he wouldn't be tempted to deliver her back to Fenwick Manor if she told him who she was. Mother might offer a reward for the return of her wayward daughter, and with a stab of regret Sophia realised her own purse had been left in the carriage when she fled. She had no way of making a counter-offer without a penny to her name, no way of persuading Fell not to make the transition from rescuer to captor.

She saw how he watched her with those piercing eyes and felt her pulse skip beneath her skin at his scrutiny, unfamiliar and yet…

Not unpleasant.

Her experience of young men was scant, to say the least—even nuns in a convent might speak to the occasional male, more than Sophia had ever been allowed. At the few rare parties she had been permitted to attend Mother had held on to her arm with cold fingers like a vice, turning her basilisk glare on any who might have strayed too near.

She wouldn't want to risk a kind man looking my way. Not that they'd have reason to.

Only Septimus would do as Sophia's intended—his malice was exactly the repayment she deserved for her part in the tragedy of almost twenty years before, the weight of guilt around her neck something she knew couldn't be escaped.

Even so Sophia had chafed under Mother's pinching grasp, longing to be among the dancing couples and perhaps flirting her fan at some handsome partner. The desire to throw off the restraining hand was always so strong, her natural high spirits aching to be allowed free rein—but she knew what would happen if she disobeyed and the prospect was enough to douse the rebellious spark that glowed deep down inside, never permitted to see the light.

She'd lapsed into silence again without meaning to, only the slight sigh of the man waiting for her reply dragging her away from the thoughts that gnawed at her.

'Your name, then? Will you tell me that at least?'

The mismatched gaze searched her face more and more doubtfully the longer she took to speak, her confusion and discomfort growing with every second she cast about for an answer. The novel sensation of being so close to a man, unchaperoned and *on his bed* of all places would have been mortifying enough without the added complication of his being so confoundedly attractive. She would have to conjure a story to explain how she came to be lying in the forest and a new name to match—both things that required more time to think than Sophia currently had at her disposal. With her cheeks burning, she blurted out the first thing that sprang into her head.

'Marie. Marie—Crewe.'

Where that flash of genius came from Sophia wasn't sure, but after a short pause Fell gave a small nod.

'Well then, Miss Crewe, as I said, my name

is Fell and this—' he jerked his head towards the dog that lay near her with its head on its paws '—is Lash. As a pair of poor bachelors we weren't expecting company, so if it's any comfort we're as surprised by this turn of events as you are.'

Surely nobody could be *quite* as surprised as she was, Sophia thought as she willed her heartrate to slow back to an acceptable speed. Opening her eyes in a strange man's bedroom was not how she'd expected her moonlight flit to end, the most intimate encounter with a male she'd ever had—but then again, what *had* she expected? There had been no plan other than to escape Fenwick Manor and its inhabitants, her movements after that as unknown to Sophia as to anyone else. Perhaps stumbling into Fell's path might turn out to be fortunate after all. For all her misgivings she was now under a roof, at least temporarily safe from the eyes of those hunting her, and for that she ought to be grateful.

The frenetic thumping of her heart under control a little more, Sophia shifted slightly higher on the bed to lean against the headboard. Fell sat impassive, awaiting a response as she settled herself, stalling for time while she groped for a plausible story. His silent presence was a curious mixture of calming and unnerving, determined patience strangely at odds with such a huge frame. Despite what could have been an intimidatingly large build there was no shadow of the subtle menace Septimus had always radiated, the difference between the two men like night and day, and Sophia's sudden appreciation for the fact brought her thoughts to a sharp halt.

No more of that. Remember what you ought to be concentrating on. The man's a blacksmith, for goodness' sake, and you are...well, yourself.

That was the truth and there was nothing more to it, Sophia acknowledged grimly. He was far below her in status, but even if he'd been an earl there was no reason a man like Fell would so much as look at her twice. Handsome and clearly capable, if any other rank he would have been exactly the sort of man Mother had taught Sophia never to hope for. A suitor with those qualities could have his pick of women— why would he waste his time with her?

Thoughts of Mother helped focus Sophia's mind, her fear rising again to stick in her throat. She would have to make the most of the chance she had been given and, to do that, she would have to lie.

'I was in service to a family in Salisbury,

as—as a maid. I had to leave suddenly and in the confusion of travelling I found myself lost in the forest, without any of my luggage and unable to find my way in the dark.'

Fell half-raised one eyebrow but said nothing to disagree, merely inclining his dark head as she spoke. For a horrible moment Sophia was sure she saw a glimmer of scepticism in his expression, although the next it disappeared back below the surface.

'A maid?'

'That's right.'

'I see. And where was it you were headed that made you take such a detour…in the middle of the night? Somehow deprived of your luggage?'

Sophia dropped her eyes to the patchwork quilt she lay on, thinking fast as dismay seized her.

You've always been a terrible liar. Yet another thing you could never do right.

'It was—I thought, perhaps…' she stuttered, stumbling over the words. 'I didn't have a precise destination in mind. I thought I'd get to Marlborough and then decide my route from there. Cutting through Savernake Forest seemed a good way to save time, but as I said, in the dark… My case and purse were left behind when I had to get down from the coach unexpectedly and, by the time I realised, it was too late to return for them.'

She tailed off, still refusing to meet his eye as she ran out of thread to spin her pitiful cobweb of a lie. There was no way he'd believe such a pile of garbled nonsense, surely, yet when he replied Sophia felt herself wilt with relief.

'Fortunate I found you, then. You wouldn't have got much further with that leg left the way it was.'

In the whirl that had spun her since she woke Sophia had almost forgotten her pain, but now Fell mentioned it she felt a renewed shard rake her. She looked down swiftly, her insides contracting briefly at the ugly stain of dried blood on her skirts. The stiff patch was as much as she could stand—any fresher and her innards would have turned, her horror of all kinds of gore so vivid even the memory was enough to make her swoon.

'Nasty wound about this long.' Fell gestured with his fingers, although Sophia's thoughts were abruptly diverted by a new dread dawning in her stomach. The only way he would know what kind of injury she'd sustained was if…

'I've cleaned and dressed it, but it'll need time to heal. Your ankle seemed as though you'd turned it, too.'

Sophia's blush gripped her entire body, roasting her in the fire trapped beneath her own skin.

He had looked. He had actually looked!

Even her eyes felt hot as she thought how Fell must have swept her skirt to the side to treat her leg, a liberty absolutely no lady of her standing would allow. To uncover something so private, so *forbidden*, went against every lesson in decorum Sophia had ever been taught. Only a woman's husband might catch a glimpse of her calves, or even a scandalous knee if he was exceptionally lucky. Certainly no lady would so much as countenance a *blacksmith*, of all people—but of course, she wasn't a lady here. In Fell's cottage it was vital he believed she was a maid—*Marie*—and surely women of the lower classes had different standards. If she let her shame show in her face he'd suspect her even if he didn't already, her safety dependent on sustaining her feeble lie.

'Oh. Well. Thank you very much,' she answered through teeth clenched in mortification, although Fell didn't seem to notice. He was too busy softly rubbing the dog's brown ears, huge calloused fingers again surprising Sophia with their gentleness. They were the same fingers that had cleaned and dressed her wounds, strong and tanned and scattered with healed burns shining here and there, and the knowledge increased the heat in Sophia's cheeks to positively scalding. It was an unspeakably intimate thing for him to have uncovered her pale legs and washed the blood from them, all carefully enough not to rouse her. A large part of her was still appalled, embarrassed, thinking she ought to be offended, but another part, secret and more scandalous than anything else, couldn't *hate* the notion he had touched her skin. He must have carried her in from the forest before anything else, she realised belatedly—his arms were like nothing she'd seen up close before, power barely contained by the scorched sleeves that covered them, and to know she had nestled within them lit a taper Sophia hadn't known existed. It was unacceptable, and distinctly unladylike, yet there it was: an instinctive and irrepressible recognition of the attractions of a good-looking man over which she found she had no control.

The man responsible for such an unfamiliar reaction shrugged his sculpted shoulders. 'Doesn't take much skill to bind a leg. I've plenty of experience doing the same for horses and they've twice as many to contend with.'

Before Sophia could decide how she felt about being compared to a horse Fell got to his feet, towering above her with his hair almost brushing the low ceiling and for a half-second she felt a twinge of fear. He was truly one of the biggest men she had ever seen, obviously more than capable of lifting her if he chose. She couldn't escape, her injury throwing her entirely into his power—yet the flicker dimmed as she saw how carefully he stepped away from her, such unfamiliar consideration for her comfort sending her pulse skipping again like a spring lamb.

'You must be half-starved by now. I'll find you something to eat.'

Fell stirred the tea leaves slowly, his thoughts too full of the woman lying in his bedchamber to notice it had begun to stew. The remnants of yesterday's loaf and the last of his cheese were already on a tray and he wondered if it would be enough to sate his mysterious guest's appetite— but that was the least pressing of the concerns that currently circled through his mind.

If she's a maid named Marie, I'm the Prince Regent.

Far from being a worldly man, even he could tell the difference between a woman of his own class and one that was…not. From the moment she'd opened those pretty eyes of hers he'd known, the look in them that of a rabbit caught in a trap. A country girl might be bemused to wake in a stranger's home, as would anyone, but her face wouldn't flush scarlet at being alone with a man, nor freeze in horror at finding one had caught a glimpse of her apparently sacred legs.

I've never known a servant with such smooth hands or a voice you could cut glass with. She's a lady and why a lady would be roaming alone after dark is something I couldn't begin to guess.

There had to be a reason for her to go fleeing through the forest and it certainly wasn't the hopelessly transparent lie she had wanted him to swallow. To tell a falsehood was to attempt to conceal the truth, which in turn meant there had to be a truth *worth* concealing—and what a gentlewoman might feel the need to hide was far beyond Fell's remit. She was frightened, though, and the spark of concern that kindled inside him at the thought was one he tried to rationalise at once. *Anybody* alone and afraid would stir his pity—if Marie, or whatever her real name was, moved him with her fearful eyes and pale face it had nothing to do with her beauty.

Fell splashed some milk into a chipped dish and placed it on the tray before steeling himself to return to his bed. A woman daintily arranged on his pillows was the very last thing he had anticipated when he awoke that morning—both disturbing and agreeable at the same time, in spite of what his stern self-control might mutter. It wasn't something he'd thought he'd ever see again, the last time he'd enjoyed such an honour now so many years ago the memory had frayed at the edges. If things had unfolded differently Charity would have been his wife long ago, but it wasn't to be and Fell attempted to dismiss the recollection with dark brows drawn into a frown.

Good enough to shoe the villagers' horses, but not to marry their daughters. A half-Roma bastard for a son-in-law wasn't what her father wanted and neither did she, in the end.

Charity hadn't cared a fig about his illegitimacy or the fact that Roma blood ran in his veins, or so he'd been stupid enough to think. It was as though she was blind to what everybody else saw so vividly and for that alone her worth was more than the rubies he'd wished he could buy for her. She had looked down deeply into the well of his soul and seen the real man inside staring back at her, her acceptance of all that he was a shower of cooling rain dousing the flames of inadequacy that had burned him all his life. She'd barely reached his shoulder, yet the power of her love had brought him to his knees, felled by the validation he saw in her eyes and finally the confirmation that he was *enough*. It was the stability he had always craved, the antidote to the poisonous whispers that had followed him since the day he was born into shame, wailing as if he already knew what future awaited him.

Young fool that he was, Fell believed every one of her sweet words.

It was only when she disappeared from Woodford without as much as a goodbye that he realised the depth of his mistake. Her father, a farmer usually humourless and grave, had laughed himself sick when Fell knocked at their cottage door and asked earnestly for her hand, promising to love her for the rest of his days if she would only be returned—but he was too late. She'd gone north to marry a distant cousin as she'd always intended, her father was happy to divulge, only passing time with handsome, low-born Fell until her betrothed could afford to take a wife. The farmer hadn't approved of his daughter's dalliance, of course, but she'd assured him there was nothing to it—how could there be when Fell was so far below her in every respect? The very notion that she might have entertained *marrying* such a creature was absurd and so Fell's heart had crumbled to dust, his dreams for a lifetime of more than just derision and scorn scattered to the winds and his only chance of ever knowing tenderness from anybody but Ma carried away like dandelion seeds in a storm.

With an irritable grunt Fell turned his back on the memories that still pained him, threatening to make an already strange day worse. Dwelling on the past wouldn't help him think what to do with allegedly-Marie, stretched out on his bed like a mermaid on a rock with her vibrant red hair tossed around her shoulders. She was too pretty by half, if truth be told—and Fell had no need of a pretty woman disrupting his quiet life. Since it had been driven home to him so cruelly that he could never hope to be worthy of a wife he had lived alone with only his dogs for company, Lash the offspring of his old bitch Queenie who had passed away the previous spring. Dogs didn't care who his father was or whether his mother could speak a different tongue. Their loyalty was unshakable, ten times as kindly as the villagers who muttered as he passed. Lash and Ma were the only family Fell would ever have, the prospect of a wife and children torn to shreds the day Charity was ripped from him. A family of his own, with a loving wife and legitimate children to bear his name was all he'd ever wanted, the chance to finally anchor himself into a place he *belonged*, among his *own* people—but that would never happen for him now, instead condemned to continue life on the fringes with nowhere and no one to truly call home.

'Mr Fell?'

The sweet voice from his bedchamber sent a flurry of something down the back of his neck, startling him with its timid civility. Usually it was his last name that hailed him, often barked or mumbled but never truly polite. Marie's manners were oddly touching—yet more proof she was not who she claimed to be.

Fell strode back to his guest with the meagre tray of food balanced in one hand, the other clutching two cracked cups. Lash hadn't moved from his position at Marie's side, his eyes closed in delight as she tentatively stroked the shaggy fur of his neck as if not sure she was doing it right.

Fell lifted a brow in mild surprise, trying to ignore the fresh colour that had leapt into Marie's cheeks at his return to the room. The bloom suited her, emphasising the peaches and cream of her complexion, so different to his own. 'He likes you. He wouldn't let most folk touch him like that.'

He set the tray and cups down on a little table beside the bed, almost missing the flicker of shy pleasure that flashed across her face. The next moment he wished he *had* missed it, as it was replaced by a small, uncertain smile that lifted the apples of her cheeks in a way too damn appealing for comfort.

'Does he really? I always wished I might be allowed a dog of my own, but Mo—'

She broke off, eyes darting to meet his in swift apprehension. Evidently she had almost let something slip, as he saw a muscle move in her jaw as she clenched her teeth together to stop any more dangerous words slipping past dry lips.

They sat together in an awkward silence for a few heartbeats, until Fell unceremoniously deposited the plate in his blushing guest's lap.

'You need to eat something. It must be some time since your last meal.'

Marie nodded, taking the lump of bread with only a slight hesitation. She ate quietly and slowly although Fell could see in her face that she must have been ravenous, his humble bread and cheese probably as delicious in her hunger as the good food she was doubtless used to.

When every crumb had disappeared from the plate Fell poured her some tea, faintly amused by her concerned glance at his battered cups. Her pretence of being a servant was falling apart before his eyes, but she hadn't seemed to realise and once again Fell wondered why she thought it necessary to play such a strange game.

'What will you do now? Seems to me you're in some difficulty, stranded with no luggage or anywhere real to go to.'

Marie paused in sipping her tea, the cup absurdly large and unwieldy in her small hand. She glanced from Fell to Lash as if the latter could tell her how to respond, but the dog's silence gave nothing away and she dipped her head to fix on the patched bedspread beneath her.

'I confess I don't yet know.' Her voice held such fresh worry and fear that it touched some forgotten part of Fell's insides, covered in dust since Charity's betrayal. Marie was like her in a curious way, the fragility they both shared shining through to make him shift uncomfortably in his seat. She was frightened, injured and all alone, with evidently no desire to return from where she had come.

And now she's in my cottage—which makes her my problem.

A stab of conscience pierced Fell's breastbone like a lance. Ma had been only a few years

younger than Marie was now when Rector Frost
had found her in the forest, terrified and all
alone with her birth pains coming stronger with
every moment that passed. If not for his kindness to a mysterious woman running from an
equally mysterious past, who knew where Ma
would have ended up, the old man's compassion
exactly what Essea had needed at her most vulnerable. Now in an uncanny twist of fate Fell
was the one to come across a young woman in
need of help, a situation that mirrored the events
of thirty-one years before in a way starkly as-
tounding.

Fell tapped his fingers on the leather front
of his apron, reluctantly following the thread
of his thoughts to their inevitable conclusion.

*You'll never be half the man the rector was,
but you should at least attempt to follow in his
footsteps. You know what you ought to do—but
will you attempt it?*

The words came out more gruffly than Fell
would have liked, but his misgivings had apparently turned his throat to sandpaper. 'You
can stay here while your leg heals, if you'd like.
Not that you've much choice the state it's in at
present.'

For a moment he thought she hadn't heard
him, her head still downturned and face hidden

by that copper wave, although when she spoke there was something in her voice he couldn't place.

'Stay here? With you?'

'Until you're able to carry on your travels.'

She looked up at him then, and his heart gave an unpleasant lurch at the quiet pain in her eyes. It was unhappiness mixed with mistrust, the sorrowful acceptance of a dog used to a kick in place of a caress. 'Ah. You're mocking me, of course.'

He frowned, taking in her resignation as if she expected nothing else. 'Of course I'm not. What reason would I have? I'm in earnest.'

Marie regarded him warily, suspicion and genuine bewilderment mixing in innocent wonder. 'Why? Why would you help me?'

'Why wouldn't I, if I'm in a position to?'

The question only seemed to increase her puzzlement. She brought a hand up to gather her hair over one shoulder, casting Fell a sideways look that quite unconsciously enhanced the pretty shape of her profile in a way most unsettling.

'But…how? How would that be possible?'

Fell swallowed, the unease already lapping at him increasing beneath her disbelieving gaze. She truly was the most beautiful woman he'd had in his cottage in almost ten years, the knowledge unwanted yet just as undeniable. It wasn't a realisation he desired, nothing of any use coming from his appreciation for the soft glow of her flushed cheeks.

She's clearly too high-born for the likes of you, even if you weren't a bastard of questionable parentage. Which you are—and won't ever forget.

Shouldering the thought aside, Fell gave the most nonchalant shrug he could manage.

'Quite easily. I'm outside in the forge most of the day so I'll not be under your feet. A bit of help with the cottage is all I'd ask in return, being as there'd be an extra body in it, but I'm not a man who wants looking after. You can sleep in here and I'll go in the forge, save your blushes.'

He watched as several expressions chased each other across Marie's smooth face, one after the other in a vivid stream of unconscious animation she couldn't control. She seemed so eager to agree, so movingly hopeful he had provided her with a way out, yet still something in her held her back.

'I couldn't ask you to do that. It would be too much of an intrusion, surely.'

Her words were polite, restrained, although

Fell sensed the desperation behind them as tangibly as a brick wall. 'You didn't ask. And there's far worse places to sleep than a forge—it's warm and, with a blanket, I'll be more comfortable in there than you will in here.'

'I'm still not sure... I would never expect you to go to such lengths for someone like me.'

'Do you have somewhere else to go? A better plan in mind? I don't believe you do.'

She blinked, eyes suddenly dropping to her hands—but not before Fell caught a glimpse of the pure relief in her face and his chest gave another wrench at her vulnerability.

'I don't know how to thank you. Your kindness... I've never known anything like it. I just don't know what to say aside from thank you.'

Fell nodded briskly, determined at least *one* of them would maintain some stoicism. Marie's shock at his concern was both touching and pitiful in equal measure—and revealed far more than she had intended. If she was so unused to the most basic civility she must be more accustomed to suffering—a notion that stirred worryingly close to the bone.

'Someone like me'? What might she mean by that? I wonder.

'Nothing *to* say. Couldn't call myself much of a man if I wouldn't help a lady in trouble.'

She gave another of those small smiles that sent a flicker through him, although she shook her head in earnest appeal. 'I'm not a lady, though. I'm only a maid.'

He inclined his head, stubbornly ignoring the warning bells chiming in his ears. There was no going back now, even if he had just made the error in judgement that flicker of something long forgotten made him suddenly fear.

'Of course you are, Marie. My mistake.'

Chapter Three

Laying his hammer down, Fell wiped the sweat from his brow with one forearm. The fires of the forge were fierce enough without the July sun beating down to heat the very air itself, not even a trace of a breeze to relieve the feeling of wading through hot soup. It was growing hard to remember the last time there had been any respite from the unrelenting sunshine turning grass to straw and cracking the dried mud of his path—certainly not during the five days since Marie had taken up her unexpected residence in his home, a turn of events he was still yet to fully understand.

His shirt lay plastered to his back and he plucked at it with a grimace, holding the damp fabric away from his body to let in some air. The leather apron fastened round his chest hardly helped in keeping him cool, either, and he untied the strings with an irritable tug to toss it across his anvil.

What I'd really like is to be in the cottage, out of the heat and possibly sipping some cold ale— neither of which I can do at present, thanks to my heroics.

It had seemed such an obvious thing to offer Marie a place to stay, Fell grunted to himself as he pushed open the forge's door and scowled at the blinding sunlight that greeted him. She'd been friendless and alone, clearly scared out of her wits and running from something she didn't want to share: all a mirror image of Ma's situation when Rector Frost had stepped in as her salvation, prompting Fell to likewise sally forth. There were two key differences, however, that had escaped his notice five days before, and now they were getting more and more difficult to ignore.

The good, kindly rector had been past sixty when Ma appeared out of nowhere, a happily married man with a compassionate wife and a house more than big enough to take on a terrified eighteen-year-old and her newborn son. Fell's cottage was tiny by comparison, already snug when only his large frame and a scrawny lurcher dog occupied it—and in his case there was no forty-year difference in age to make his appreciation of Marie firmly paternal. She was in her early twenties by the looks of it, only a handful of winters younger than himself and, despite his best efforts, he couldn't manage to remain as frankly oblivious to her charms as Rector Frost had been to Ma's.

Damnation. Why couldn't I be an old man— or, better yet, why couldn't she?

Fresh sweat prickled on his forehead and at the back of his neck, an aggravating tickle that did nothing to ease the tension in his shoulders. At least out here in the blistering yard or cloistered in the hellish heat of the forge he was safe from his unsettling guest. Her leg prevented her from moving much, instead confining her to the cool shadows of the cottage and out of his sight for much of the day. It was only at mealtimes he saw her really, when she would present him with a plate of bread and cheese and a mug of ale, but never anything more elaborate than that…hardly surprising if she didn't have the first idea of how to cook, being either the most useless maid that ever lived or the lady Fell suspected. She would have had somebody to do all those tedious chores for her, never needing to learn how to take care of herself or anybody else if the unblemished skin of her hands was anything to go by.

And I'm still no closer to understanding what she meant by 'someone like me'. As far as I can tell she's got nothing to be ashamed of—the reverse is true and there lies the trouble.

Fell ran a finger around the collar of his shirt, feeling the unpleasant wetness of his nape. He caught sight of the pump standing in one corner of the yard, the sudden urge to place his head beneath the spout gripping him as tangibly as a fist, the longing to feel cold water drenching his soot-dusted hair now all he could think of. It would be a blessed relief after the roar of the fire and the buzz of too many thoughts that currently spun in his mind, the presence of Marie in his home an unfortunate reminder of everything he would never have for real. A woman in his cottage was something he had wanted for years, a wife to love and children a product of the union that would cement his place in the world—but Charity's cruelty had taught him the folly of that dream, something a half-Roma born with the taint of bastardy should never set his sights so high as to wish for. Even now, almost ten years after her laughing escape, the sting of her harsh lesson left a bitter taste on his tongue and he couldn't think of her without a wrench of his insides. If even a farmer's daughter considered herself too good for him a woman such as

Marie must be in another world entirely, beautiful and untouchable and more proof of the necessity for Fell to turn his face away from the pursuit of love. There was absolutely nothing to gain from noticing the different hues of copper and gold that shone among her hair, or the way her green eyes darted away from his so he might not catch her watching him with an expression he couldn't quite read. She wasn't for him and he wasn't for her, or anybody else for that matter, his background something no power could change. Charity had laid that fact out quite clearly and the memory of her pretty, lying face made him flush anew with the pain of regret.

He was at the pump without really knowing he had walked towards it, unfastening the top few buttons on his shirt with practised fingers. He had to bend almost double to fit his head beneath the spout, but the sensation of the first drops of cold water falling on to his hair and neck was a relief for which he would have gladly concertinaed himself ten times. It ran over him in soothing rivulets, drenching the clammy material at his shoulders and running in a crystal stream down his chest to cool where bitterness had threatened to seize his lungs in a punishing grip. There was no fighting the way of the world, he thought as he scooped a handful of water to rub over his heated face. Things were as they were and he had little choice but to accept the cards he had been dealt.

A sudden squeak from the direction of the cottage prised open his eyes, stinging from the mix of sweat and water he wiped from them. It sounded a little like a startled mouse—although when he saw where it actually came from he couldn't help but allow his lips to curve.

Marie dithered halfway down the cracked path leading from the back door, leaning heavily on a stout stick and her face the colour of a poppy field—simultaneously scarlet, yet green about the gills. Directly behind her Lash proudly offered up the unfortunate rabbit he held in his jaws, blocking her retreat from the evidently unexpected, mortifying sight of Fell's damp, unbuttoned shirt and chest scattered with drops of water that glittered in the sun. Each awkward, ungainly step she hopped away from Lash's macabre gift brought her closer to where Fell stood, watching their dance with growing amusement, the dog following eagerly, although politely confused by her lack of delight. Trapped between a rock and a hard place, poor Marie looked as though she didn't know which way to turn and in the comical absurdity of it Fell couldn't resist.

'He wants you to take it,' he called to her helpfully, although she didn't seem to appreciate his efforts. Marie glanced over her shoulder at him, eyes skimming the open front of his shirt as if by their own volition before she could drag them away and her face flaring hotter in embarrassment so strong it was palpable.

'I'd—I'd really rather not!'

Biting back a smile, Fell ran a hand through his wet hair, flicking droplets to the ground to soak into the dried mud.

'Are you certain? He'll have caught that especially for you, you know. I knew he liked you.'

'I'm sure I'm very grateful, but...do you think you could ask him not to stand *quite* so close with it?'

Marie hobbled back another painful step, still clutching her stick and hurriedly snatching her bright skirts away from Lash's trophy. The problem of her missing luggage had been easy enough to fix: Ma kept a few old dresses stowed in a trunk beneath Fell's bed along with the handful of valuables she didn't want to take on the road. She wouldn't mind Marie borrowing a couple, Fell knew with certainty, and it was oddly pleasing to see the younger woman shuffling about in the vivid colours of a Roma rather than her own muted neutrals even if the dresses were a fraction too long. Rich reds and sunny yellows suited the pallor of her skin and flaming tresses of her hair, a distinctive shade Fell couldn't recall the last time he had beheld—and shouldn't try to, he reminded himself sternly, determined not to dwell on anything to do with his disturbing guest any more than was humanly possible.

Still determined she should claim her present, Lash advanced again and the object of his affections staggered back another pace, awkward in her alarm and evidently not paying enough attention to where she stepped. Her stick slipped on a raised stone and she dropped it, crying out sharply as her injured leg suddenly bore her weight and for a moment seeming as though she might crumple to the sun-baked ground.

'Careful!'

Before he had time to think what he was doing Fell found himself at her side, one hand on her arm and the other at the slim curve of her waist. He hauled her upright, just catching the surprised stretch of her eyes before her face creased into a pained grimace.

'I fear I shouldn't have done that.'

The hand at her waist felt as though it was on fire, so much did it scald Sophia's skin beneath the thin fabric of her gown, and despite the agony in her leg she couldn't escape the heat that radiated from Fell's grip to ignite her racing heart. She might as well have been caught in a flaming vice for how much she could have torn herself away from him, both the strength of his grasp and her own shameful reluctance to move away holding her firmly in place.

'Probably not. That'll set you back a couple of days, I shouldn't wonder.'

Fell shook his head resignedly—at her clumsiness, no doubt, she thought with a hot rush of embarrassment—but didn't release her from his hold. Instead, all the breath left Sophia's body as in one smooth movement he gathered her in his arms and lifted her, steadying her against his chest where the unbuttoned shirt proudly displayed the expanse of honed muscle so mesmerising the first glimpse of it had made Sophia blush to the very tips of her ears. Now she found herself *touching it*, actually coming into contact with the still-wet skin Fell had doused with cold water, coarse damp curls mere inches from her face that felt so hot she now feared it might melt away entirely.

'What were you doing out here? Your leg needs rest.'

She felt Fell's voice rumble through that chest

as he carried her towards the open kitchen door
as easily as if she were a sack of feathers, each
word vibrating in her ear to make her flush
anew. Her own voice was unfortunately squeaky
when she tried to reply, her throat as dry as a
desert as the sensation of Fell's sculpted arms
around her almost robbed her of the ability to
speak.

'I thought it felt a little stronger today so
came to see if you wanted a drink. It's so fearfully hot outside and with the fires lit the forge
must be unbearable.'

Fell lowered his head as he ducked through
the cottage door, bringing his stubbled jaw
down to almost touch Sophia's face. She could
have turned and kissed him at that distance,
so close were his set lips to hers, and the very
idea of doing so sent a sharp, unladylike thrill
right through her breastbone to pierce the softness within.

Sophia stiffened in his grasp, her spine turning to marble at the dangerous direction of her
thoughts.

*Don't be ridiculous. He'd be horrified—and
I'd sooner lose my mind than do something so
clearly unwanted.*

Still, the urge to reach out and trace the hard
line of his profile hovered at the edge of her

consciousness, an instinctive desire she shied away from in alarm. If there was a less appropriate reaction to being so close to a blacksmith Sophia certainly couldn't name it, her scandalous enjoyment of resting against a warm, worktoned chest something she never knew could stir in her quiet soul. Even the smell of him was tempting, a combination of coal soap and smoke that danced around him as Fell carefully placed her down on one of the low benches beside the kitchen table and turned away, his attention already moved on to the task at hand.

She watched as he took the rabbit from Lash and inspected it closely, her revulsion at the sight tempered by worrying thoughts that nipped at her composure.

Not since the death of her father had Sophia known what it was to be treated with the gruff kindness Fell had shown her since he'd scooped her from the forest floor. He hadn't once raised his voice or seemed resentful at being made to sleep outside and, on more than one occasion, had even deigned to ask how her leg was faring, far more than she would have expected from her own mother, let alone a relative stranger with no reason to care. It was frighteningly tempting to think she might abandon her pretence in the face of Fell's apparent sympathy, his consideration for her a shadow of the warmth she'd ached for so hopelessly for so many years— yet the dangers that lurked made her hold her tongue.

Fell might be friendly enough while he had nothing to gain, but how was she to know he wouldn't drag her back to Mother for the promise of a heavy purse? Surely he wouldn't turn down the prospect of a handsome reward for the sake of Sophia's pleas—what man would choose her happiness over a pile of coins, or be moved by the sight of her tears? Nobody was above acting out of cruelty or selfishness. Sophia knew from bitter experience it was safer to assume Fell was like the rest, putting his own interests above those of the young woman who expected nothing different. Perhaps it was unfair to tar him with that brush, having so far only treated her fairly, but it seemed so unlikely anyone would break the mould of Sophia's understanding. She was far more able to believe in the wickedness of people than the notion they might be something better.

Don't be foolish just because he showed you some decency. In your desperation for tenderness you'd put yourself at risk of discovery, all for a man you've barely known five minutes.

Sophia frowned, almost too consumed by her

thoughts to notice Fell rolling his sleeves up to the elbow. The movement unveiled his forearms, scattered with black hair, and she felt another prickle of that heat in her cheeks.

It's not just his kindness you've a weakness for, though, is it?

It was a ridiculous thing for her to notice, she chided herself with swift discomfort. All the legitimate worries, guilt and fears that circled in her mind day and night *should* have made it impossible for her to register anything else, yet for some accursed reason the solid shape of Fell's arms called to her, impossible to ignore and unsettling in the extreme. It wasn't proper or decent for a lady to acknowledge a man even *had* arms, but her eye didn't seem to grasp that message, even occasionally straying to visit Fell's shoulders or daring a flick towards his unique face.

The mismatched colours of his eyes was something that grew more fascinating each time they fixed Sophia with their uncanny scrutiny, strange and intriguing—and far more attractive than any blacksmith should be allowed. Sleeping in his bed was almost too intimate for words, the idea of fitting her body into the hollow made by his frame something that didn't bear thinking about.

'You can watch if you like. It might be useful for you to learn how to prepare a rabbit for eating.'

Fell glanced at her sitting near the table, a trace of another grin flickering on his lips to make her blink. He had the most engaging smile she'd ever seen, no trace of the cold malice of Septimus's or Mother's angry sneer. It was a smile to gaze at, to appreciate the soft upward curve roughened by a chin full of dark stubble…

She brought herself up short before her mind could wander any further off course. Probably the last thing in the world she wanted, aside from to set foot in Fenwick Manor, was to have anything to do with what was about to happen at the kitchen table and she swallowed down a wave of queasiness at the thought.

'Thank you, but I think not. I've never been able to bear blood—I believe that's what made me faint in the forest the day you found me. The very notion makes me feel quite light-headed.'

'You might wish to turn around then. I don't want you stretched out insensible under the table.'

Sophia spun hurriedly as Fell reached for a knife gleaming in its wooden block. As if confused by her squeamishness Lash came to sit at her feet, peering up at her as she reached to stroke his ears with an unsteady hand.

'It doesn't trouble you, obviously.'

From behind her came a grunt of agreement. 'Not in the least. All my dogs have been good hunters and as soon as I could be trusted with a knife my mother taught me how to deal with their gifts. The odd rabbit made us a bit more popular in the rector's kitchen when winters were lean.'

The sounds at her back made Sophia wish she could stop up her ears, but the embers of her curiosity glowed brighter than her disgust. Fell hadn't spoken of anything personal before, in fact barely stringing three words together over the past five days, and the chance of learning something more about the man who intrigued her so despite her best efforts was too tempting to ignore.

'Your mother taught you? Is that not unusual?'

She heard the soft sound of Fell's shirt moving as he shrugged. 'She had no choice but be the one to teach me how to be a man. Practically everything I know came from her.'

'Not from your father?'

There came an unpleasantly moist noise that made Sophia's insides twist.

'No idea who he is.'

Unseen by the man behind her Sophia's brows contracted in a frown. How could such a thing be possible? She must have misunderstood. The identity of one's father was one of the most important things in deciding one's place in the world, the family name key to fortune and reputation. Her own papa had been both handsome and rich—no wonder Mother had wanted to keep him all to herself, not willing to share him even with the child they created together. If Sophia hadn't come along things would have been so different, so much better for all concerned, a truth reiterated to her so many times she couldn't remember a time she hadn't known it.

'Surely you must. Your mother *must* be able to recall the name of her husband, even if you never met him.'

Fell gave a dry laugh, finding some grim amusement in her words. 'How can I put this delicately enough for a lady's maid? I was born on the wrong side of the blanket, Marie. My mother was a young Roma girl who had the misfortune to meet a man who put a baby in her belly without intending to marry her and we've both had to bear that shame ever since.'

Sophia's eyes flew wide as a flood of pure,

burning mortification swept over her like a wave, slamming the door shut on any coherent response she might have made.

Stupid girl!

Mother's venom rang in her ears, the constant refrain never more appropriate than at that moment. How had she stumbled into a conversation about *legitimacy*, of all things, the most taboo, unmentionably vulgar subject no lady should ever entertain? A Romani mother would account for Fell's name and the pleasing distinction of his hair and skin, an interesting discovery Sophia would gladly have learned more about, but the circumstances of his birth was something entirely different, a secret a man of her own class would have taken to his grave.

When she didn't reply Fell filled the silence with studied indifference that didn't fool her for a moment. 'I've asked Ma about my father many times, although she's never been willing to discuss as much as his name. She was—is— the very best of mothers, but I won't pretend her silence hasn't irked me something fierce over the years. If she desires to keep her past a secret, I've no choice but to assume she has good reason. She's been both mother and father to me and I'd defy any man to do better.'

Sophia took a breath, attempting to force some of the blood from her cheeks back to her brain. Shock and distinctly upper-class horror still ran through her at Fell's confession, but with great effort she managed to tamp it down. It wouldn't do for him to see her prim surprise, perhaps more suited to a lady than Marie the maid.

Carefully disguising the unsteadiness of her voice, Sophia chanced a nod. 'She sounds like a singular woman. Does she live close by?'

'She is that and, in truth, I've no idea where she is at present.' Another noise Sophia would have been happy not to hear came to make her shudder. 'The Roma are like the wind—impossible to pin down and never sure which direction they'll move in next.'

He appeared at her shoulder, reaching for a seasoned-looking pot standing on the range, and Sophia angled her face away to avoid a glimpse of his hands.

'You don't move with her?'

Fell retreated again, but not before she caught the shake of his head. 'She always struggled with living in one place and as soon as I was old enough I told her she could leave the village without me. I've made a life for myself here—not much of one, but it's mine. I built the forge myself with my own two hands after the old smith I was apprenticed to died and it's the one thing I've ever been proud of. It's where I go to forget that I don't truly fit anywhere else and it's my biggest sorrow I'll never have a child to pass it on to when my years are done.'

Surprise almost made Sophia turn around, only catching herself in the nick of time. Why would he assume he would never have children? He was still young and certainly comely enough to tempt a woman to wed him—a realisation that made her blush all the more.

'Surely you've plenty of time to marry and have a family of your own, if it's something you want so very badly.'

There came another of those dry laughs, this time with precious little humour, and although his voice was steady Sophia could have sworn she caught a whisper of stubbornly concealed sadness. 'It's the thing I want the most in all the world, yet I know it's not to be. Do you imagine there's a queue of fathers beating down my door for their daughters, or Woodford ladies lining up to wed the illegitimate son of a Romani maid? The villagers scarcely speak to me, let alone consider me a match for any of them. A Roma woman wouldn't settle to village life either and I'd never be so cruel as to ask it of her.

In the absence of a third option I've reconciled myself to remaining a bachelor. At least that's peaceful enough.'

She heard him drop something into the pot and replace the lid before the sound of water splashing into a bowl suggested he was finally—mercifully—washing his hands.

'And you? Do you have much in the way of family?'

The question hit Sophia squarely in the chest and she hesitated before answering. Sitting in the calm shade of Fell's cottage with a dog at her feet and a bright gown on her back she could almost have pretended there was no sad little Sophia Somerlock, only Marie Crewe. It was so tempting to deny Mother existed, to dismiss her as though she had never been at all—but her claws were sunk too deeply into Sophia's soul, her continual cruelty shaping Sophia's very sense of self, and even miles away her daughter still shuddered beneath her spiteful shadow.

'I, too, have only my mother. My papa died when I was six.'

It was Fell's turn to pause. When he spoke, there was gruff sympathy in his voice that made Sophia finally twist to face him in confusion.

'That must have been a terrible thing for such a young girl.'

He regarded her steadily and she saw she'd not been mistaken. Genuine compassion softened the lines of his weathered face, real feeling Sophia could scarcely comprehend. She'd never seen such pity directed at her before—it was always Mother who demanded consolation, insistent that nobody mourned Papa as keenly as her. Sophia was never allowed to show her sorrow or seek solace from her grief in anybody else—how dare she when she was the one who had spoiled everything by being born, when it was all her fault Papa lay in the churchyard, his grave crowned with flowers it was part of her penance to tend? She deserved no comfort and the look in Fell's eyes unsettled her more than he ever could have known.

If he knew the truth of what had happened, there's no way he would look at me so. He would turn in disgust and his revulsion would be my just deserts.

She flexed her hands from the tight fists they had clenched into without her noticing, nail marks marring her palms. So often her body acted of its own accord, finding painful little ways to punish her when the crushing weight of guilt became too heavy to bear. Small bruises, scratches and scrapes were forever appearing on her milky skin as if from nowhere, always the work of her own spiteful fingers and always ready to strike.

'I suppose it was. I confess my life was never the same again.'

That much is the truth, she thought bleakly as Fell released her from his gaze to fix it on the scarred table.

While Papa lived the worst of Mother's jealous malice had been contained, only seeping out in poisonous drips when his back was turned and Sophia was left unprotected. Once he was in the ground there was nothing left to stem the flow and she had been drowning in it ever since, the cause of her father's untimely demise and never able to forget it. It was no wonder no man would ever want her for anything other than her fortune and the Thruxton name that had been thrust upon her: how could anyone be expected to love her, when even her own mother could not? How would anyone love her when she'd been a blight on so many lives that might have been happy without her?

Her confusion and sorrow must have formed a rigid mask on her face, for with another keen glance Fell artfully changed the subject.

'That rabbit had a beautiful pelt. I can make you

something from it, if you've a liking—although I can't imagine a maid having much chance to wear furs.'

She peered up at him standing beside the table, face inscrutable again now the sympathy was hidden behind his usual brusqueness. There was real goodness in him, she realised with dawning wonder, the kind she had never dreamed might be shown to her and didn't for one moment think she deserved. She'd lied to him to keep herself safe and had kept up that lie despite his kindness—all because of her fearful heart, now beating faster with both guilt and a growing appreciation for Fell she couldn't understand.

The memory of her wardrobe, packed with expensive clothes, back at Fenwick Manor flitted through her mind to interrupt such thoughts and made her suppress a grim smile. Her collection of furs was the envy of all who saw them, proof of the wealth Mother was so eager to display. Septimus would have showered Sophia with gems, gowns and sables—and whatever horrors he saw fit to mete out on his trapped, friendless wife. A rabbit-fur stole might seem a poor thing in comparison to the luxuries she was used to, but she would rather that than a hundred gifts Septimus would lay at her feet if he were to discover where she had fled.

'You're so kind to offer, but I think you're right—what reason would a maid have to wear furs?'

Chapter Four

Sophia peered through the low branches of the trees that screened Fell's cottage from the rest of Woodford Common, more small thatched houses set a short distance away and grouped together on either side of the rough road as though to deliberately exclude the forge. From her hiding place she could watch the villagers going about their business without being noticed and the scene unfolding so captured her attention she could hardly tear her eyes away.

Careful not to be spotted, Sophia craned her neck to follow a young lad carrying a load of wood, his feet fairly swimming in a pair of boots far too big for him as he scurried across the cobbles. He was passed by two women with baskets over their arms, chattering before dropping polite curtsies to an elderly man inspecting the rose climbing his front porch. A small girl stood in another garden, fiercely beating the dust out of a rug, while her mother juggled pegging washing with holding a baby, her face pink, but even from a distance her smile was clear to see.

Wherever Sophia looked there was activity, strangers living their lives with unselfconscious zest that she both wondered at and envied. They all looked to have such *purpose*, so busy and seemingly happy with their lot—there wasn't a fine gown or expensive coat among them, yet from the earthy shadows she could see more contentment than she ever recalled noticing in any overcrowded ballroom or stuffy parlour while drinking endless tea. Compared to the villagers' existence her former life seemed so stunted and bland, for all its undeniable privilege devoid of the colour and liveliness she now saw all around. Part of her longed to limp out from the trees and shyly introduce herself, the cheerful energy of Woodford calling to her neglected spirit to make her wish she could join in, but the sensible majority of her mind stopped her before she could make such an ill-advised mistake.

It was essential they caught no glimpse of her as she recovered, her leg growing stronger, but still bound with rough cloth and sometimes needing the support of a stick. By pure luck she'd stumbled upon a host who by his own admission the villagers didn't often speak with, his home concealed by the trees currently sheltering her from the midday sun. With her distinctive flaming hair she was all too easy to identify and the fewer people aware of her presence the better. There was still the danger Fell might be tempted to give her up for a purse provided by Mother or Septimus, and the discomfort that thought brought her every day was something Sophia could have very well done without.

More evidence of the stupidity Mother said I'm known for. What reason would Fell have to favour my wishes over a heap of guineas, when one choice has no value and the other so much?

It was a question that taunted her and one she had no wish to answer. Of course, there was only one logical reply, although Fell's behaviour confused her at every turn. Tiny little considerations that to so many would go unnoticed were more pleasant to Sophia than Fell ever could have guessed—she had not known what it was to be treated without contempt since she was a child of six. She drank it in as eagerly as a parched flower might drink in rain, the likewise arid desert of her soul amazed and grateful for such a monsoon of small kindnesses—yet she could not allow herself to lose control. It would be all too easy to have her head turned by Fell's decency and believe he might be somehow different, that he might see something in her worth more than the disdain she'd endured almost her whole life. Some determined part of her would always hope for such acceptance, a stubborn gleam that refused to be completely extinguished even in the face of Mother's dislike for her *useless disappointment* of a daughter.

A sharp pain in her arm made Sophia look down, surprised to see her fingers digging into the skin without knowing she'd moved. Little half-moon indentations marked where her nails had been and she rubbed at them with a frown, trying to dismiss the unhappy memory of her mother's face when she had spat those words at Sophia's bowed head. How old had she been then? Sophia wondered absently. Fourteen, perhaps? Fifteen? About the age when a girl was finding herself along the road to womanhood, emerging from the chrysalis of a child and unfurling her unsteady wings. Mother had sought to clip Sophia's immediately and the scorching malice had increased ever since to keep Sophia firmly beneath Lady Thruxton's boot. The lively spirit that had once made Papa laugh had been resolutely crushed until only a hidden flicker of it remained, the fire in Sophia's belly doused with icy water poured by her mother's own hand.

Just the thought of Mother was enough to make Sophia's palms prickle and her heart quicken beneath her dress, green today with flowers embroidered on the bodice and tucks to give shape to the skirt. It was pretty despite its simplicity, far less elaborate than the gowns she'd left behind, and running her fingers over the hand-worked petals helped distract her from the rapid flit of her pulse.

I ought to return to the cottage. There's nothing to be gained by standing here, wishing I could introduce myself to people who wouldn't want to know me anyway.

With a final deep, calming breath Sophia straightened her shoulders and turned for the little house behind her. As soon as she limped out from the shade of the waving trees she felt the heat seize her, sunshine glaring down to warm the lopsided curls pinned determinedly to the top of her head. Without a maid to help her, her hairstyles were becoming more and more haphazard by the day and she couldn't help a grimace of dark, frightened amusement at imagining Mother's disgust.

Hair half-down and wearing a Roma dress—
even she'd be lost for words if she saw me like
this.

'Afternoon, Marie. Have you been out?'

A glance towards the forge showed Fell leaning against the doorframe, hammer in hand and
sweat gleaming on the brow furrowed in enquiry. The by-now-predictable flurry of interest that stirred the hairs on the back of her neck
murmured to her, the same as it did every time
she laid eyes on his broad shoulders and the hint
of coarse hair she saw at his unbuttoned collar, but she set it aside to offer a hesitant smile.

'Not really. I just stepped into the garden to
take the air, although the heat makes it hardly
refreshing.'

'You're not wrong. No whisper of a breeze
today.'

He closed his odd eyes with his face turned
towards the sun, giving Sophia the opportunity
to watch him for a moment without fear of being
seen. With the weighty hammer dangling from
one scarred fist and his frame almost filling the
doorway he was an alarming prospect, huge and
dark-haired and somehow untamed—yet she recalled the note of sadness in his voice when he
had confessed his desire for a family, a glimmer

of vulnerability that she hadn't thought such a formidable outside would conceal.

Surely those village ladies are too fastidious by half. If I were a woman of their class, I'm not sure Fell's parentage would be an insurmountable obstacle.

The thought made her blush, but that didn't stop it from being the truth, she would have to admit as she noted the pleasing swell of Fell's bicep hardly hidden by the singed sleeve of his shirt and the delightfully tawny cast of his skin. Surely nobody looking at him could deny he was attractive, in a rough-hewn sort of way, and the kindness he had shown her might be agreeable to anyone. His illegitimacy—Sophia flushed to even *think* such a word—was unfortunate indeed, but his Roma mother seemed far less of a consideration. It was an interesting rather than undesirable facet to Fell's identity, the depictions of Romani life she had read about and seen in picture books more romantic than anything else. There was no cause to dislike the travellers that she could see—none of them had ever wronged her at any rate, which was more than could be said for the aristocrats she had borne hostility from for as long as she could remember. Perhaps Woodford was too quick to judge Fell on things he couldn't change, denying him the chance of a family he had accepted he would never now have—but that was none of her business. Fell's lack of a wife was not her concern, something she had no reason to consider in any way. As soon as her leg had mended sufficiently she would leave his cottage and continue her journey into the unknown, the uncomfortably intriguing blacksmith fading to a mere memory she'd have no cause to revisit, certain she would vanish from his thoughts the moment she was out of sight.

Fell opened his eyes unexpectedly quickly and Sophia immediately switched her gaze to the sun-baked ground, cringing away from the possibility he had caught her studying him so intently. Instead, however, he seemed to be peering over her shoulder at the tree-lined lane at her back, shading those strange eyes with his hand to see more clearly.

'Looks as though we've some visitors, although I've not seen them here before. Need their horses shoeing like as not.'

Sophia turned to see for herself, just catching a glimpse of two men on bay horses still some distance from the forge—before recognising one of them with a strangled gasp as though suddenly fighting for air.

No. Please, heaven—no!

Mother's groom would be identifiable at a hundred paces even if Sophia hadn't seen him for twenty years, the sight setting her breath to claw at her throat. In his youth, a hoof to the face had left a curving scar across the left side of Phillips's jaw, drawing his mouth up into a permanently grim smile even Lord Thruxton had seemed to find unsettling. Phillips's devotion to Mother was endless and deep—he'd been with her since she was a girl, giving years of the unquestioning service Lady Thruxton always felt was her due as a beautiful woman dripping with wealth. It was no wonder she had sent her most loyal servant to hunt down her ungrateful failure of a daughter: nobody could match Phillips in his determination, no doubt trusted to drag Sophia home by her hair if the situation required.

Sophia took a sharp step back, feeling her leg shriek with pain, but too fixed on the men riding towards her to pay it much mind. They hadn't seen her yet. Phillips's attention was on the man riding beside him, one of Fenwick Manor's stable lads, and she felt a flicker of desperation crackle through her like lightning in a storm. If she could reach the cottage before they turned in at the forge, she might be able to hide, perhaps escape the terrifying thought of being

forced to return to face Septimus's cold rage.
It was only a few steps to the open front door
with wisteria climbing each side, Lash lying
across the threshold like Cerberus guarding the
gates of hell…

*But what of Fell? Won't he give me away as
soon as he discovers who I am?*

The notion seized her chest in its icy grip and
she turned her frightened eyes to him, hopelessness and despair swirling as she watched his face
cloud with sudden suspicion. He was no fool—
she knew he saw the frozen fear in her expression and the flit of his gaze from her to the men
growing closer showed the immediate link he
made between the two. There was no way she
could pretend their approach played no part in
the blanching of her face or skitter of the rapid
pulse he could see at her throat, but with no time
to attempt anything more to save herself Sophia
was left with no choice but to pick up her skirts
and limp agonisingly towards the cottage as
fast as she could—not a word passing between
her and Fell, but one last look of frank pleading
hanging in the air as she turned and fled.

Fell watched Marie hobble away, new caution
rising with each ungainly step she took towards
the safety of his house. It didn't take a scholar

to understand the men who were almost upon him were people she knew and had no wish to see and he unconsciously tightened his grip on the hammer still hanging from one fist. That final glance holding such stark fear and an entreaty he didn't yet understand put him on his guard at once, concern starting to simmer at the sight of her frightened face. Whoever they were Marie was afraid of them and he found he disliked the thought of her distress—as well as the prospect of someone from the past she had run from finally catching up with her when she had thought herself safe.

'Lash. Here.'

The dog had woken as Marie clumsily hopped round him and now he got to his feet, coming to stand motionless at Fell's side as though sensing his master's unease. Fell patted the dog's wiry neck and together they watched the two strangers draw nearer and dismount, the older man with the scarred face clearly in charge of the young one who nodded at Fell a little nervously with a swift glance at both the hammer and the dog.

Arranging his face into a look of mild enquiry, Fell stepped out of the forge's doorway and into the sweltering yard. 'Is it shoes you're wanting?'

The scarred man removed his hat for a moment to mop his brow with a handkerchief, squinting at Fell against the glare of the sun. Even without a disfigurement he would have had a discomforting face, unfriendly with a hardness about the eyes that quite suddenly made Fell's mind up for him. Whatever these men wanted, whoever they were, they wouldn't be getting near Marie—she must have shrunk from them for a reason and the air of hostility he could sense coming from the man before him was enough to convince him of that reasoning's soundness.

'No. We're looking for someone. A young lady.'

Fell slightly raised one eyebrow with a trace of a grin. 'Ah, well. Aren't we all, friend? Aren't we all?'

Out of the corner of his eye Fell saw the younger man conceal a small smile behind his hand, although it slipped from his pink face at his superior's withering look.

'It's a *particular* lady we're searching for—a Miss Thruxton. In her twenties, red hair, green eyes. We've reason to think she may have come this way. Have you seen anyone of that description?'

Pretending to consider the question, Fell scratched behind Lash's ear.

Miss Thruxton, in truth, is it?

The door to the cottage was still ajar, lying in Fell's line of sight over the newcomers' shoulders, and he caught the most fleeting glimpse of Marie concealed behind the frame. She'd be able to hear every word, no doubt listening with her heart in her mouth and standing rigid with dread, until he saw her peep out from the shadows and fix him with a desperate gaze that almost made him flinch from its naked terror.

'There's a generous reward for any information regarding her whereabouts. She's a simpleminded girl, not capable of clear thinking, and it'd be a kindness for her to be found.'

'I see. Ran away from home, did she?' Fell nodded as if interested, all too aware of the frozen audience unseen by the other two men.

'Aye. If she'd a speck of sense she would have stayed where she was, but as I said—she's a foolish girl.'

Fell chanced a glance back at the doorway to the cottage. Marie still peered round the frame, staring with eyes huge with fear and pleading and mutely shaking her head with such passionate entreaty Fell felt himself struck by her vulnerability all over again. Even if the scarred man's story hadn't been an outright lie—*simpleminded, is she? It seems nobody told her that—*

he still would have paused before handing her over, the panic on her face something painful to behold.

With his hand still resting on Lash's head Fell shrugged his broad shoulders. 'Afraid I can't help you. Perhaps you'll have better luck in the next village.'

'Are you sure? We have it on good authority she was last seen heading in this direction.'

'I think I'd remember a woman like that. We don't get many flame-haired beauties passing through Woodford Common.'

He kept his gaze firmly on the man in front of him even as he bit the tip of his tongue at his misstep. His private opinion of Marie's prettiness had come spilling out of his mouth before he could stop it and he could only hope she'd been too gripped by fear to have caught his glowing description of her charms.

The scarred man held Fell's eye for a long moment, his younger companion shuffling from foot to foot behind him. Beneath his fingertips Fell felt Lash's hackles raise slightly at the beat of tension stretching out in taut silence and wondered distantly if he would need to call the dog off—but then the stranger nodded and turned away, both visitors swinging up on to their horses again.

'Come on, lad. We'll stop in at my cousin's house before heading to the next village. If she came this way, no doubt he will have seen her.'

Fell watched as they turned their mounts' heads for the lane, suddenly wanting nothing more than for them to disappear back the way they had come. Far from answering the questions that swirled around Marie, those hunting her had just raised more and Fell knew he wouldn't now be able to rest until he learned the truth from her own lips.

Just before they rode out of sight the man with the scar turned in the saddle and called back at Fell over his shoulder, his voice so cold it sent a curious shiver down Fell's back despite the glaring sun.

'If you do happen upon her, just remember this: Lady Thruxton of Fenwick Manor will pay handsomely for the girl's return—whatever state she's in. She only has one daughter, after all. Good day to you.'

'Drink this.'

Fell pushed a glass of gin across the kitchen table towards where the woman sat staring down at her lap. When she reached to take the drink he saw how her hand shook, sending ripples across the surface as she lifted it slowly to her lips. She grimaced at the first tentative swallow and set it down again, still avoiding his gaze with her face turned slightly away.

'So. Not Marie Crewe, after all?'

There was a slight pause before she shook her head, drooping autumnal curls gleaming in the light spilling through the kitchen's small window. She didn't volunteer anything further and they sat together in silence, Lash's sigh of contentment as he stretched out on the floor the only sound in the stillness of the room.

'Would you like to tell me who those men were?'

Another shake of the head was the only reply.

'But it was you they were looking for?'

Still nothing.

Fell sat back in his chair, fingers finding the stubble on his chin and rubbing lightly. It was like getting blood from a stone, the mysteries of the woman sitting opposite no closer to being revealed.

'Are you with child?'

That question received an immediate response. Not-Marie's head came up at once, eyes wide with horror once again, although this time of a very different kind.

'Absolutely not!'

Fell lifted one shoulder, relieved she'd found

her tongue at last. He had begun to fear the scarred man had been right and Marie—or Miss Thruxton, apparently—wasn't too quick off the mark. 'No need to take on. I'd be the last person to judge you if you were. It just seemed the most obvious reason for a young woman to flee from a good home without even telling her ma where she was going.'

She looked at him unhappily, suddenly reminding him of an animal caught in a snare, and with a flicker of surprise he felt the urge to hold out a comforting hand to her, to enfold her in his strong arms again and reassure her that he wouldn't cause her harm. Instead he swallowed the urge and washed it down with a mouthful of gin, nodding at Not-Marie to follow his example.

'Drink up. I think you should tell me your story now and I'll have the truth this time, if it's all the same to you.'

The taste of gin lingered unpleasantly, but Sophia had more important things to concern her as she wondered hopelessly how to begin. Her hands still trembled and her legs felt weak with pain and distress, her heart leaping as with each breath she tried to order her thoughts. Phillips's face swam before her each time she so much as blinked, a nightmare she had hoped would never be made flesh. Only the fact his attention had been fixed momentarily on the stable lad beside him had spared her from his notice, giving her time to flee. Seeing him riding towards the forge had been one of the most frightening moments of her life and now Fell wanted her to somehow put her horror into words.

Giving *anybody* an insight into the wretched existence she'd left behind would shame her to the ground. Admitting even her own mother couldn't manage to *like*, let alone *love*, her was a horrible prospect, made worse by it being Fell to whom she'd have to lay bare the truth. Some ridiculous part of her had grown too fond of him, she would admit, and now shied away from letting him know how much she was reviled by those who knew her best. But he had done her a great kindness in shielding her from Phillips and for that she owed him an explanation, even if it showed her failings as both a daughter and a human being.

She took a breath, debating whether to draw another sip from her glass to steady her ragged nerves.

'I suppose there's little point in concealing it any longer. My name is Sophia Somerlock, of Fenwick Manor near Salisbury.'

Fell shot her a narrow look, although his tawny face was alight with curiosity that lent appealing animation to his features. 'I know of the place. Very grand it is, too. But your name—is it not Thruxton?'

'No. Mother insisted I take my stepfather's name after they married, but I will be a Somerlock in my heart until the day I die.'

Her glass had found its way back to her hand by some mysterious force and she took another drop, wincing at the acrid taste. She'd never tried something so vulgar as gin before, but she couldn't argue with its power to loosen the tongue.

'I left the manor after my mother decided I was to marry my stepfather's nephew, the heir to the Thruxton family fortune. I wasn't informed until all the arrangements were put in place and my feelings about the match were not consulted.'

'Aha.' Fell nodded thoughtfully. 'He wouldn't have been your choice?'

'I think he wouldn't be any woman's choice if they were acquainted with his true character.' The image of poor Jayne Thruxton, Septimus's doomed first wife, flitted through Sophia's mind to make her shiver. She still didn't know for certain what had happened behind the closed doors of their marriage and prayed now with every fibre of her being she would never find out first hand.

'But why run? Why not just refuse?'

'That wouldn't have been an option. If I'd gone against Mother's wishes…' Sophia tailed off for a moment. How could she begin to explain the force of nature that was Mother? She held all who knew her in her thrall, charming those she deemed worthy into acting as she wished while terrifying others less fortunate. Her conduct towards her own daughter was in a league all its own, nobody else seeing the particular streak of cruelty reserved solely for her only child—and nobody else as deserving of it. 'There *is* no going against her. Fleeing was the only thing I could do if I wanted to avoid being forced into marriage.'

'Why would she seek to force you into a marriage you so clearly didn't want?'

Because she hated me first for daring to be born, then more for what I did to Papa, and seeks to give me the punishment I earned.

Sophia swallowed.

I think that would be a revelation too far.

It was a fair question, yet even in the depths of her unhappiness she couldn't bring herself to answer with the whole truth. It would shame her to dust and then she would never be able to meet Fell's eye again.

'I am an expensive disappointment with more failings than I can count. As a result I cannot blame her for finding it hard to love me—there's so little there to prompt affection. If she'd chosen a less offensive match I would have accepted to please her, but Septimus was a step too far even for me.'

'Did she *tell* you that you were a disappointing failure? Your own mother?'

At Sophia's nod Fell's handsome features twisted, although she hardly noticed. To her dismay she felt the sting of hot tears creep up behind her eyes and she blinked rapidly to hide them. The stomach-churning horror of being so nearly discovered merged with hopelessness to raise a lump in her throat no dry swallow could dislodge, despair and confusion so bitter she could have choked on it. The prospect of a life spent looking over her shoulder was so bleak it made her want to allow the tears to fall—but there *was* no other path and with only a moment of hesitation Sophia took her glass and drained it without tasting a single drop.

Fell watched her force the drink down without judgement, chin resting on one battered fist.

'You could marry. You could take some other man as your husband; surely then you'd be safe.'

'I could not.' Sophia shook her head, her voice hoarse from the burning mouthful of gin, but still quavering with determinedly suppressed emotion.

He doesn't understand. He doesn't know me well enough to see what a laughable suggestion that is.

Only somebody unaware of Sophia's true worth could say such a thing, a person flatteringly—but entirely wrongly—assuming a man could ever want her for herself. Her face was passable and her figure even pleasing, Mother had once been so generous as to sniff, but her character, talents and learning were so lacking no man would surely dream of asking her to marry him without the prospect of her family fortune sweetening the deal—a blunt fact Sophia had never thought to question. It was a prospect so unlikely she might have smiled, had her face not been a glazed mask of misery, pretty enough but concealing the wickedness Mother had insisted lay behind.

'With no fortune or family, who would take me? Why would any man choose to bind himself to someone so utterly lacking in all manner of things that make a good wife? If I waited for a man to offer his hand, I'd be waiting the rest of my life.'

She looked down at her lap where her cold fingers twisted together so tightly it hurt her, almost missing the look that skipped across Fell's face like a pebble skimming atop a lake. It was unreadable and nothing she could name, although his eyes on her raised the fine hairs on the back of her neck in a wave of sensation she couldn't ignore.

He sat back in his chair, both hands clasped behind his dark head and strange gaze shifting to roam the ceiling as he apparently lost himself in thought. In silence Sophia waited for him to speak, the time crawling by as desperate unhappiness swelled inside her chest until her ribs felt as though they might crack beneath the strain. Now she had laid her situation bare for Fell to see it seemed more real, even more hopeless, and Sophia could see no way out.

She was startled by Fell's unexpected movement. Suddenly, as though needing to act before he changed his mind, he sat smartly forward again and tossed his own drink back in one smooth gulp, setting the glass back on the table with a decisive clink.

'As far as I'm concerned nothing's changed. You can stay until you're fit enough to travel, if you wish, although I know my cottage is a good deal too poor for a lady. But I won't give you up.'

He rose swiftly to his feet, brushing his hands together as though the matter was settled and Sophia wasn't blinking up at him in naked surprise he could hardly have missed. 'I need to return to the forge and sitting here talking won't make many shoes.'

It was such a rapid veer from still contemplation to brisk activity Sophia couldn't quite catch up, confusion lurching inside her even as Fell strode towards the door. She stared after him for a moment before surging upwards herself, limping across before he disappeared into the sunlight.

'Wait, please—wait a moment. Don't you want to discuss this a little more? When you offered me sanctuary it was when you thought I was someone else entirely...' Sophia turned her eyes to the ground, shame washing over her. She'd lied to him, taken him for a fool, and she could scarcely blame him if he wanted her out from under his roof. 'I wasn't honest with you and for that I am sincerely sorry. I would understand if you'd rather I left.'

Fell turned on the threshold, one hand still resting on the door. Outlined by sunshine he seemed bigger than ever, solid and immovable—and so suddenly *safe* it took any further words from Sophia's mouth. He had protected her, even when he had no cause to, showing more concern for her welfare than even her own flesh and blood.

He was silhouetted against the sun and she couldn't make out his expression—perhaps that was what gave her the courage to ask the question that burned on her tongue.

'Why didn't you tell them?' Her voice was quiet, almost afraid what his answer would be. 'Why didn't you turn me over for the reward?'

A taut pause bridged the gap between them, Sophia waiting with shallow breath and Fell filling the doorway with his powerful frame. When he finally murmured a reply it was almost too low for Sophia to catch—although the hand that reached out to touch her bare arm in silent assurance spoke louder than any words, the brush of his fingers against her skin lighting a sudden furnace in her gut.

'One look at your face told me you were afraid. I'll not be the reason a woman is compelled to do anything she doesn't wish to.'

His touch was as light and as fleeting as a butterfly on a blossom, the merest whisper of contact born out of concern, yet Sophia felt her entire body spring to life as though a streak of lightning had struck to ignite her very core. Every nerve thrilled to feel the warmth of his fingers dancing the length of her arm, each hair stirring in the wake of his gentle hand's feather-like touch. It was like nothing Sophia had experienced before, stranger and more *wonderful* than anything she could remember, and the joy of it turned her mind to warm toffee.

Nobody had touched her with anything close to affection in above sixteen years, not since Papa had stroked her flushed cheek on the day he died. He had been the last to look at her with the rough compassion she now saw in Fell's face as he stared down at her, turned slightly so the sunlight illuminated the craggy lines of his nose and jaw, and the notion spun unending circles of confusion. All she could do was watch as Fell cleared his throat with self-conscious brusqueness and turned to step outside, muttering over his shoulder as he went.

'I've work to do now if you'll leave me in peace. Those shoes won't make themselves.'

Chapter Five

Sophia sat with her knees drawn up to her chin as she stared into the empty darkness of Fell's bedchamber, the blankets beneath her still neat and undisturbed. She hadn't even attempted to sleep, the idea of rest impossible while Phillips's sneer haunted her and the sensation of Fell's hand on her skin still tingled in every nerve. If Mother could see her hunched into such an unladylike pose she would be excessively displeased—but she didn't even know where Sophia was, thanks to Fell's intervention, and again Sophia felt relief so sweet she could almost taste it on her tongue.

But today bought only a short respite. I still need to decide what to do when the time comes for me to leave this cottage and surely that cannot be too far away.

Fell's misguided suggestion swam back through

her thoughts, executing another lap around her head. It was a ridiculous notion born out of his complete—and merciful—misunderstanding of what kind of woman she was, but that didn't stop it from returning time and again to niggle away with a voice she couldn't quite dismiss.

He truly seemed to think my marrying some-body else was a viable option. Perhaps I should take his error as a compliment.

What kind of man would agree to take her with no money, no good name and no tangible benefit from the match? Septimus would have gained all three: the Somerlock fortune would become his with its heiress as his bride, bring-ing with her the continuation of the Thruxton name. He would have had heirs from her, too, another generation to mould in his own image and the passing of his spirit down the ages, never to be forgotten even if his cruelty ought to have been buried by the sands of time.

What would those children have been like? Sophia wondered with a sudden chill seeping beneath her borrowed nightgown. Would they have taken after their father, the boys hand-some and the girls beauties, but both concealing malice beneath their perfect façades? Perhaps Mother's essence would have prevailed, a child born cold and angry and never satisfied with its lot, or by some miracle a glimmer of Papa's gruff kindness might shine through, some small consolation for her while bound to Septimus for the rest of her life.

Would they have had your eyes, Papa, or perhaps our red hair?

The idea almost made her smile for a moment before the usual suffocating guilt descended to coil about her neck. She was the reason Papa would never see his grandchildren, her yearning for it the height of hypocrisy. If she hadn't done what she did, she might not be in this position now, a lady depending on a blacksmith for help...

Sophia lurched upright so quickly she felt her neck jar, but she paid it no heed as she sat wide-eyed in the quiet of the night, frozen with the sudden flash of inspiration that illuminated every corner of her mind like sunlight through a window. It was as though she'd lit the fuse on a stick of dynamite and swallowed it, the following explosion so powerful Sophia could scarcely breathe.

Fell wants children, a family to call his own—might he consider me to provide him with one, in exchange for saving me from a fate like a living death?

She brought a hand up to feel where her heart

danced, leaping wildly as if spurring her on as the idea unfurled itself before her. Hadn't he told her himself, only a few days previously, how he longed for the little ones he feared he would never have? The sorrow in his deep voice had been so clear to her then despite his attempts to hide it, the memory sparking a vivid combination of compassion and hope to writhe in her stomach. He had been so sure a wife would never come to him, so determined his future included nothing but his lonely forge... Was it possible he would listen to a scheme from which both he and Sophia could profit, albeit in very different ways?

She had so little else to offer but the prospect of an heir, Sophia thought as she licked at dry lips; a legitimate son or daughter to fill Fell's cottage with the light and laughter of a child. With no money her fertility was the only bargaining chip she had left, the only thing she might trade for her freedom from Septimus's malignant grip. Fell might even grow to tolerate her in time, after she had placed a couple of warm bundles in his arms, and that was surely the best a woman like Sophia could hope for. He would never love her, of course, but nor would anybody else, and it was surely a less risky gamble to place one's bet on a man capable of basic decency if nothing more.

Slowly, as if frightened that to move would break the spell of the idea glittering before her, Sophia swung her legs down from the bed and reached for her cloak. The instinct to dress before leaving the room muttered to her, but she ignored it, terrified any delay would make her lose her nerve. Unless she acted *now*, forced herself into motion *that very moment*, she might hesitate and think the better of her ludicrous plan and then she might never voice the tentative suggestion growing louder and louder inside her head.

He won't accept. Of course he won't. But if I don't ask I might never know for sure...and I can think of no other way to escape the reach of Mother or the threat of a new name thrust upon me that I never sought or wanted.

If Fell had been any other man, she would never have dared dream he might even hear her without laughing, she thought as she staggered through the darkened cottage towards the back door on legs weak with apprehension. A gentleman of her own class would turn up his nose at once, surely rejecting Sophia's pauper proposal without a second thought—but Fell was no gentleman, instead a fatherless blacksmith with almost as much to gain from the match as Sophia. If he had any other offers she wouldn't have stood a chance among them; she could only hope, as she pushed open the door and stepped out into the moonlit yard, that Fell was as desperate to escape the path laid out for him as Sophia wished to turn from her own.

Steeped in silver, the forge waited silently for her approach, neither encouraging nor discouraging her from limping heavily up to the door and taking hold of the wrought-iron handle. Not a sound came from within, only the lightest hiss of a breeze through the trees and the occasional melancholy call of an owl suggesting Sophia wasn't entirely alone in the warm night. It would have been so easy to stand for hours feeling the air gently sift through her hair to cool her heated skin, but that wouldn't take her any closer to the outcome she both hoped for and feared, the only chance of salvation she could think of.

With her heart racing so fiercely she was surprised she couldn't hear it Sophia quietly opened the door and peeped inside. For a half-second she couldn't see Fell anywhere in the room scented with charcoal and ash, still stifling from the now-doused fire and heat of the day—until pale moonlight flooding in from one unshuttered window lit his sleeping form stretched out beneath a workbench, his eyes closed and bare chest rising and falling with calm, even breaths.

The sight wrapped a hand around Sophia's throat and squeezed tightly, for a brief moment distracting her from the chaos already running riot inside her. The forbidden glimpse she had caught of Fell's impressive chest on the day she'd stumbled upon him at the pump had hinted at what lay beneath his shirt, but to be confronted with it so starkly was something else entirely. Any genteel lady would be shocked by such a vulgar sight, yet Sophia found herself quite powerless to tear herself away, almost relieved when Lash uncurled himself at his master's side and sat up, the movement waking Fell and forcing Sophia to avert her eyes. Even with her gaze fixed firmly on the rough floor, however, she couldn't shake her awareness of the uncovered breadth of his shoulders, or the torso scattered with hair that surely should have shocked rather than intrigued.

Out of the corner of her eye she saw him shift on his thin mattress—then sit up sharply, his hand flying out for an enormous hammer lying close to where he slept.

'It's me!' Sophia stepped backwards in swift

alarm, arms held up in front of her face. 'It's Sophia!'

She heard him exhale sharply, then a heavy thud as the hammer was replaced on the ground.

'What the devil are you doing in here?' His voice was still thick with sleep, but the next moment quick concern rushed in to replace his bemusement. 'Is something the matter? Have your mother's men returned?'

A little braver now he was unarmed, Sophia shook her head in the dim light. 'No, no. Nothing like that.' She hesitated, steeling herself to continue. 'I… I wanted to speak with you.'

Fell peered up at her in blank, bleary-eyed bafflement. 'Now? You want to speak with me now?'

At her shy nod his incredulity increased, furrowing his already crinkled brow. 'It couldn't wait until the morning? What time *is* it?'

'I don't know. I haven't yet slept.'

Sophia watched him run a hand over his tired face, still confused but with a gleam of concern that gave her the smallest glimmer of hope. He didn't seem annoyed she'd disturbed him, more puzzled, and puzzled was better than she might have expected. Without irritation he might be more receptive to hearing her plan in its entirety, maybe even willing to consider it despite all odds.

'You haven't yet slept. On account of what happened this afternoon? Or because of what you wish to speak to me about?'

'Both. They walk hand in hand with each other.'

Fell scrubbed at his strange eyes with the heels of his hands, evidently bewildered by his night-time visitor's cryptic murmur. 'I'm a working man, Miss Somerlock, and I need rest. Perhaps you might stop talking in riddles so I can go back to sleep.'

'Very well.'

With her legs still shaking Sophia stepped fully inside the forge and closed the door behind her, folding unsteadily on to a tall stool set at the side of Fell's bench. He rose from the floor to sit across from her, wearing only a pair of old breeches and a suddenly wary expression that with a dart of that *something* she saw enhanced the sharp line of his jaw. Her chest felt clenched in a vice and her stomach full of snakes that coiled uncomfortably, the slight nausea of nervousness circling in her gut, but there was no going back now—no other choice but to set her proposal free to face Fell's judgement, either the making or breaking of a future free from fear.

One deep breath didn't help her find her tongue, so she took another and another until the vice beneath her breastbone loosened just enough to allow her to speak.

'I have an idea to put to you. One I think might suit us both.'

Fell crossed his sculpted arms across his chest and waited, head held slightly to one side, for her to continue. The wariness hadn't left his look, but even in the moonlight Sophia could see it was tempered with a cautious curiosity that gave her courage to go on.

'You suggested I take a husband to save me from my mother's scheming and the match she would make for me. I… I would like that husband to be you.'

Fell didn't move a single muscle, sitting as still and as quiet opposite Sophia as a statue carved from stone.

She would smile in a moment.

Any second now.

She would break into a laugh at her jest and he might join her with a huff of his own, the butt of the joke, but at least breaking this uncomfortable beat of tension that made the very air in the forge feel as though it were suffocating him with each breath. *Of course* she wasn't in earnest, playing some ill-advised prank he didn't understand, yet she gazed at him so hesitantly it was almost as though—

'I know I have few charms to tempt you, but I'd hoped you might at least consider it.'

Sophia's fingers twisted in the hem of her cloak and she looked away quickly, flustered and embarrassed, yet risking a glance back to read what she could in the blank amazement of his face.

Hellfire. I think she's in earnest.

He stared back with the parted lips and wide eyes of someone struck smartly over the head with a heavy object—which was exactly how he felt, as the gears in his mind began to slowly turn again and the enormity of Sophia's declaration hit him like a kick in the ribs.

'You want to marry *me*? *Why?*'

Looking pale and strained in the moonlight, Sophia swallowed hard as if with great difficulty. 'It occurred to me a union between us might fulfil both our desires. I would gain a husband to keep me from a forced marriage, a husband who has already shown me such courtesy and concern for my wellbeing I would never receive from anyone of Mother's circle. In return you would have a wife to give you the legitimate children you long for, but thought would never be born to you. That would be the understanding: my safety in exchange for a family of your own.'

She broke off, chest heaving now with barely contained anxiety Fell found it uncomfortable to see. He wanted to reach out and touch her, a gentle brush of his fingers against her skin to calm her as he had only hours before, but all the strength seemed to have left him and he could only sit in stunned silence as Sophia pressed the back of one hand to her doubtless flushed cheek.

For some stretch of time neither of them spoke, Fell's mind too full to find any words and Sophia apparently waiting with wordless dread for his reply. Only Lash seemed in any way unmoved by the bizarre conversation taking place above him that Fell might have thought was a dream if not for the growing ache in his head, a pain as though the rapid flit of his thoughts were pinging around inside his skull.

Is she truly offering me the chance of a future? To finally have children to love and a family I might belong to with no secrets or shame?

It was all he'd ever wanted, the most cherished wish of his lonely heart—yet good sense and bitterness stopped him in his tracks before he could be carried too far by ridiculous fancy.

When he had pictured himself with a wife it

had been Charity he'd imagined, sweet-voiced and bonny, but certainly no lady. Even she had been too good for him in the end and the knowledge that Sophia sought his hand under duress only emphasised the truth he had known since Charity had vanished from his life, leaving behind only the sting of rejection.

He wasn't worthy of a wife and most definitely not one like Sophia. She only wanted him out of desperation, bartering for her life like a farmer at market, but with herself as the livestock for sale. It would be shameful for him to accept, akin to buying an unhappy woman with no other choices left to her, and that he would not do. Of course she didn't have tender feelings for him—he would never have expected her or anyone to stoop so low—and he wouldn't doom her to a life at his side, to be snubbed and cast down because of his own selfish desires.

'It can't be. You've done me a great honour by asking, but I think you know that can't be done.'

He saw Sophia's face fall and immediately regretted how the faint gleam of hope was extinguished from her countenance. She truly seemed as though she had wanted a different answer, inexplicable as the notion was, and the knowledge he'd disappointed her was decidedly unpleasant.

Fell leaned across the narrow bench to catch Sophia's downcast eye, his voice unwittingly gentle in his undeniable desire to spare her distress.

'Think what you're suggesting—really *think*. You truly believe you could stand to be a wife to me, living in a cottage and bearing my children? Despite the differences between us and how far above me you are in every respect? It would be a mistake for you to take me as your man. You wouldn't be able to endure it.'

Sophia cast him a swift sideways glance, lifting her chin a fraction so her head no longer drooped on her slender neck.

'I have considered my actions carefully. You have never shown me anything except kindness and I believe if we were to marry we might find some accord between us.'

'Accord…aye. Perhaps. But that won't stop you being a lady and me a Roma bastard, begging your pardon, and say what you will I can't see a lady deigning to stoop so low as to share my bed.' The picture those last three words conjured was one Fell set aside at once, the prospect so suddenly tempting it alarmed him. Pretty, dainty Sophia Somerlock in his bed was surely something any man might want, himself included—but *that* was not an image he had any reason to entertain. 'The very idea must disgust you.'

Even in the dim light he saw Sophia's cheeks colour with well-bred embarrassment, but to his surprise she met his eye, still shy but now with an underlying hint of determination that was absurdly attractive.

'Is it that you doubt my word? You think I offer those terms to trap you without intending to honour them?'

Fell shook his head, caught a little off guard by the faintest streak of challenge he had never suspected Sophia possessed. It flared into life and died again in the blink of an eye, but it was enough to make him wonder if there might be more to the anxious, self-doubting woman than he had thought—a question more intriguing than he liked. 'No. I believe that *you* believe you're sincere. I don't doubt your intentions, but I think on our wedding night you would re-alise how distasteful it was to as much as *kiss* a blacksmith hardly worthy of looking at you and you would curse yourself for your mistake.'

For a moment Sophia merely sat, straight-backed and elegant as any high-born lady taught good posture since she could walk; but then she answered, so quietly Fell barely heard her even in the silence of the night.

'You don't know I would find it distasteful.'

'No? You think otherwise, do you?'

He leaned forward a fraction more, readying himself to dismiss Sophia's objections with the frank truth. They were from different worlds and possessed such strikingly unequal value a match between them was laughable, something Sophia must *surely* realise. He didn't even know his father's name, courtesy of Ma's damned silence that had raised his hackles more times than he could count. She was too good for him even if she thought otherwise, and nothing she could say would convince him—

The last glimpse of Sophia Fell caught before she closed the narrow gap between them was the surprising determination in her eye. It was the look of a woman fighting for her life, so resolved despite her fears he felt a surge of respect well up inside him she more than deserved— and then her lips settled over his and his mind emptied of anything other than raw shock and the wonder of feeling soft warmth where he had never thought to feel anything ever again.

It was a chaste kiss, a little hesitant and clearly unpractised, yet something in its innocence touched Fell somewhere in his chest to make his unsuspecting heart rail against his ribs. He felt Sophia's breath coming quickly and knew her pulse must be bounding as hard as his own—or even more so, obviously unused to the sensation of pressing her mouth to another's and feeling her blood begin to heat beneath skin suddenly alive in every nerve. Naked amazement gripped Fell and wouldn't let go as the urge to sweep the bench aside and draw Sophia into an embrace washed over him, a powerful instinct shouting to be heard above the roaring in his ears. She was so close and yet so untouchable, forbidden and yet waking desires inside him he had never thought to feel again... Even the scent of her was exquisite torture, soap and rosewater drifting from the flaming hair he wanted nothing more than to sink his hands in and rake with fingers unsteady with longing.

Her uncertainty was delightful, so vulnerable in its naivety it was as though a bolt was wrenched loose from Fell's usual cynicism to unleash the weakness kept so firmly inside. Not since Charity had swayed in his arms had he felt anything even close to what coursed through him as Sophia's lips gently ghosted his own, leaving stars in their wake and a whole heap of awkward questions he had no wish to answer. She drew him out, delving deeper to expose the weakness within like a diamond surrounded by rock, stirring the hidden yearning he had banished to the shadows for fear of the hurt it could bring.

She drew away before Fell wanted her to—although when he would have had the strength to break the kiss he didn't know. It could only have lasted a moment, a few seconds of contact at the most, but it might as well have been several years for all the head-spinning fog through which he now stared, mute with confusion, at Sophia's scarlet face. He wanted to say something, *anything*, but his ability to speak had been stolen by Sophia's unexpected decision.

'Is…is that proof enough that I will be able to keep my promise?'

If her voice had been any more stilted Fell wouldn't have been able to understand what she'd said. Her mouth barely moved, apparently half-frozen with disbelief at her actions and her hand when she reached to press it against the bodice of her nightgown shook so hard Fell caught the movement even in the gloom.

Still reeling, he lifted his own hand to his lips, feeling the place Sophia had touched and changed everything between them in a matter of seconds. The arguments against her proposition hadn't changed, yet for the life of him Fell suddenly couldn't quite grasp why they had been so important.

Don't be a fool. One kiss won't change the fact I'll ruin her life if I marry her.

The stern mutter in the back of his mind spoke up to make its feelings undeniably plain and Fell steeled himself against a flash of disappointment so intense it took him by surprise. Of course the little voice was right. Despite her protestations Sophia couldn't possibly know the fate she was inviting for herself; he would have to guard them both against it, even if the pull to surrender to her will tugged ever more strongly.

Unfortunately for his good intentions Sophia chose that precise moment to fix him with huge, imploring eyes that swept aside all reasoning like a tower of cards.

'You would be saving me. *Please* don't let me fall to those who would cause me nothing but harm.'

He sat back in his seat, suddenly robbed of all certainty by the desperation in her face. If he refused Sophia, he would be abandoning her to the future she longed to outrun, even if his reasons were noble. Her life with him might be difficult, but surely it was for her to decide whether that was preferable to whatever waited for her back at Fenwick Manor and the fiancé she had left behind.

Imagine what would have become of Ma if

she'd been left to face the world alone. I of all people should know how much of a difference the kindness of a stranger can make to a life.

The thought made him shudder. If Rector Frost hadn't taken Essea in, giving her sanctuary from the darkness that snapped at her heels… Sophia would always be more than he deserved, the kind of wife a low-born creature like himself could only dream of, but that seemed to matter less and less the more he reflected on the consequences of turning her away.

She doesn't have to love me. She only has to keep her word, as I'd hoped Charity would. This might be the only chance of a family I'll ever have and all other thoughts aside I should be grateful to her for even offering this chance.

Fell rubbed at his aching eyes, suddenly almost too tired to think. Through the open window the faintest glimmer of dawn had begun to bleed into the horizon, drawing to a close the strangest night he had ever had.

'You've truly given this every serious thought? There's little chance you'll change your mind come morning when the light of day shines on what seemed like a good idea in the dark?'

On her stool opposite Sophia gazed at him

with a face as solemn and serious as a judge, the graveness of her look adding years to her young features. 'I'm quite sincere.'

He believed her. It was the oddest feeling to have so much instinctive trust in the word of another and yet there it was: a declaration of her intentions that he knew, somehow beyond any doubt, she would hold to until her last breath.

Fell ran his hand through his hair, still disordered from the sleep he had no hope of resuming. There was only one thing left to say and he delivered his judgement with finality from which there was no turning back.

'Then I suppose I'd best not argue with my betters. If you're truly in earnest—I agree. And may heaven help us both.'

Chapter Six

Sophia felt the unpleasant sensation of every eye following her as she moved down the cobbled street, her audience's curiosity regarding the mysterious newcomer growing with each limping step she took. It was a relief to duck into the sanctuary of the grocer's shop and take a moment to collect herself, her breath quickened by both the effort of walking and the feeling of inquisitive stares boring into the back of her skull.

Fell followed her inside and flicked her a small, swift smile that managed to twist Sophia's stomach despite the nerves already coiled there. When not dressed in his work clothes he looked smart—or as smart as a man with soot beneath his nails could look—and the power of a well-pressed shirt to enhance the charms of an already handsome male wasn't lost on her.

'You look flushed. Did the walk from the forge tire you?'

'A little, I confess. I'll be glad to rest my leg for a moment.'

The curve of his lips increased a fraction, lifting the corners of his unusual eyes. A woman in the queue in front of them had subtly shifted position to catch a glimpse of Sophia, but now turned away again hastily at Fell's enquiringly raised eyebrow.

'You'll have plenty of chance for that. The grocer considers anything less than two hours of conversation with each customer a personal slight.'

Sophia only nodded, the anxiety pooling in her core threatening to overcome her courage. It had taken every ounce of bravery she possessed to leave the cottage and hobble through the middle of Woodford Common, every step requiring new determination. The stark, faintly unfriendly stares would have been bad enough without the accompanying fear any one of the villagers might recognise her or suspect she didn't belong, the prospect of a reward surely tempting to those with no reason to resist it.

She had taken precautions, of course, to foil anybody with dangerous intentions. The first time she had seen her hair in the glass after washing it with the compound Fell provided she'd stopped and stared, open mouthed with shock at the stranger gazing back at her—the pungent mixture of willow bark and vinegar had turned her distinctive mane from copper to black, and when combined with a little pencil through her fair brows she could have been another person entirely. Set in papers each night to encourage a reluctant wave the ebony tresses hung heavily down her back, another bright Romani gown contrasting with their darkness. All things considered, it would be difficult to identify Sophia as a lady born and bred in a manor house, but fear still gnawed at her as she smoothed down the skirt of her loaned dress.

If somebody was to see through her, to wonder where she came from, all might be lost. Mother and Septimus would be upon her before she could as much as draw breath to scream, their malice doubtless increased tenfold by her daring to disobey...

'Stop your fretting. Nobody here has a clue who you are and you'll raise less suspicion if you're seen out and about behaving as though you belong.'

It was as though Fell had read her mind, hunching slightly to murmur into her ear. The feeling of his breath against her neck cast an alarming ripple of delight through her body, softly stirring sinew and nerve to make them sing the melody his presence provoked with no effort at all. Ever since her rash action of a week before, when she had lost her head and lurched forward to kiss him, her body's unconscious awareness of him had flowered into full bloom, his every movement capturing her attention and making her want to curve towards him like a moth to a flame. She didn't *want* to feel such an unfathomable attraction, heaven knew, yet there was nothing she could do to stem the desire to touch him again, to feel the warmth of another person she'd never known until that night could be so sweet.

And now we are to marry, as soon as the rector reads the final banns. Less than a fortnight and then he will be my husband and I his wife— I still can't believe he agreed to it.

Sophia slid him a sideways glance, taking in the sharp lines of his profile as he fiddled with his cuffs. He seemed too big to be folded neatly into the tiny shop with shelves stacked and goods hanging from the ceiling, far more suited to the free-ranging space of his forge or yard, and she was once again struck by a combination of dread and wonder that it was him to whom she would soon be bound. All her life she'd assumed her husband would be a man of Mother's choosing, some uninspiring, well-bred gentleman Sophia would have to learn to tolerate—and who would certainly never love her. At least Fell was not malicious or unkind, contrasting completely with Septimus's cold cruelty, and perhaps in time they might even become something like friends. A few stares from the villagers seemed a small price to pay to ensure her safety from the Thruxtons' persecution, although it still remained to be seen what life as Fell's bride would truly entail.

Still with the unpleasant sensation of eyes on her Sophia watched as someone passing the door caught Fell's attention and his dark brows drew into a frown.

'That's Mrs Lake. I wanted to catch her about her grey mare—I'll be back in a moment.'

Sophia stiffened in sudden alarm as Fell made to move away. She would be left alone among the strangers who peered at her with sharp curiosity she took for dislike. Almost from the first step she'd taken out of the safety of the cottage she'd been aware how the villagers glanced at Fell, some dismissive and others merely cool, but none much friendlier than that. She didn't want to stay there in the crowded shop to face their interest alone and besides...

Any one of them could speak up and spoil ev-

erything. It would only take one person to see through my disguise and then I'd have to start running again. Didn't I overhear Phillips say he had a cousin in this village?

She took a breath, trying to force herself to release her set jaw, but then a spark kindled beneath the skin of her wrist and she glanced down in surprise to see a large hand resting where her pulse now leaped.

Fell eyed her for a moment before dropping his voice lower, delightfully intimate in its deep murmur. 'There's nothing to fear. I wouldn't leave you otherwise.'

Sophia nodded, but nothing could distract her from the heat suddenly radiating from that hand to creep higher along her arm, raising every fair hair as it went. If his touch was supposed to calm her it had completely the opposite effect, instead rallying every nerve to react to the light pressure setting her ablaze.

I must put a stop to this—and quickly.

The perturbing reaction of her body whenever Fell as much as brushed against her was becoming too worrisome to ignore. When she had been nothing but a temporary guest in his home it had been bearable, if unsettling, but now their association was to deepen she would have to fight harder against the pull of that unthink-

ing weakness for his ironic smile and the way
his odd eyes crinkled at the corners in harmony
with the curve of his lips. *He* would never have
a similar penchant for *her*, she knew without a
doubt; why would he, when she brought nothing
to the table other than the ability to give him a
child? She was under no illusions he was marrying her for any reason other than to gain a family and any fonder feelings she might entertain
for him would be pure foolishness to indulge.

And yet…

*It's so difficult to remain impartial when each
day he shows himself to be better in every respect than any man I've ever known—excepting
Papa, of course. Fell agreed to the marriage so
he could become a father, yes, but also in part
to save me from my fate. How many other men
would make that sacrifice and take a woman
with no money or real value to shield her instead of collecting a reward?*

The more Sophia allowed those kinds of
thoughts to circulate through her mind the more
confused she became, in turn finding it all the
more difficult to remain unmoved by the small
kindnesses Fell showed her each day. It was the
tolerance and warmth she had longed for since
she was a child, crying out for it in the lonely
confines of her room. Fell's attentiveness was

dangerous, drawing her closer to a man she couldn't hope to have, and unless she managed to rein herself in Sophia knew she would soon wish she had tried harder to free herself from its grip. Even his parentage didn't seem to matter to her disobedient emotions. Where others were scandalised and repulsed by his illegitimacy and Roma blood, Sophia couldn't bring herself to mind. Perhaps once she, too, would have had stronger feelings, but all she could see now when she looked into Fell's tawny face was the man himself—strong, capable and willing to stand with her in her distress. His background seemed irrelevant when set against the flesh-and-blood person they described, a blacksmith surely the equal of a penniless disappointment of a woman below him in every way other than status.

Fell retreated in search of his quarry and Sophia watched him go, striding head and shoulders above everyone else in the shop—including the cluster of women standing near the door, who followed his exit with sharp eyes and dissolved into rapid whispers that made Sophia swallow a groan.

Out in the burning heat Fell shaded his eyes from the sun and cast up and down the street, alert for any hint of which way his prey had walked. Mrs Lake had suggested she might be selling her steady grey horse when Fell had seen her in church the past Sunday and he wanted to be the first to put in an offer. He'd shod Bess since she was little more than a foal and her sweet temperament might be a good match for Sophia. A married man with a family needed a dependable horse, after all—a thought that made Fell unsure whether to smile or frown.

A married man with a family. I never would have dreamed that would be my future.

It was simultaneously the most wonderful and terrifying prospect Fell could imagine and he felt the weight of it settle across his shoulders like a heavy cloak. Ever since Sophia had come to him like a spectre in the night he had struggled to believe their bargain, convinced he would wake at any moment to find none of it was real.

Mrs Lake had apparently disappeared from the face of the earth and with a grunt of annoyance Fell turned back, noting as he did the increased scrutiny that followed him. There could be no doubt it was Sophia's sudden existence that piqued the fresh interest in him as the village curio. To the residents of Woodford it must seem as though Sophia had appeared from nowhere, a black-haired beauty unexpectedly among them just as had happened thirty years before; no wonder there was so much muttering and eyes hastily averted when Fell caught them following his soon-to-be bride.

She could almost pass in that dress and with her hair made so dark. A long summer spent in the sun rather than a parlour will tan her skin and in time I'd challenge anyone to prove she wasn't at least part Roma—in that spirit she thinks she has to hide, if nothing else.

Walking back through the grocer's open door and out of the dense heat he felt another flicker of admiration, twin to one that had flared as he strode beside her from the forge into the village. Sophia had been clearly afraid as she waited to see if she would be unmasked, but had kept her composure, braving the weight of the stares on her and responding with nothing but a polite—if shaky—smile. There was more courage lurking beneath that quiet exterior than he'd first thought, Fell would admit, and it was with the embers of his growing respect for her glowing brighter that he joined her in the barely diminished queue.

She angled her head away at his approach as if to hide her face, immediately putting Fell on his guard. Sophia didn't speak, but one look showed her hands tightly gripping the handle of the basket she held, her chest seeming to rise and fall more quickly than might be comfortable.

'Is something amiss?'

'No, no. Not at all.'

Still her fingers maintained their painful lock on the basket and Fell caught a fleeting flick of a glance in the direction of a group of women standing nearby.

The village gossips. They've been ogling her half to death—I'd wager a guinea.

Sophia's mouth was set in an unhappy line and her face was pale as he gritted his teeth on his irritation. The nosy busybodies couldn't help themselves, he knew from bitter experience, and he'd expect nothing else from them; but he disliked that they had brought a downward curve to Sophia's lips and found himself reaching for her before he had time to consider the wisdom of such a thing.

'Come on. I'll take you back and return alone later.'

The fabric of her dress was smooth beneath his fingers and a contrastingly jagged shard forced its way between his ribs the moment he touched her. It was a flicker like a stray spark escaped from a firecracker, taking him by surprise—or so he told himself, a lie he couldn't for one second sustain. In truth, the desire to once again feel Sophia's warmth had taunted him ever since she'd stolen all sense from his mind with the gentle movement of her lips on his, the feelings she had unleashed dangerous but more enticing than Fell could believe. It was foolish to indulge them and could lead to nothing but trouble, a fact his accursed weakness for her shy smile didn't seem to understand.

She started a little, eyes fleetingly widening at his touch before dropping away to fix again on the heads turning in their direction. A new hint of colour crept into her cheeks, but she didn't pull away—instead seeming to draw a fraction closer as if to accept his protection, a glimmer of hesitant trust in him that made Fell's heart leap in both confusion and pleasure.

I suppose I needn't read anything into that. Anyone might cling to a man my size for safety, especially if he's skilled with a hammer.

He drew her closer to the gawping group and guided her limping steps between them, offering a curt nod to any inclined to return it. They weren't even through the open door before he heard the muttering start up, voices lowered, but still easy enough to understand in their ravenous hunger for gossip.

'So? Do you think she's—?'

'Another like him? Could well be. Looks like one at any rate.'

'We'll be overrun before long. First his mother appearing from who knows where, leaving us with the fruit of her shame to go off running about the country again, and now a wife for him just the same. It's disgraceful.'

'We'll see how soon after the wedding comes the first child; I'd bet it'll be a swift confinement, if you grasp my meaning. The apple won't fall far from the tree and that lad was never likely to amount to much with his parentage in the gutter.'

Fell felt the muscles of his face tighten at the hissed words that hit his back in stinging flecks of malice. As always the temptation to answer their slander gripped him, but he forced himself to resist, the wisdom Ma had passed on to him years before surfacing at the front of his mind.

Never give them satisfaction. Words are all they have and the only person who can give them the power to hurt is you.

The memory helped calm him a little, although his anger only dimmed rather than disappeared. It was very well for Ma to say such things, but wasn't she at least partly responsible for the whispers that swirled about him in the first place? If only she'd reveal his father Fell wouldn't seem quite so mysterious and worthy of comment, the uncertainty surrounding his lineage confusing for him and fascinating to others…

There was silence at his side and he glanced down to see Sophia turning to look back at the whisperers. The pink spots on her cheeks glowed brighter and a new crease of her brow nipped at him somewhere in the last unprotected place in his chest. She was clearly thinking something, although what was happening beneath those black tresses he had no way of telling.

And so now she knows the truth.

She would have heard the whispers eventually, but still shame lapped at him like icy waves to think graceful, ladylike Sophia now knew without any shadow of doubt how low he stood in the eyes of the world. The hissed words of his neighbours mercilessly illustrated how far beneath her she was stooping in marrying him, just as Charity had always secretly felt, and it was as though somebody had removed the foundations of his already precarious pride to send it crashing to the ground. All of a sudden he wished more than anything she hadn't witnessed his humiliation—then felt alarm spread through him at how much he realised he cared what she thought. Guarding himself for so long against the wounds words could inflict had left him too jaded to waste time with such sentiment, or so he'd thought; the notion of Sophia somehow intruding into the carefully guarded part of him still vulnerable was worrying in the extreme.

He unconsciously tightened his grip on Sophia's arm, attempting to help her over the threshold and away to escape—but found she didn't move.

'Wait a moment.'

Before Fell could reply she stepped back towards the muttering group, cheeks still burning, but a spark of something moving in the depths of her green eyes he couldn't quite place. He could only watch as the women fell silent at her approach, unfriendly as a gaggle of suspicious old geese.

'Please excuse the interruption, but I couldn't help overhear. Am I to understand you're well acquainted with the Barden family?'

The leader, a bitter creature Fell recognised as a Mrs Cairn, drew herself up to her full height in offended dignity. 'Why, no, indeed. None of us has the smallest connection to them.'

'Not friends at all?'

'Of course not!'

Still mystified, Fell saw Sophia's half-smile.

It was a little uncertain, but the strange light still danced and with a rush of shock Fell realised it was the faintest pinprick of challenge—another intriguing hint of the hidden spirit beneath the controlled exterior. 'Oh. Forgive me. I assumed from your manner of speaking that you must be an intimate acquaintance.' She paused to give a rueful shrug as though dismayed by her own foolishness and Fell saw he hadn't imagined that fascinating glint of irreverence. 'Imagine my surprise to find your conversation therefore based on no knowledge, truth or reason whatsoever. I shan't take up any more of your time. Good afternoon.'

Without waiting to see the outrage on Mrs Cairn's face Sophia turned and stepped smoothly away, one hand finding the crook of Fell's elbow and bearing both of them out into the sunshine. Behind them the voices rose again at once, but this time Fell hardly heard them, too transfixed by the quiet satisfaction that flitted over Sophia's features to pay them any mind.

'What was *that*?'

Sophia allowed him the swiftest of upward peeks, cut off abruptly by the sweep of fair lashes as she looked away. The high colour at each cheekbone was the deepest Fell had seen there although she ignored it with a shake of her head. 'I didn't care for what they were saying. It was unforgivably rude.'

'Aye, well. I can't disagree with you there.'

He lifted his hat and pushed the hair back from his forehead with the brim, busying himself so Sophia might not see the utter surprise that wreathed his face.

Did she...speak out for me?

He couldn't remember a time when anybody had challenged the slander spread about him on his behalf. Ma would simply sail past with the confidence the villagers found so offensive, far too secure in herself to pay any mind to the whispers that followed. That it would fall to Sophia, of all people, to take up his cause was something he never would have expected— surely she was too mild for that, too careful in concealing whatever flare of temper might lie within that quiet soul?

'You'll have to get used to that kind of talk if you're set on wedding me. It won't ever stop— and it won't ever grow kinder, no matter what you do. It's as well you learn that now.'

Sophia still looked away, only the top of her hand-me-down bonnet visible to Fell's searching gaze, but there was no mistaking her wariness at what he realised too late could have sounded like a rebuke. 'Are you angry? Would you rather I hadn't said anything at all?'

'Of course not. I just…' He cast about for the right words, surprise and confusion clouding his mind to make it damnably hard to think. That fleeting gleam of light in her usually guarded eyes had spun him like a hurricane, leaving him unsure which way was which and stumbling for the path. 'I wouldn't want you to expect anything to change. This is my life— and it will soon be yours. I'd rather you were prepared.'

To his relief the bonnet bobbed up and down in a short nod. 'I understand and I'm glad I didn't irritate you with my lapse of control. My mother would have been beside herself if I'd spoken like that in her hearing. It's just the sort of insolence she wanted to knock out of me.'

Fell couldn't help a wry huff of a laugh despite the uncomfortable sensations executing swirls in his stomach. 'Unsuccessfully, apparently.'

'I'm not so sure. Certainly not for want of trying.'

He looked down at the edge in her voice, but still only a straw brim peered back, shielding Sophia from his concern. From that angle he could see nothing but the tip of her nose and a few raven waves that gave nothing away about whatever was running through that busy mind.

What was it she said her ma called her? An expensive disappointment? Fine words for her own daughter.

Whatever had made her run from Fenwick Manor had evidently left its mark, a thought Fell found he disliked. Probably he shouldn't want to know what mysteries Sophia carried within her that made her the way she was, so unsure of herself and concealing a glint of spirit she seemed determined to suppress, but there was no denying Fell's interest in the past of the woman who was to be his wife—and his growing desire to help her see *he* at least could be trusted not to harm her in the way he feared she imagined.

They had almost reached the forge with their strange combination of long strides and ungainly shuffle and as they neared the familiar sight of his cottage tension still coiled in Fell's chest. Anger at the muttered malice towards his mother echoed to combine with his amazement Sophia had spoken against it, an action he couldn't deny—however much he tried— thrilled him as much as it astounded. She'd set aside her usual caution and put herself out for him…although *why* she'd bothered was something he had no way of knowing.

Aside from to ask. Which I have no intention of doing.

He opened the gate he'd wrought himself many years ago, back when he'd been so foolish as to believe it would please Charity each time she turned up the path to their cottage. The memory of her face the first time she'd seen it appeared out of nowhere to catch him unawares, abruptly twisting his insides in momentary pain before fading back into nothingness. The pang was sharp, but he was almost glad of its sting—it reminded him of the folly of hoping for a woman's love, a reminder he was in danger of needing now more than ever with Sophia hobbling at his side. It would be all too easy to lose his head again with such temptation before him, another woman he would need to guard against letting get too close and opening himself back up to the inevitable rejection that had followed him all his life. The only beings who might ever love him for himself were Ma and Lash, he knew with certainty—the former he hadn't seen in months, having left to travel wherever the road took her and the latter now padding towards him with a wiry tail swaying in welcome. *They* were who he should look to for affection and for confirmation he wasn't a wastrel, not a beautiful high-born lady bound to him by fear of her future and a bargain struck for the convenience of both.

'Afternoon.' Fell ran his fingers over the sun-warmed fur of Lash's head in the reflexive movement of a lifetime of practice. The dog squinted up at him with a pink-tongued grin and turned to greet Sophia, nudging her with his long muzzle until she, too, traced the contours of the brown markings by his ears.

'Hello. Did you miss me?'

Sophia's voice was returned to normal now, the curious edge of bitterness left behind on the sweltering road through the village. Whatever she had been thinking at the mention of her mother had been enough to make her shrink a little, unhappiness Fell found he wanted to protect her against, just as she had leapt so unexpectedly to his defence against Mrs Cairn and her coven.

Too intent on her face, Fell didn't realise their hands had met until Sophia withdrew her fingers from Lash's fur with almost guilty speed, snatching her hand away from the dog's head as if he'd tried to bite her. A fresh blush rushed in to chase away her pallor and Fell felt similar heat climb his own neck at the realisation it was her fingers he had stroked by mistake, entirely too absorbed by the complex thoughts turning his brain to custard to pay attention to his movements.

I ought to be more on my guard, he chided himself, watching as Sophia backed away with uneven steps and her hands held to her chest. *If I didn't know better, I'd think I did these things on purpose.*

She stopped just outside the cottage door, throwing him a fleeting look over her shoulder that caught him somewhere beneath his ribs.

'I truly wish they hadn't said those unkind things about you and your mother. I don't know much of your history, but I know enough to re-alise there's nothing of the gutter about you—in fact, far from it.'

Before he could reply Sophia flipped up the latch and stepped over the threshold into the shaded calm of the cottage, leaving behind only an impression of a bright skirt, black hair gleaming in the sun—and a man filled to the brim with hopeless confusion.

Chapter Seven

Ten days passed in the blink of an eye.

The moss-covered gravestone was cool beneath Sophia's trembling fingers as she traced the letters carved into it, feeling the worn contours of a name long since ceased to be spoken. It wasn't one she recognised, but something in the shape of the grand cross-shaped stone reminded her of another grave she had once visited regularly, over twenty-five miles away now, but never to be forgotten. She stood alone in the morning sunshine, not another soul to be seen stirring in the village or on the rough road between the squat old houses, and she cut a solitary figure who might have been the last person left living on earth.

Oh, Papa. How I wish you were still here, today of all days. I might take courage in having you beside me as I walk down the aisle.

Woodford's quaint little church stood proudly before her, but her legs felt too weak to take the final few steps inside. Somewhere behind the old oak doors Fell waited for her, tall and silent beside the rector who would finally bind her to the blacksmith for the rest of her life—and save her from the fate she would run to the ends of the earth to avoid. In less than an hour all *those* worries would be over and she would be Fell's wife, leaving her with an entirely different set of problems to find answers to.

If Papa was still alive, though, I would never have needed to flee in the first place. Mother wouldn't have married Lord Thruxton and my life wouldn't have been blighted by the prospect of Septimus as a husband.

The harsh truth was unavoidable and Sophia squared her shoulders to bear the wave of grief and shame that rose to claim her. There was no getting away from it: she was to blame for all that had happened, as Mother had always said, and the price to pay was a lifetime of guilt slung around her neck.

He should be here. But he's not and it's my fault—and will continue to be my fault whether I loiter here or no.

She took a deep breath, feeling the air fill her burning lungs and press her ribs against the bodice of her dress. It was nothing like the gown she'd always assumed she would wear for her wedding; in her girlish dreams Sophia had been draped in gauzy white, a veil shimmering from her hair and expensive silk gleaming as it caught the light. Instead she was in fresh blue muslin with no headdress to speak of, only a few cornflowers scattered among her black tresses in simple beauty as though she was a country maid born and bred and not a lady desperate to escape a hopeless past.

No giggling bridesmaids accompanied her up the church steps nor proud father escorted her on his arm. It would be a wedding like no gentlewoman had before and yet Sophia couldn't bring herself to regret its lack of glamour. Luxury and wealth had done nothing to bring her happiness, she thought as she gathered all her courage to grasp hold of the heavy iron handle and cast open the door—perhaps by some miracle she might find some here, in occupying the arms of a good man even if not his heart.

Come, then. Take a final glance at the outside world as Miss Sophia Somerlock. I pray as Mrs Barden life might be kinder—and I must endeavour to deserve it.

Fell's back was turned to her as she stepped into the quiet peace of the empty church, the calm silence a soothing contrast to the wild thrum of her pulse. Over two hundred years of whispered prayers and murmured blessings filled the space with a feeling of serenity Sophia clung to like a child might its mother, drawing strength from the stillness as she paused just inside the door. The distance from the porch to the altar seemed suddenly so much more vast than it had the previous Sundays at the reading of the banns, when each week eyes flicked in her direction and lips muttered who knew what gossip at her retreating back. Now it stretched out before her, with no father beside her a lonely journey she had no choice but to undertake all alone. None of the villagers had gathered for the simple service, only the rector's wife and a man Sophia vaguely recognised as a church deacon quietly sitting in the front pew to act as witnesses. It wouldn't have mattered if every seat had been filled, however, for all the notice Sophia took. That long walk and the man waiting at the end of it were the only things she could think of, all else falling by the wayside as anxiety swirled inside her like a crashing tide.

He'd heard her enter, she knew from the hardly perceptible stiffening of Fell's shoulders as he waited for her approach—a subtle movement that caught her eye at once, so attuned was she to every shift of his intriguing frame. It was something she was powerless to control, the instinctive reaction of her body to Fell's presence; a more poetic soul might have described it as a dance of desire, the way she felt herself curve towards him with helpless longing she could hardly restrain. As his wife that longing might finally find an outlet, but still the danger to her heart warned her to stay on her guard.

Recall why this wedding is taking place. Even if Fell seems to tolerate me better than Mother would have thought, that doesn't mean he feels anything for me beyond friendship and pity for a woman in need.

Rector Birch had peered up from his lectern at her entrance and now regarded her impatiently from beneath his heavy brows. Evidently he wished to begin the ceremony as quickly as possible, but there was no chance of that while the bride loitered so fearfully at the end of the yawningly empty aisle. He frowned slightly and Sophia tried to spur her stubborn legs into stirring, but they wouldn't obey and for a horrible moment she wondered if she would ever move again. The passage through the church was just so long, so barren in its friendless length—how could anybody be expected to traverse it alone, she thought with desperation, with nobody there to offer a steadying hand—?

Fell looked over his shoulder and took in the set pallor of her frightened face in one swift glance. Apparently that was all it took to make up his mind for him, as with only the briefest of hesitations he strode the length of the church and held out his arm.

Sophia glanced from the straining sleeve in front of her—crisp, white and scarcely containing the muscle beneath—to the rector's frown and back again, her voice a hiss of alarm in the silent church. 'What are you doing?'

'You've no father here to give you away, so I'll do it myself.'

'You intend to give me away…to yourself?' She peered up at him, the mention of Papa a brief sting as she fought the urge to seize hold of the burly forearm and hold it tight. 'Is that not a little unorthodox?'

Fell shrugged, his heart-stopping smile of wry amusement suddenly the only thing Sophia could see in the sunlit space between them. 'Isn't *everything* to do with this wedding?'

He was right. Nothing in what was about to happen was something either of them could have foretold and yet there they were, about to step out into the unknown and take whatever future might be destined for them. All she could say for certain was that with Fell's help she would escape Septimus's wrath and would in turn strive to be the best wife she could— unorthodox, but necessary, and a slim escape from the misery she knew she deserved.

With tentative fingers she took his arm and felt her face flush rosy as she settled her hand over the swell of muscle. Very soon she would be able to reach for that bicep as often as she chose, if she were only brave enough to do so, and the thought was one that stayed with her as together the lady and the blacksmith marched forward to meet their fate.

Fell hardly heard Rector Birch as he tonelessly ambled through the service, as usual more interested in his own voice than anyone else's. All Fell could truly concentrate on was the pale face of the woman beside him, her eyes demurely cast down and her pretty lips barely moving as she all but mouthed her vows—giving the name Somerlock, not Thruxton, both to honour her father and escape those with evil intent. Both sounded just as sweet to Fell, although she could have been saying *anything* for all the words were able to penetrate his wonder.

He hadn't seen her all morning, deliberately

keeping out of the way as she performed the fe-
male mysteries of a bride on her wedding day,
and now she was before him the most curious
lump seemed to have risen in his throat.

If I thought she was lovely before, she's man-
aged to surpass herself today.

The blue dress wasn't one he could recall
having seen Ma wear, perhaps hidden at the
very bottom of the trunk of folded gowns. It
fitted across the shoulders and bodice as if it
had been made with Sophia in mind, dropping
from beneath her ribs to form an azure puddle
at her little slippered feet. Cornflowers winked
at him from among her shining hair, the only
ornamentation she wore and yet needing nothing else to enhance the raven waves. She didn't
look high-born and haughty. Instead, she suddenly struck Fell as something he'd seen in one
of Rector Frost's books many years ago now, but
a picture that had lodged itself immovably into
his mind. It had been an illustration of an angel
with wings outstretched, her clothing simple
and her serene face lit by light that seemed to
come from within herself. Sophia's face wasn't
quite as tranquil, small white teeth occasionally worrying at her lower lip as if in anxious
thought, but her porcelain beauty was the same
and it made Fell swallow to realise she, too,

seemed bathed in some unearthly glow. Perhaps it was the sun streaming through the windows above—or perhaps it was something else, the beauty of her face and the equally good heart he knew beat inside her, lending radiance to the woman only moments away from becoming his wife.

I never thought the day would come when I'd stand up and pledge myself to another, not since Charity slipped through my fingers like water. It's a shame Ma isn't here to see this miracle— I don't think she'd believe it, either.

He stole another glance at Sophia out of the corner of his eye, drinking in the clear line of her profile and solemn crease of her brow with something like wonder. Now the moment was upon them it seemed like a dream. Surely the idea of a woman like Sophia joining with him for ever was something too strange to be true— but it was she who had suggested it, he thought again with frank disbelief, and she who had chosen him as her future. Together they would start a family based in truth, without secrets and shame lurking in the shadows, a prospect that made his insides twist sharply and without warning. Sophia would never love him or feel the dangerous stirrings that taunted Fell whenever he saw her smile or watched as she gently stroked Lash's ears, but she was prepared to give him the most precious gift and one thing he had always wanted: legitimate children and people he could call his own.

Her sacrifice might drive away the tension Ma's visits brought with the reminder that he was neither fully Roma nor otherwise, the question of his heritage perhaps somewhat soothed, and for that he resolved to repay Sophia time and again with the kindness she'd apparently never known. If his feelings for her were blossoming from regard to something more, he would make sure she never knew it—only unhappiness for both of them the reward if he were to let his disloyal weakness slip.

Rector Birch nodded at Sophia's whispered vows and turned to Fell, only half-listening to the words that would unite two people from completely different worlds to try to make a new path together. It was a service the rector had performed more times than he could count, although Fell had no doubt the older man's attention would be more acute if he knew how unusual a couple stood before him. Sophia's humble disguise had served her well, however, as there was no trace of recognition that all was not as it seemed as Rector Birch gestured for Fell to produce the ring.

A flicker of self-conscious apprehension passed over him as Fell retrieved the band from the pocket of his waistcoat and weighed it in his palm, not for the first time wishing it was more elaborate.

She must be used to wearing jewels I've never seen the like of, he thought as he looked down at her flushed face, even now a little uncertain at his hesitation.

Sophia's eyes followed every movement, seaglass—green stretched wide as he straightened his fingers and allowed her to see what nestled in his palm.

Her darkened brows rose in surprise and her mouth formed a perfect circle at the gleaming gold ring sitting in his warm hand. For a moment she simply stared, before that emerald gaze fixed on his and he saw a hundred unspoken questions flit through it like wind-tossed leaves. If his heart hadn't abruptly leapt up into his throat at the disbelieving appreciation he saw in her face, he might have smiled. Instead he was unable to move as much as a muscle made rigid by the shy delight stealing in to replace her uncertainty. Whatever she'd been expecting it evidently wasn't this: a perfect, dainty ring forged by his own hand from pure gold, the most exquisite thing he had ever made for the most deserving woman he could imagine. The precious metal had been costly to buy, it was true, and infuriatingly fiddly to shape, but every second of frustration was washed away when he took Sophia's slender hand in his own and slipped the ring on to the third finger as if she had been born to be its mistress.

He heard a tiny sound escape her at the touch of his hand and felt a corresponding rush of confusion at the expression that skittered across her face, half-pleased and half-shocked, as though somehow disturbed by the feel of his skin against hers. He wanted to ask her what it meant, that glimmer of *something* nameless but tangible that now hung in the air between them, but the next moment to his shame he realised he didn't dare. Sophia's reaction might be nothing at all, a gleaming haze like a mirage and just as deceptive, and he shouldn't try to coax something from her that would only disappoint his foolish hopes. Perhaps he'd been wrong to pour so much of his heart and soul into her wedding band, yet no reward could be greater than the quiet pleasure with which she moved her finger back and forth to catch the light, the ring a glittering ornament on a woman with no need for such gilding, so brightly did she already glow.

A sensation like fire fled through Fell's

nerves to thrill in each sinew, making it all the more difficult to fight the growing desire to seize hold of her tiny hand again and pull her closer. Soon he would be able to do just that if he chose—but the idea of alarming his bride filled his mouth with a sour taste he tried to swallow back down.

That would frighten her for certain—and I will not have my wife regard me with fear.

All the same, the longing to capture her in his arms called to him insistently, wheedling and whispering his name—until Rector Birch muttered the words that sang in his ears and Sophia turned to him with determination that sparked a fresh blaze in the depths of his chest.

'…and so I pronounce you husband and wife. You may now kiss the bride.'

The rector sounded mildly disapproving, not entirely convinced of the propriety of allowing a Roma bastard to kiss his equally questionable bride in the sanctity of a church, but Fell had no attention to waste on anything other than Sophia's flushed face. The rector, the witnesses, the empty pews and the peaceful stillness of the ancient church were nothing but indistinct shadows as Fell took Sophia's peach-soft cheek in his hand, bent down—and settled his mouth on hers.

It was a relief to touch her, to feel her warmth against him again as he had that night in the moonlit forge when she had come to him and set in motion the events that would change his life for ever. He brought his arms around her without even realising he had moved. Of course the changes had begun before that, he realised distantly somewhere in the back of his mind, too intent on drinking in every second of contact between his lips and hers to allow for any distractions. He hadn't known it at the time, but surely the real beginning was the moment he found Sophia in the forest, her eyes wide with fear and the wan beauty of her face piercing his defences like an arrow. How could he have guessed that same woman would become his wife, now bound to him until parted only by death?

Sophia swayed slightly in his arms but didn't pull away, accepting the gentle questing of his lips with a tiny sigh that dropped dynamite into Fell's chest. The relief of kissing her again should have helped quench the flames that leapt inside him yet that breath only stoked them higher, not enough cool water in the world to douse the conflagration that raged while she stood within the circle of his arms.

He felt the creep of one tentative little hand on the flat muscle of his back and couldn't suppress a shudder of sensation at the exploring fingers roaming a landscape left bereft of touch for more years than he could count. The last woman he had held against him and breathed in her scent had been Charity, who returned his kisses with robust enthusiasm; Sophia was more hesitant, still so inexperienced and unsure, but there was a curious spark beneath her innocence that made her go on, finally surrendering entirely to Fell's clever mouth and half-swooning in his firm embrace. The little hand explored higher, ghosting over lean ribs and tracing the stacked column of Fell's spine while he held her close, the secret lines of her slender body separated from him by only the flimsiest of blue muslin and smouldering beneath his fingertips.

Something inside him stirred like a wild animal waking from its winter sleep, raising its head and blinking in the first sun of spring as he summoned his courage to drop a hand to her waist and feel its heated span with a burning palm. Still Sophia didn't flinch from him, a realisation as startling as it was welcome—wasn't she shocked to find him so ardent, her high-born sensibilities offended by his commoner's advance? Perhaps he ought to break the kiss before he strayed too far and discovered the limits of his new wife's tolerance, before the working of his tender lips prompted a frown rather than green eyes closed in something akin to enjoyment—

But no action on Fell's part was necessary.

'I imagine that's quite enough, Mr Barden.'

At the sound of the rector's affronted voice Sophia froze in Fell's arms, her languid posture straightening at once and eyes snapping open to stare up at him with mortification that couldn't have been more clear. Her face flooded scarlet and she took an unsteady step back, shattering the connection between them and pressing one hand to the front of her heaving bodice to lay flat against where her heart—if it was anything like Fell's own—must have been bounding in a rhythm all its own. With her lips still parted, pink and petal-soft, and her breath coming quickly she looked so irresistible Fell could have elbowed the rector aside and taken her face in his hands once again.

But I won't.

Fell swallowed down what felt like a lump of broken glass trapped in his dry throat and tried to force a smile for the brand-new Mrs Barden.

Whatever just happened was surely a result of the moment and one I took too far.

Sophia might not have pushed him away, but that didn't mean she'd appreciate a repeat of his actions, straying as they had dangerously close to uncovering the forbidden desires of Fell's heart. Now they were man and wife and would have to live together it was more vital than ever he kept his true feelings towards her hidden, the unveiling of sentiment Sophia would never return only making living together unbearable for both.

She's my wife now and I am her husband, but I can never forget how little I deserve her—or hope she might ever come to truly care for a fatherless blacksmith with nothing to offer but the safety of a wedding vow.

Sophia barely lifted her eyes to his as they signed the register, her hand quaking a little as with a stroke of the pen she threw her life into his keeping. His own fingers were more steady, the bold signature Rector Frost had helped him to devise as a young lad standing out proudly in glossy black ink on the page that tied him to his refined new bride. The witnesses signed likewise and then it was done: in less than an hour Fell had gone from a single man to a husband with a whole world now opened up before him, the prospect of a family to call his own now within his grasp.

The woman to thank for his good fortune hovered at his side like a periwinkle ghost, her face pale but for two bright spots of colour that blazed on her cheeks. She glanced across at him, a swift cut of her jade eyes, and he could have sworn he caught a glimmer of relief pass over them as she saw his reassuring smile.

It's my job to care for her now, starting from this moment—I could begin by helping her to stop looking like a rabbit caught in a snare.

If she felt a stab of regret for what she'd just done, there was no way back now, he thought as with a nod to the rector he held out his arm. Both he and Sophia had signed their existence into the hands of the other and they had no choice but honour that commitment, regardless of any uncertainties and fears that might swirl inside two stomachs. The gentlewoman and the half-Roma would have to learn to deal together, and the look on Sophia's countenance told Fell she had just reached the same conclusion.

'May I escort you outside, Mrs Barden?'

Her blush deepened, but Sophia slipped her hand into the crook of Fell's arm and allowed him to lead her back up the aisle he had guided her down not long before. She still limped a little on her injured leg, but her back was straight, her shoulders square with the perfect poise of a fine lady, and for the first time Fell felt a rush of pride suffuse him that caught him unawares.

By what miracle did he have holding his arm an elegant woman with a kind heart, who might pass those qualities to his sons and daughters? Surely there was no man alive that could look at Sophia and not feel a pang of envy for her husband, a notion Fell had never considered. For the first time in his life his position might inspire jealousy, a realisation so novel he had to fight the desire to utter a dry laugh.

He pushed open the heavy door of the church with a flourish and drew Sophia out into the blinding summer sunshine. The light glanced off her silken hair and he stopped to admire it, wishing he could run his fingers through the sun-warmed strands when he heard his name called in earnest.

'Barden! Barden, will you come with me to Down Farm? It's a matter of urgency!'

Both he and Sophia turned to see a young man running towards them on the road that led out of the village to the fields beyond, kicking up clouds of dry dust as he hastened in their direction.

Fell drew his dark brows together, regarding the man as he drew alongside them with his face red and breath escaping in short pants.

Winters the farmhand? What does he want? Any simpleton can see this isn't the moment.

'I've just been wed, Winters. Surely you wouldn't expect me to come on my wedding day.'

'You have my sincerest congratulations—and you too, Missus—' Winters nodded breathlessly at Sophia '—but it can't wait. The Downs' gelding has fallen and his leg looks a fright: the only person who might save it is you.'

Fell hesitated, suddenly caught. Any other villager wanting a favour would have fallen on deaf ears, but Winters was amiable enough and the idea of a suffering animal was something different altogether. Under normal circumstances he would have left at once, but with Sophia at his side he felt torn.

I can't go running off on our wedding day, yet the life of the Downs' gelding hangs in the balance...

If the young horse's leg was irreparable he would be killed, a sad end to a life so full of promise and a prospect that clawed at Fell's throat.

Sophia made his mind up for him. With a half-smile she disengaged herself from his arm, the place where her hand had been now curiously empty without her touch. 'You go, Fell. It sounds as though you're needed more at the farm than at the cottage.'

'You're certain?'

She nodded, the pretty colour flooding her cheeks only making her more beautiful in the hazy sunshine. 'Of course. If anyone can help that poor creature, it's you.'

There was no time to stop and enjoy Sophia's words; all Fell knew was they filled the space behind his breastbone with heady warmth where once there had been nothing but an achingly lonely void. Her confidence and unquestioning belief in him took him by surprise in the very best of ways—as did that knowing smile—but with Winters waiting restlessly for Fell to follow him there was nothing to do but take Sophia's hand and gently press a kiss on to her knuckles, that glow increasing until she was like a poppy in a garden.

'I'll return as soon as I can. I bid you good afternoon—Wife.'

Chapter Eight

Snakes turned somersaults inside her as Sophia sat by the dying embers of the sitting-room fire and watched her wedding ring glint in their orange glow. The sun had finally dipped out of sight behind the trees that hid the cottage—*her* cottage, now—and the only light came from the fireplace as Sophia took another breath to steady the lurching of her heart.

A wife at last, only not to the man I was intended for—and he can never touch me now.

The enormity of what she had done that afternoon circled her like a savage pack of wolves, the images of Mother and Septimus clawing their way to the forefront of her mind to make their displeasure known. Mother's face was dark with insurmountable rage in the shadows of Sophia's thoughts, elegant features drawn into a mask of ugly fury, and Septimus's cold anger made her shudder as though a cold breeze had swept the room. Even beyond their reach the thought of their reactions bothered her, although nothing could blot out the other object that occupied her crowded mind. At one time it would have been unthinkable for anything to surpass her fear of those left behind at Fenwick Manor, but the events of the day had worked magic to help her look beyond those terrors and focus on someone else entirely.

Fell.

His kiss still tingled on her knuckles as she gazed down at the ring he had wrought himself, huge hands surely struggling to make such a delicate piece and a testament to his skill. Each time she twisted it to feel the smooth metal brush heated skin she recalled his look of concentration as he had slid it into place, a slight crease appearing between his dark brows that she longed to trace with gentle fingertips. Already she had found it difficult to stand at the altar beneath the weight of her apprehension and the desire to curve just a little closer to her new husband, one she'd had to fight hard against; and when he had taken her face in his hands as carefully as if she was made of fine china her legs had almost buckled entirely, only the unshaking scaffold of his arms keeping her upright in his embrace.

She shivered now at the memory of how softly his lips had roamed her own and lifted a finger to touch where a ghost of that sensation still lingered. If Rector Birch hadn't intervened, who knew how long Sophia would have stayed rooted to the spot in dazed delight as Fell taught her a lesson she hadn't known that she hadn't known: how good it could feel to be beneath the spell of a handsome man with a clever mouth and hands big enough to cup the entire span of her scalding waist. It was a lesson she'd learned gladly at the time, although as the afternoon wore on into evening Sophia's misgivings increased with the lengthening shadows.

He'll be back soon and then we will have to begin it, our life together, starting with what happens tonight.

Her cheeks burned hotter than the stirring coals at the thought of what was to come when Fell's heavy footsteps returned from Down Farm. He would claim his rights as a bridegroom on his wedding night, just as she had sworn he could on the night she had brokered their engagement…whatever *exactly* that would turn out to mean. More fortunate young brides might have been tactfully informed by a loving mama of what to expect, but Sophia had no such thing, only the vicious entity that was Mother, and Lady Thruxton would sooner have thrown her best pearls into a river than do anything to help prepare her daughter for what was to come. All Sophia's knowledge—and there was precious little of it—was vague at best, only that sharing a bed was a necessary evil all women must endure for the making of children like those she had promised Fell as payment for her safety. Aside from her promise it was essential to ensure the unquestionable validity of their marriage, husband and wife in action as well as in name, and having come so far there was no way Sophia could fall at the final hurdle of escaping from the fate Mother had wanted for her.

The mantel clock ticking companionably in the silence showed past ten and, despite the unease in her stomach, Sophia felt her eyes growing heavier. The day had been long and draining in its high emotion and, with a nervous glance at the cottage's front door, she rose to her feet. Fell should have returned long ago; something must have happened to delay him and sitting up all night in front of a cold fire would do nothing to dispel the apprehension making a nuisance of itself. She might as well retire to bed and await her fate in comfort, she thought as she crossed the darkening room—if not with an easy mind.

By the time a quiet knock came on the bed-chamber door Sophia's eyelids had drooped and the first whisper of sleep had begun to call softly, but the gentle tap sliced through the silence like a knife and she sat up at once, heart leaping to bound inside the confines of her ribs.

'Fell?'

The door opened, the tell-tale squeak of the hinges barely audible to Sophia above the sudden rush of blood in her ears as Fell stepped noiselessly inside, carrying a guttering candle that cast rippling shadows across his tawny face.

'I'm sorry I was away for so long. Everything that could have gone wrong did and there was no possibility of me leaving before now.'

Sophia nodded, her throat contracting into a tight knot and her pulse skipping as Fell placed the candle beside the bed and peered at her through the gloom, odd eyes glittering in the feeble light.

'Are you well?'

Again, no words were willing to present themselves and Sophia could only incline her head in what she hoped was agreement. Beneath the scrutiny of Fell's mismatched gaze her nightgown felt curiously inadequate to shield her, too thin to hide the lines of her body from him, yet she couldn't summon the power to haul a blanket up to cover herself. In the heat of the summer night she'd kicked them away, so it was with nothing but a wisp of linen between them that Sophia watched her new husband begin to unbutton his now rumpled shirt.

'I can't pretend that's how I imagined we'd spend our wedding day—you alone here and me up to my elbows in things I don't think you'd appreciate my describing.'

'Think nothing of it,' Sophia finally managed to croak out. Possibly she should have ventured something more, but her attention was too fixed on the downward progress of Fell's hands on the buttons of his shirt to muster a better response. With each movement another sliver of hard chest was unveiled, a mesmerising display Sophia couldn't seem to drag her eyes away from. The dull beat of her pulse increased another notch, racing against itself as finally the shirt hung loose and Fell shrugged it off with a roll of his sculpted shoulders.

'Even so, I'll find a way to make it up to you. Not the best of starts for a marriage, I think you'll agree.'

Fell flicked her a smile that made any chance of reply impossible and bent to take off his boots. Once those were removed all that would be left to follow were his breeches…a realisation that sent Sophia hurriedly curling on to her side with her eyes set firmly on the wall beside her head and blessing the darkness of the room to hide her scarlet cheeks.

In the light of the dancing candle Fell glowed like a bronze statue, shifting shadows playing across the peaks and valleys of work-honed muscle and tempting Sophia to stare with un-ladylike fascination. Once the breeches joined the shirt crumpled on the floor there would be nothing left to hide, a thought both intriguing and terrifying that dried her throat as though she'd thirsted for a week.

There came the sound of final rustling behind her and then the bedchamber was plunged into full gloom with the extinguishing of the candle. Sophia felt the mattress dip as another body lay down on it and closed her eyes briefly in a silent prayer for the wisdom to know what on earth to do next.

They lay together, neither speaking into the silent night. Sophia felt every sinew tense as she listened for any movement at her back, any tell-tale sign of her husband's approach, but the unfamiliar warmth of another person in her bed was the only indication of his presence, creeping towards her to run a soft finger down the length of her spine as she waited, barely breathing, for his advance.

But none came.

Sophia allowed the moment to stretch out like a delicate thread, pulled tight as a bowstring in the quiet room. The only sound was that of Fell's steady breathing, its calm regularity something Sophia envied as her own breaths came shallow and swift.

Is something amiss?

With an unpleasant thrill it suddenly occurred to her that he might not even be intending to make an advance—a mortifying thought that made her freeze further. Could it be he shied away from the idea, steeling himself to do something he had no desire for? Her mind reeled back to revisit the church, when he had taken her in his arms and set his lips across hers to send a burst of wild flame beneath her heated skin. He hadn't seemed disgusted then at least, something that should give her courage; so with her heart in her throat she forced herself to roll over and turn to him in the darkness, cutting the bowstring of silence with stubbornly swallowed fear.

'You needn't worry for me. I know what we must do.'

She could have sworn she heard the raising of a dubious eyebrow.

'Do you?'

'Of course. To secure our marriage so nobody may try to unpick it later. And I remember my promise to you…the children.'

There was a pause. Now her eyes had grown used to the darkness Sophia could just make out the shape of Fell's fine profile silhouetted against the moonlit curtain, his firm jaw and curling black hair making her fingers clench on the desire to reach out and touch.

'I know you're still a maid. I didn't want to frighten you and I know this must be a difficult step. For a lady to lie with a blacksmith…' He tailed off, the outline of one solid arm coming up to rest behind his head and throw the contours of his chest into hypnotic relief. Lying this close was a temptation like nothing Sophia had ever known, her hands itching to trace the geography of muscles she'd so far only been able to stare at with eyes that refused to turn away.

'I'm not afraid.' Her voice rose a little on the obvious lie and she heard the soft swish of Fell's hair on his pillow as he turned his head in her direction.

When he spoke it was so gently the nape of her neck prickled with sensuous delight. 'It needn't be a duty, something you dread. It's necessary for the reasons you gave, aye, but if you allow me I can show you there are far worse things to endure. You might even find you enjoy it.' He stopped, seeming to want to say something more—and then every nerve in Sophia's tense frame exploded with sensation as a warm hand found hers and the thumb swept across her knuckles to leave a blaze of heat in its wake. 'May I?'

Sophia bit back a gasp at the touch of his skin, reigniting the fire that had leapt within her at his kiss in the church. The embers of it had glowed in her stomach ever since and now, with every pass of his thumb over the sensitive ridge of her knuckles, the ashes were stirred back into crackling flames that burned her from within. She stared wide-eyed through the gloom, just able to make out Fell's equally intense gaze locked on her face—and spoke the only word necessary to unleash the full force of the conflagration's fury.

'Yes.'

As soon as the word dropped from her lips Fell's hand was on her waist, his palm pressed to the warm curve draped in thin linen. His thumb now brushed the lowermost rib that encased her pounding heart and the movement would have made her sigh had Sophia not gritted her teeth to restrain it.

For a moment she was afraid Fell had heard how her heart slammed against her breastbone with each beat, for he stilled with his hand in place and his eyes seeking hers in the darkness.

'I'll not hurt you, Sophia. You can trust me for that, if nothing else.'

She tried to reply, to find some answer for the reassurance so unexpected and touching, but the strong fingers had found their way to her back and were drifting over the joints of her spine like explorers traversing a strange land. Their relentless march moved higher, capturing the crest of her shoulder and along the white length of her neck to trail sparks behind them, not stopping until they reached her cheek and cupped it with gentleness it still surprised her to find Fell possessed. She couldn't help a shiver then, knowing what was to come next—but it was one of pleasure, not disgust, and when Fell's lips came down to touch hers every other thought was chased from her mind to leave behind only the instinctive desire for more.

Her arms reached for him as if they had a will of their own and something inside her leaped at the low rumble she heard come from his throat as her hands made contact with his bare chest. It was warm, and hard, and so broad Sophia could hardly comprehend it, the terrain beneath her fingertips sculpted by hammer and fire no pampered gentleman could boast. His other hand slid between her waist and the mattress and pulled her closer, shrinking the gap between them, but not for a moment breaking the movement of their questing lips.

Like two halves of the same puzzle they fitted against each other with effortless ease, legs tangling in the blankets kicked to the end of the bed, but neither with a thought to spare for something so irrelevant as comfort when the most primitive longing seized each in its grasp and squeezed until both sets of lungs were burning.

Somewhere, shoved into the darkest recess of Sophia's pleasure-drunk mind, a note of caution attempted to battle against the blissful dance of Fell's lips on her tingling skin.

Perhaps some restraint might be better.

The voice was almost lost in the roar of blood that coursed through her veins as Fell's hand slipped from her waist to cradle the intimate plane of her lower back and draw her closer still.

Recall this is a necessity for him and not a

choice. It would be unwise to show true depth of feeling when it cannot be returned.

The voice was right. Of course it was. The murmured warning rang true, but Fell chose that particular moment to deepen the kiss and drink Sophia in as though she was all he needed to stay alive, a lifeline for a desperate man with nowhere else to turn. Try as she might to heed the cautious mutter, Sophia couldn't stop her mouth from opening wider to allow the tip of Fell's tongue to trace its contours, a skilful flutter that dragged a gasp from her and set him smiling against her flushed lips. It was a mistake to display her longing for his touch so brazenly, pitted as it was against the knowledge no man would care for her if he knew the truth of what damage she'd wrought all those years before, yet all good sense fled from her as she trembled in the blissful prison of Fell's arms as though she suffered from an ague.

He drew back and she caught the vague shape of his hand moving to run through his tousled hair, the breath she felt on her cheek now fast and uneven. She could smell the good scent of him, the unique clean musk of a man closer and less decently dressed than ever before, and the stirring in her innards increased tenfold.

'Can I—?'

Fell's voice was low and hoarse, the want in it making every hair stand on end as he took the hem of Sophia's thin nightgown in his fingers. Even in the depths of her desire some part of her marvelled at his restraint, this consideration for her feelings surely few men would show in the grip of such a moment, and she could do nothing but nod wordlessly for him to continue his breathless exploration of her unmapped skin.

He drew her nightgown up over the swell of her hips, following its progress with the softest graze of his fingertips that made Sophia buck quite unconsciously against the granite column of his body. One hand still anchored the small of her back, making escape impossible, but Sophia had no wish to flee the sensations that overcame her as with a fluid movement Fell slipped the gown over her head and flung it in the vague direction of the floor.

With nothing now between them Sophia heard Fell's ragged sigh, the untamed sound of it tearing at her and sending fresh heat to shatter any last thought of restraint. Both arms came around her now, Fell's lips seeking her own once more with renewed passion that would have taken her breath away had she any to spare, and she gloried in the scalding pressure of his hard chest on hers. Every movement, every heartbeat, every breath brought her closer to the man she'd watched for weeks with a growing fondness for which she'd had no name—but as she lay with him in the warm night with his hands drifting to count her ribs she knew what it was.

I think I may be starting to love him.

She stilled, eyes flaring open in the darkness to make Fell's fingers pause in their journey sliding upwards across her heaving ribs towards somewhere much more interesting.

'Is something wrong?'

She heard the note of concern managing to fight its way through the fog of Fell's desire, his consideration for her comfort only reinforcing her sudden realisation. Even with a naked woman in his arms his courtesy won out, his worry for her so unfamiliar, yet the very thing she'd longed to experience since she was a little girl.

'Shall I stop?'

Sophia hesitated, the new truth she couldn't deny ringing alarm bells to chime above all other thought. She was playing with fire now, walking a fine line between keeping her promise to Fell and allowing her blossoming feelings to hold sway and surrender to the pleasure of being held in his strong arms. A truly sensible woman would break free, put distance between herself and the man who would never love her back—but instead with all the courage she possessed Sophia took Fell's hand and placed it where her heart fluttered like a bird in a cage.

'No.'

I can worry about that in the morning. For now, I just wish to enjoy tonight.

With hazy sunlight filtering through the curtained window Fell buried his nose further into the heap of rose-scented hair spilling across his pillow. The warm shape in his arms stirred and without thinking he gathered it closer against his chest, fingers skimming a soft-skinned stomach that quivered at his touch. Usually Charity would giggle at his tickling fingertips, but this morning she seemed strangely quiet beneath his wandering hands…

Because it isn't her.

Fell's eyes snapped open to take in the dyed black tresses and glowing face of Sophia, worlds apart from the last woman he had awakened beside. She peeped up at him from amid the rumpled blankets, uncertainty flickering in the depths of her sea-glass eyes as she scanned his for any clue as to his thoughts.

I'm glad she can't see into my mind. I'm not sure she'd appreciate what she found there.

His pulse skipped faster as the events of the night shuffled themselves back into order and presented themselves to him again, a flicker of disbelief underlining each memory that passed through. Opening the bedchamber door to see Sophia's candle-lit face peering back at him from the bed; how her eyes had stretched wide with flattering—and unexpected—fascination as he unbuttoned his shirt; the soft words she'd murmured to give him leave to approach and finally…

Finally, quite frankly the purest, most natural experience of his life, when his uncertain new wife had melted like butter into his embrace and he had felt her beneath him, all around him, everywhere as though consumed by her essence. She'd kept the promise he had wondered if she would be able to endure and gone further than he ever could have dreamed, her breathy sighs and the sensation of short nails gripping his shoulders coming back to him to stir his insides. He could still feel their sharp pinch now, lying in the warm untidiness of the messy bed—but that wasn't what bothered him as he mustered a smile for his waiting bride.

I think I'm in trouble.

A new feeling was slowly rising, gradual but insistent as a dripping tap. Just like a stray drop of water the puddle was small now, but left unchecked it would spread and deepen until it became a river and, the same as Fell's weakness for Sophia, after last night in real danger of becoming a flood. Her sweet surrender to him in the darkness might be the final nail in the coffin of his determination to remain immune to her unwitting charms—for his own good.

'Good morning. Did you sleep well?'

Sophia's cheeks flared, the dusky colour calling for Fell to run a finger over their softness as he had only hours before as she clung to him in wordless abandon. The thought made the stirring in his innards all the more intense and he had to take a moment to collect himself before he replied.

'I did. It's a welcome change to sleep in a bed again after weeks on the forge floor.'

A hesitant smile curved Sophia's lips and she tucked the blanket round her a little tighter, fastidious as any lady arranging an expensive gown. 'Well. You won't have to go back to doing that now, I think.'

It was an innocent enough remark, but one that found its way through his defences like an arrow to a target. She spoke as a real wife would to her husband, as if sharing a bed was the most normal thing in the world, and once again Fell was assailed by the surprise that overwhelmed him when he woke to find Sophia nestled in his arms.

She isn't repulsed by my presence—not now and not last night. She had every reason to find our intimacy unpleasant and yet...unless she's a very good actress, she seems...curiously unmoved...

Slowly more details of the hours before dawn crept back to filter into Fell's mind, a procession of pictures and sensations he had to take care didn't show on his face. It was true—Sophia hadn't been disgusted by his approach, only a little shy as might be expected of any maiden, and had even seemed to respond in kind to the advances he'd ventured. He could scarcely believe how natural it had felt to embrace her, carefully drawing her out with gentle caresses to make her sigh—he'd held himself in readiness to stop at her command, but it hadn't come, instead allowing him liberties he never dared dream he might be granted. A more sentimental man might wonder if somehow, against all the odds stacked against them, they might have forged a connection in the warm summer night—but the idea of such a thing was too tempting to allow. Surely only disappointment awaited Fell if he continued down that path?

'You could bear me to stay another night? I'm honoured.'

That ready blush kindled once again, but Sophia merely shrugged. 'Isn't it normal for a husband and wife to share a bed? I always thought so from my parents' example.'

'That's my belief, although I understand wives aren't always as gracious about it as you. A reason for me to be thankful—at the very least *my* wife won't insist I continue to sleep on a hard stone floor.'

He pushed himself up to lean back against the wooden headboard, careful not to allow the scant cover of the blanket to slip too far. The undulating shape of Sophia hidden beneath it drew his attention at once, a delightful landscape of hills and valleys he had traced with burning hands only hours earlier, and he clenched his jaw on the desire to reacquaint himself with its secret lines. Away from the anonymous cloak of darkness Sophia would object, surely, the dimness of the night having led her into behaving in a way she'd never countenance in the stark light of day.

'*Are* you thankful?' Mercifully oblivious to the ungentlemanly wanderings of his mind Sophia gathered her hair over one pale shoulder and shot him a suddenly serious glance that showcased her pristine profile. 'You don't regret our marriage? You're quite sure?'

Fell avoided her searching look, his eye landing on the ring winking at him from Sophia's third finger, catching the light that struggled through the curtain. It was a tangible reminder of the step they'd taken together, a joint leap of faith into the unknown, and he slowly shook his head.

Perhaps he *should* regret taking Sophia as his wife. Certainly it was a dangerous move, one that had already affected him more than he liked—or should allow. The lesson Charity had taught him muttered in his ear at Sophia's shy gaze, something innocent and perfect and far too good for the likes of him.

I can't allow last night—and my own foolish weakness—to blind me to the truth. If Sophia guessed my feelings, she'd be disturbed and rightly so; I've nothing to offer but safety from what she ran from and a man like me can't expect anything more.

That made sense. And yet...

She offered him the chance of a family, children who would return his love without hesitation and help heal the tension between him and Ma. For all the risks involved in taking Sophia as his bride that rosy future was something he couldn't turn away from, the answer to the prayers of a lonely boy grown into a man still crushed beneath the weight of his own inadequacy and questions about himself he couldn't answer. Sophia was like an avenging angel sent to save him from his fate—his saviour and potential downfall rolled into one, his passion and his pain with no way of separating the two. The confusion their night together spun was something he would have to work through, the illusion of them having made a connection surely just that. How could it be otherwise, when Sophia represented the very thing Fell knew he would never be worthy of having in truth?

'Of course not. Do you?'

'No.' Sophia twisted her hair into a loose braid, the turn of her head suddenly obscuring her face so he couldn't make out the expression on it. 'I don't regret a thing.'

Chapter Nine

Fell wiped his forehead and with the toe of one boot nudged the rotting tree he had just floored. Many had been damaged by a vicious late-summer storm that had torn through the forest the day before and now they leaned down precariously, dangerously unstable and threatening to keel over with the slightest breeze. Thick boughs lay scattered among sodden leaves and more than one tangle of roots pointed accusingly at the sky, a gaping hole in the ground yawning where the tree had once stood. The once-peaceful forest was now a maze of hazards and until he'd made it safe again Fell had requested Sophia kept away—giving him time to think about things he'd long since imagined settled.

She returned my kisses in the darkness of the night and didn't pull away, and even now she has a smile for me whenever I enter a room. Of all the things I expected of our marriage I never saw this.

But memories of smiles and kisses were by no means all that conspired to make Fell's life complicated.

Thoughts of Sophia's soft words had haunted him ever since she'd uttered them—*I don't regret a thing.* They'd been a throwaway comment, surely, and no more than that—yet he couldn't seem to master the pleasure they stirred at the back of his mind. The unexpected compliment was like a soothing balm for his riled soul, far more pleasant than it had any business of being for all it was damnably confusing. If he was sensible, he'd forget every word and maintain his defences, too canny to fall into the trap even if temptation called to him with determination growing by the day. Sophia's kindness—for couldn't that be all it amounted to?—might so easily trick him into believing she felt more for him than she ever could and surely he'd be a fool to offer sentiment there was no way she'd return.

For the rest of the morning and into the afternoon the sound of metal on wood rang through the trees, echoing around the forest to startle birds and send squirrels scurrying back to their dreys. It was only when his stomach gave a growl of complaint that Fell realised it was long past time for dinner, too absorbed in the rhythm of stacking and chopping to notice how much time had passed or that the clouds above had darkened further into stormy menace. Even so, it took the first drop of rain falling on to his pushed-back hair to make him straighten up and lay his axe across his shoulders, straining against the handle to stretch the tight muscles of his aching back.

He cast an eye over the rough piles of wood, making a note to return later with a barrow to collect them. For the time being he hefted as much as he could carry beneath one arm and turned for home, axe dangling from his free hand as easily as a child might swing a doll. Rain began to fall all around him, pattering through the canopy with increasing force until the heavens opened in earnest and a distant grumble signalled approaching thunder roaring in to accompany the downpour that soaked the back of Fell's shirt. He lowered his head and ploughed onwards, boots stirring the wet leaves underfoot. It wouldn't be long before he reached the cottage and then he could dry off before the sitting-room fire, steam rising from his damp curls as they shone black in the light.

If the sudden flit of a woodpigeon somewhere off to the side hadn't caught his eye, Fell might have missed the wildly tilted tree. Instead he *just* saw it—teetering drunkenly, the ancient oak looked as though it might topple any moment and an unpleasant tingle threaded down Fell's spine at the thought.

Anyone walking beneath wouldn't stand a chance, Sophia included. That tree would come down right on top of them and there would be nothing anyone could do to help.

With a sigh lost to the stirring forest he set down his armful of wood and strode over to the oak, eyes narrowed against the sting of rain. Spending the time to chop through another thick trunk was the last thing he wanted with his stomach growling louder by the minute but the alternative didn't bear thinking about. It would be on his head now if somebody was hurt and hunger was no justification to leave a death trap where anyone might stumble beneath it.

'Good thing I told Sophia not to go walking,' he muttered to himself as he hauled the axe on to his shoulder and looked the tree up and down, deciding where to land the first blow. It was vital he chose the right place to guide the trunk down safely, its huge weight more than able to crush him into the forest floor. Carefully calculating the angle of its descent, he marked the spot with the edge of his axe and then began to swing in earnest, sweat growing on his brow to mingle with the unceasing rain.

The tree was old and took a long time to surrender to the axe, but bit by bit Fell cut through the rings, each telling a year of history in the oak's long life. He felt a glint of regret at having to bring it to a close, but the risk of leaving the tree standing was just too great, so precariously did it hang over a path often used by those passing through. Each swing brought it closer to falling until eventually the trunk gave an ominous crack and the tree began to move, so slowly it was hardly noticeable at first, but for the swish of its wet leaves catching those around it.

Fell stood back to give it room, following its unhurried lean forward with practised eyes. Any moment now it would pick up speed and come crashing down among the moss and soaked grass, a hulking beast of wood and bark quite capable of ending his life in turn if Fell didn't treat it with respect. Fortunately for him he knew better than to stand in its way and surely there was nobody else out in such a storm to be caught in the path of a trunk whistling through the air with deadly force—

But for the bright red dress Sophia was wear-

ing Fell might not have seen her. As it was he
barely had time to watch her emerge from the
scrub and peer around from beneath her soggy
bonnet before her eyes grew round and she
stood quite still, rooted to the spot and gazing
upwards in paralysed terror as the oak swept
through the rain and hurled itself towards the
very place where she stood.

'Sophia!'

His cry rang out above the snarl of thunder
overhead, but he hardly realised he'd shouted
her name as he threw himself towards her. All
he knew was he had to reach her, push her out
of the way even if it meant harm to himself—
and as he closed the space between them and
flung her bodily to the side he thought he could
at least die peacefully in the knowledge he had
traded his life for hers.

Sophia lay on the ground, one cheek pressed
to the cold earth and her arms flung out like a
child's discarded doll. Fell's shoulder had caught
her square in the belly, forcing the air from her
and leaving her gasping for breaths that came
short and painful.

Where is he? Surely he didn't—?

She wrenched herself to her knees, feeling
her head spin with the movement, but pushing

the sensation aside. Mere feet away the knotted trunk of the mighty oak lay defeated on its side, a jagged wound showing where Fell's axe had brought it tumbling down. There was no sign of him, however, and with the coldest dread Sophia scrambled through the mud on her hands and knees to look among the fallen tree's tangled branches.

'Fell? Fell, where are you?'

The leaves were glossy with rain as she parted the boughs and looked desperately for any glimpse of Fell underneath them, searching for a glimpse of white shirt or curling black hair. Sickening fear and a slow creep of hysteria climbed up to choke her, horror and disbelief mixing to make her shake her head in instinctive denial.

No. No. This can't be happening. Not again. Not after Papa.

Could it be? Sophia gritted her teeth on her terror and ripped the branches back with frantic strength. Had she truly caused the death of yet another man she cared for?

She should have stayed away. If she'd listened, done as she was asked, Fell wouldn't have had to leap in front of her and save her from certain death—just as Papa had in a different way, leaving Mother a bitter widow with yet more reason to loathe her unwanted only child. It was history repeating itself in the cruellest way and Sophia felt her fingers grow numb as shock and terror turned her blood to ice.

Why didn't I stay in the cottage? Why did I come to look for him when the rain started?

Fathomless guilt and despair enveloped her in a suffocating cloak and she stifled a desperate sob, still tearing through the branches. Her hands were scratched and sore from the rough bark, but she didn't spare a thought for the pain, their sting nothing compared to the agony of never seeing Fell's smile again.

A low groan made her freeze.

Two long, tanned arms bound in a torn shirt reached out from beneath the trunk, hands digging into the wet ground for grip. The rest of Fell followed them, mud-spattered but miraculously unharmed, and Sophia stared up at him from her crouch on the churned earth as he straightened up with a wince.

'Lucky for me that ditch was there. You'd have been able to use me as a rug otherwise.'

A strangled cry fell from Sophia's lips and she lurched to her feet. Fell stood large as life before her, fully intact and only a little rumpled from his fall, and without thinking she threw herself into his arms.

'I'm sorry. I'm so sorry. You could have… *I* could have…'

She knew she was babbling, but couldn't seem to stop as hot tears spilled down her cheeks. Relief bloomed like a flower, although the choking grip of guilt and fear didn't relax for a moment, sinking its claws into her heaving chest and wringing out each breath.

'You could have died!'

Some distant part felt Fell's arms come round her and cradle her gently against the front of his tattered shirt, her tears soaking into the already damp linen. The rain that fell all around them hadn't ceased, although Sophia hardly noticed it pattering down on her uncovered head, her bonnet lying on the ground where Fell had thrown her out of harm's way. All she could do was cling to him with shaking hands and relish the knowledge that he was alive. He was warm beneath his shirt and his heart beat strongly where Sophia pressed her ear against his broad chest.

Raw emotion ran its course as she and Fell stood together in a wordless embrace, both wonderful and terrible at the same time. Relief so strong it could have brought her to her knees still washed over her like a cool stream, but the spectre of guilt loomed ever larger, its dark presence eclipsing all else until there was nothing it hadn't overwhelmed.

I so nearly struck again with my folly. Just like before.

She stepped back, reluctantly breaking the contact between their bodies, and at once felt the chill of a breeze flatten her wet skirts to her legs. Weak with distress, Sophia wavered, grateful when Fell took her arm in his firm grip but cursing herself for needing his help yet again. Was she always to be such a burden on him, just as she had been for those at Fenwick Manor? It appeared so—without speaking he reclaimed his axe from the ground and turned them both for home, steering Sophia through the trees like a patient dog retrieving a stray sheep.

Each step she took towards the cottage was agony, but not because of the old injury to her leg. Walking with Fell through the grey murk of the storm conjured memories she never wanted to revisit of the first time she'd felt such insurmountable guilt, almost twenty years before but living inside her each day like a malignant force. The awful, life-shattering wrong she had done in the past had almost repeated itself in the present, a ghastly mirror image of the tragedy she'd caused before. Mother had never let her forget her sins and surely Sophia didn't deserve to—she was dangerous, a walking curse, and Fell had no idea what kind of woman he had allowed into his home.

His hand was warm on her arm, but nothing could chase away the chill in Sophia's gut. She didn't dare look up into his face, too frightened of what she might find there to risk a glance.

Perhaps I ought to tell him. He should know what he married, no matter my own shame. It's the least he deserves after all I've done and might again in my foolishness.

She kept her focus on her hands as Fell stoked up the sitting-room fire, although out of the corner of her eye she watched him thrust the poker into the flames. His shirt was soaked through and showed every rough-hewn contour of muscle underneath, a sight both intriguing and painful as she wondered if she'd ever be permitted to touch them again.

With the flames leaping in the grate Fell dropped into his worn chair opposite the sofa where Sophia hunched. The light danced over his skin, glowing bronze in some places while others were thrown into shadow.

'I asked you not to walk in the forest.'

Sophia flinched. Back at Fenwick Manor she would have known exactly what came next. With another sickening rush of dread she screwed her eyes closed, certain what was about to happen and knowing there was no escape. The rage would come now, a blistering stream that would echo for miles and bring tears to run down her blanched cheeks. Mother possessed such a talent for reducing Sophia to nothing more than a sorry heap of remorse, every mistake rewarded by a punishment that always began in just this way, with Sophia trapped and unable to run from the venom about to cut down to the bone.

Her heart was beating too hard and too fast to hear Fell's words, to begin with hidden beneath the rushing of blood in her ears. Waiting for the shouting to start was almost as bad as the punishment itself, a moment that stretched on with horrible menace Mother always seemed to enjoy—

But it didn't come.

'Next time I ask you not to go there, please listen. It was for your own safety and my peace of mind. I'd rather not have to dig my wife out from beneath a fallen tree.' He raised a wry brow that dropped into a frown at Sophia's frozen face.

'Don't be kind to me. I don't deserve it,' she almost whispered into her lap, lips dry and fingers locked tightly together. 'I could have killed you.'

Fell scoffed, stretching his legs out more comfortably towards the hearth. 'It was a mistake. An unfortunate one, I grant you, but a mistake none the less and one I don't think you'll make again.'

Sophia looked up at the nonchalance of his tone, eyes seeking his in the flame-lit sitting room. He looked back, watching her carefully now with a quiet wariness the shake of her head didn't diminish.

He doesn't understand. He's staring straight at me and doesn't truly see.

'It may well happen again. I don't know how or when, but I have a talent for hurting those around me and I never seem to learn. In that respect my mother was quite correct.'

Her actions would have been deadly. Mother had always said Sophia lacked a brain in her empty head and she'd just been proven right once again. There was nobody to blame but herself for what had occurred to tear her family apart, Sophia knew, and she deserved every moment of wretchedness Mother had ever heaped upon her for causing the death of her own father.

Every time she called me useless or stupid

*she was correct. I was a blight on her life and
once I explain Fell will surely think the same.*

'Ah. Your dear, sweet mother. She had more
wisdom to share, did she? Was this as kind
as the other compliment she paid you?' Fell
crossed his arms over his chest, looking for all
the world as though it was Mother in the wrong
and not Sophia.

She twirled the hem of her apron hard between cold fingers, red marks appearing as she
spoke. 'It might not have been kind, but it was
true. I should never have walked out after you
told me not to… I'm so *stupid*. Stupid, useless—'

The apron left sore ridges on her knuckles
and she rubbed at them absently, almost glad
of the pain that flared beneath her fingertips.
It didn't seem fair for her to escape unscathed,
even if she had to administer the punishment
herself, although when Fell leaned towards her
she stilled.

He held her gaze intently, mismatched eyes
boring into hers as if he would hypnotise her
with his stare. 'You made *one* mistake. Nobody
should be cast off for ever because of one mistake and it most certainly does not make you
stupid or useless.'

Somewhere deep down inside her something
stirred. It was the faintest, most unfamiliar sen-

sation and it took her by surprise, its novelty casting a ripple of confusion across the surface of her strained emotions.

What is it? Certainly nothing I can name.

Nobody had ever spoken to her of redemption before, not even once in the long years of her torment. Fell's sweet words were a temptation like no other, so strange and unexpected and yet inviting beyond belief, flying in the face of everything she'd always been told.

Not stupid? Not useless after all?

The desire to believe in them gripped her mercilessly and held on tight. They *couldn't* be true, but the dangerous pleasure of Fell's naive assurance was intoxicating, the stirring inside her growing as he waited for her reply.

'You might not be so sure after I tell you my story.'

Fell slumped back again, clear frustration written across his face. 'Why do you think that? Because of some nonsense of your mother's? I can't imagine what you think you did that was so very terrible it should mark you for life.'

Sophia gripped one hand in the other to stop herself from sinking her nails into the skin. There would never be a better moment to confess to her husband *exactly* what terrible thing she'd done and yet she still shied away. It would shame her to nothing and lay bare the worst, the *very* worst mistake of her entire life, but Fell had been willing to give himself up for her and he couldn't be allowed to remain ignorant of how little she deserved his chivalry. His belief in her would be put to the test and she could only hope he wouldn't withdraw completely when he learned the truth.

She took a breath, heart pounding with sick fear, but her lips betrayed her all the same.

'What if I told you I killed my own father?'

Fell had taken hold of the poker again, meaning to stir the glowing flames, but he stopped with it hanging from one scarred fist.

'Your father? What do you mean?'

'Just what I said. By my actions I killed him—or as good as.'

'That can't be true.'

Sophia swallowed hard, seeing the horrified set of her husband's features and almost wishing she could bite back the words. It was as though she'd opened Pandora's box, however. They were out in the world and couldn't be put away again, only this time there was no hope left behind to balance the other evils that escaped.

'What happened?'

The poker lay forgotten on the floor as Fell

turned to her, disbelief in every line that she wished she could keep for ever. Surely once he had heard her story he wouldn't want to sit before her any longer, no doubt retreating to the forge or elsewhere she couldn't follow, and she would have to rely on her memories for the picture of his face showing anything other than shock.

'Are you sure you want to know?'

'I am.'

Fell's voice was low, although Sophia was sure she caught a note of caution creep beneath its deep cadence. She risked a swift glance at him sitting on the other side of the fireplace, huge and immovable in his chair and his face set like a granite carving as he waited for her to begin.

She laced her fingers together on the bright skirt of her gown and surrendered to her fate. There would be no going back once she started, no pulling away from the memories of the life she'd left behind that still reached for her with spectral hands. But it was her own fault she had to tell this tale; nobody else had almost claimed Fell's life that afternoon, or left havoc in her wake many years before.

'I've never had an easy relationship with my mother. She loved my father to distraction and always resented my being born as a rival for his affection. Although she hid the fact from him, I always knew I was to blame for her troubles; I was an unwanted embarrassment to her, so spirited she didn't like me to mix with the children of our society in case I shamed her. It was so lonely in that big house all alone for much of the time. Papa travelled a lot and Mother didn't like to spend time with me, understandably, so despite her orders I sought out companionship wherever I could find it. I had more courage in those days.'

The fire flickered in the grate and Sophia kept her eyes trained on the whirling orange tongues. Rain still hurled itself against the windows and a far-off rumble of thunder made Lash whine uneasily at her feet.

'My only friend was a gardener's little girl. Her name was Letty and I met her one day quite by chance in the grounds around our home. It was wonderful to have a playmate at last, even though we both knew we had to keep our games a secret—Mother would have been outraged I'd befriended a servant, although I confess I received more comfort from poor Letty than I ever did from my own mother—' She broke off, a thin twist of a smile curving her dry lips. A picture of Letty's wan little face swam before her as vividly as if it had been days since she'd last seen her and not fifteen years and more, every detail still fresh in her mind. 'But you must be wondering what this has to do with Papa.'

Out of the corner of her eye she saw Fell's nod. He sat so still he might not have been real, some figment of fancy if not for the tapping of one apprehensive finger on his knee.

'For some months all was well. My new friendship remained undetected and for the first time in my life I knew what it was to have someone to talk to, someone to laugh with who didn't seem to notice my many flaws. Letty and I would meet most days in the gardens and we would play with my dolls and make up stories and all the other things I'd always longed to do with a friend of my own—until eventually, of course, Mother found out. I was punished most severely and the gardener lost his job, which Mother made sure I knew was entirely my fault.' Sophia hardened her jaw for a moment as the memories came back, painful and raw. 'We pined for each other and I felt overwhelming guilt for what happened to her poor father. You can imagine my delight, then, when Letty sneaked in to see me one last time and yet again I disobeyed Mother's orders to go down and meet her—although she left me with a gift neither of us had foreseen. Scarlet fever.'

The tapping finger halted abruptly although Sophia barely noticed. Still focused on the leaping flames her eyes had dimmed, her vision smudged at the edges with what she realised far too late were burning tears.

'Papa returned from business abroad the day I was confined to my bed. He took one look at my burning face and was back in the saddle at once. Mother tried to persuade him to send a servant for the doctor instead, but my father insisted on going himself, terrified at the thought of losing his little daughter and riding far too quickly and recklessly in his desire to fetch me a cure.

'I'm told my mother's screams when she saw his body carried home were so loud it set our foxhounds howling. I was too delirious with fever to hear them, but I'll never forget her face when she told me I'd killed my papa or the knowledge that if only I'd been less headstrong, done as I was told by those more sensible than me, he would still be alive. She made sure I knew it was all my fault and I have lived with that knowledge ever since, while Mother made it her life's work to break my disobedient spirit and make my days as miserable as possible.'

She forced the last of the tale out between teeth clenched against rising grief and shame like a physical blow. If she'd been alone, she might have surrendered and allowed her cry to burst forth, but with Fell in the room so silent and watchful instead she swallowed it like bitter poison that burned all the way down.

For a while neither rigid figure moved an inch, both suspended by the horror of Sophia's words. What flared in Fell's mind Sophia could only guess, her own emotions shrunk to the shard of agony trying its best to lodge in the space between her ribs. Now he knew the truth of her existence surely there was nothing else he could feel for her other than perhaps pity and distaste so strong a lesser man might have broken his promise to her and thrown her into the street.

'Nonsense.'

Sophia peered through beaded lashes, startled by Fell's harsh mutter. 'What?'

'I said nonsense.'

He rose suddenly to his feet and before Sophia had a half-second to react there he was, sitting beside her on the sofa and reaching for her with hands she'd feared she might never feel again.

'Is that truly what you were taught? That

what happened to your father was in any way of your causing?'

His battered hand came to rest on hers and Sophia felt her heart leap up at the entirely unexpected contact. Whatever reaction she'd imagined Fell would have to her story certainly wasn't this—his warm fingers skimming atop her knuckles and an earnest look in his eye. There was no censure there, she saw, with amazement, only sympathy and understanding that confused her beyond measure, stoking her already undeniable weakness for him into full flame. That compassionate look drove a spike of sweet longing deep into her tight-wound chest, surely the only man alive capable of distracting her from the worst of her fears.

'How can you doubt it? You heard my story. I am to blame.'

Still hardly able to believe what she was seeing, Sophia watched Fell shake his head, as firmly and decisively as if he had the power to make the final judgement.

'You are not. Can't you see? It was a tragic accident and nothing more. If we were to follow your mother's logic as to who to blame, the culprit would be her: if she'd spent more time with you, allowed you to have friends, you might not have been forced to take comfort in a gardener's child. If anyone is culpable, perhaps it is herself.'

Sophia felt her eyes widen, behind them still aching with unshed tears. What Fell suggested was close to sacrilege; any criticism of Mother was unthinkable and to imply she might not be the paragon of virtue she had always maintained…

Her thoughts must have shown in her face, as with a wry smile Fell reached up and, so gently it almost halted Sophia's mind in its tracks, wiped a stray tear from her lower lashes with one thumb.

'I know you don't believe me now. I know you think I'm wrong. But will you do me the favour of thinking about what I say? You might even find some sense in it, if such a thing could be believed.'

She swallowed, breathlessly aware of the soft curve his thumb had sketched over her flushed and sensitive cheek. Agitation still flared inside her, disbelief and uncertainty circling like vultures, but from beneath came the faintest flutter of that same stirring sensation he had provoked in her before.

What is it? I didn't know then and I can hardly tell now, either.

The flames dancing in the grate cast half of Fell's face into shadow, but still she caught the gleam of satisfaction there at her hesitant nod. It was the only reply she was capable of making, so dizzyingly did the carousel of her thoughts spin, but it seemed enough for him for now and the stirring grew stronger as with a jolt of amazement Sophia finally realised what it was.

Do you know, I think it's hope. No wonder I couldn't recognise it before.

For longer than she cared to admit she'd lived in the darkness, cowering beneath the shadow of Mother's cruelty and guilt that never released her from its grip. With one touch of his hand Fell had given her reason to think twice, cautiously as though she feared what she might find—but still a notion before now she never would have dared entertain. Nothing could come of it, she was sure...and yet...

He didn't flinch away from me. If nothing else, I ought to be grateful for that.

Strange warmth drifted slowly outwards from Sophia's racing heart to seep through each vein, chasing away where once there had been only ice. Fell's kindness in the face of her deepest shame was nothing short of wonderful, a blessing she still wasn't sure she deserved, and the window into her thoughts must have been crystal clear for her husband as he carefully traced her cold hand.

'Just think it over. You needn't say anything else now. Only...' He trailed off, the smallest suggestion of another smile making Sophia's jangled nerves sit up and take notice.

'Only?'

'I wouldn't mind experiencing a little of that spirit you said you once possessed. I think it would be a beautiful thing to see, no matter what you might have been told.'

Sophia couldn't help a shaky laugh. 'Are you sure about that? Even now you know the trouble it caused?'

'I am. I saw a glint of it that day in the village when you intervened with Mrs Cairn on my behalf and let me tell you—it was nothing of which you should be ashamed.'

He stretched upwards, both arms reaching above his head and a wince crossing his rugged face. 'Now if you'll excuse me I think I'll go to bed. It's been a long day and I ache like nothing on earth.'

Sophia nodded. A sideways glance showed a slice of honed midriff wink from beneath his muddied shirt, still stained from the accident that could have killed him, and the sight and thought sent two very different thrills through her she had no hope of separating.

How glad am I that it did not. There are no words to give thanks for his escape.

Still, that glimpse of the secret geography of his muscles managed somehow to slip past her lingering horror and speak to the part of her so vulnerable to its charms. After the events of the day she wanted nothing more than to be close to her husband, to revel in his warmth and celebrate the simple pleasure of being alive. His goodness in the face of her distress only increased his virtues, another layer of *rightness* laid over him like a cloak. In the darkness of their bedchamber she could fit herself along the broad length of him and feel the sense of safety his presence gave her and in that moment there was nothing she wanted to do more.

Just when I thought he couldn't be more dangerous to my resolve he goes and outdoes himself. How am I to maintain my composure when he threatens it at every turn?

He smiled down at her and Sophia felt her heart turn over in her chest at the dimple half-submerged beneath dark stubble. How was she to resist that face? Or harden herself against the kindness that insisted there was more to Sophia than she herself believed?

The answer, of course, is simple. I cannot.

'I think I'll come with you.' She carefully avoided his gaze, flushing to the very tips of her ears, but powerless to stop her wayward tongue. 'An early night is just what I desire, too.'

Chapter Ten

Sparks leapt from Fell's hammer each time he brought it down on the length of metal bent over the bick of his anvil, the sound of iron on iron making his ears ring. It helped to drown out the ceaseless thoughts that looped through his mind—but only slightly. Nothing could completely obliterate the unwelcome words and pictures that currently assailed him, giving no quarter despite how firmly he tried to set them aside.

Her face when she told me of her father. The tears that welled up in those emerald eyes.

He clamped the glowing horseshoe with a pair of tongs and with a rough movement plunged it into the quench bucket. Normally the hiss and bubble of heated metal hitting cold water was one of his favourite sounds, but with the memory of Sophia's distress hanging in the air he could find scant pleasure in his work.

He'd been careful to conceal his horror and rage at her pitiful tale, determined to wipe those long lashes dry and see if he could coax a smile back to trembling lips. In the velvet night that followed he had seemed to succeed, Sophia drawing close to him and their joining together careful as if to avoid causing her more pain. Only out of Sophia's view did he allow himself to think about her mother's malice, his anger at her conduct towards his wife burning inside him like molten glass.

What the hell can she have been thinking, telling Sophia it was her fault her father died? Of all the vile lies I've heard that must be the worst.

Her vicious harpy of a mother stirred his fury past all endurance, her cruel words something he understood all too well. The power of a spiteful tongue had made itself known to him when he was but a child, the wounds it could inflict festering over the years to leave deep scars. With such venom spat at her, and at only six years old, it was no wonder Sophia had expected him to rage at her mistake and seem surprised when he did not, accustomed as she was to treatment that made Fell's hackles rise. He knew what it was to be taunted and scorned and found the notion of Sophia suffering similar pain almost unbearable.

'It's the first thing we have in common. Shame it had to be something so unfortunate,' Fell remarked darkly to Lash, the dog considering him gravely from his spot beside the open door. It was the habit of a lifetime for Fell to consult his dogs on all manner of things and several generations of scruffy lurchers had found themselves as his only confidants. As a young lad many of the village children had shunned him, encouraged by their mothers not to play with the bastard of the Roma girl Rector Frost had seen fit to take into his household. The dogs were often his only companions in the absence of anyone else—another experience he and Sophia shared, and which once again thinned his lips into a tight grimace.

Who would have thought a high-born lady to be so friendless and unwanted? It's a wonder she bore it as long as she did.

A bold flash of admiration sparked into life. She had endured life at Fenwick Manor for far longer than most would have been able, showing a different kind of strength to the more obvious obstinacy of his own. To withstand ill treatment day after day and still set one foot in front of the other showed a resolve Fell respected, a quiet tenacity in the face of unrelenting unkindness that she didn't deserve—even if Sophia would beg to differ. Clearly she had believed her mother's ridiculous accusation that she'd been the cause of her papa's sorry fate, the claws of such a horrific idea tearing her soul to ribbons and leaving her sure she was a monster. Perhaps she might consider his suggestion to the contrary—or perhaps he had intervened too late, the idea of her carrying her shame for the rest of her life piercing his chest like a knife.

I want her to be happy. If I could only help her see she's worth so much more than she thinks...

Fell held the shoe up and inspected it in the sunlight streaming through one unshuttered window. The rain hadn't lasted long, but had left its mark on the yard: deep puddles stood in the muddy, rutted ground and the air was scented with the dense freshness that always followed a storm. Under other circumstances he might have walked the forest, taking in the new life breathed into the scorched leaves and brown grass, but the thought of Sophia's unhappiness the day before made him pause. He found he didn't want to leave her, the desire to stay close at hand in case she needed him unable to be denied.

The pain in her face was something he never wanted to see again. Somehow she had gradually crept into the very centre of his heart and now unwittingly lived inside him, enhancing each day with her mere presence in his life. After Charity's rejection a measure of fear still prowled through Fell's soul, although surely Sophia was a different kind of woman entirely, possessing none of the laughing cruelty of the first he'd loved… But still his insecurities ran deep, a lifetime of shame and uncertainty as to his very sense of self something he couldn't quite shake.

'To confess my feelings for her would still be a mistake. The very idea is madness. Don't you agree?'

Lash said nothing, although by the way he wisely twitched his ears Fell could tell he understood.

'Precisely. I might only be setting myself up for a bitter disappointment and I don't feel inclined to taste another.'

Again Lash didn't reply—although this time somebody else spoke up from beyond the door.

'Talking to your dogs again, Barden? Why doesn't it surprise me you speak the same language?'

The familiar mocking voice made Fell turn and when he laid eyes on his visitor it was with a swift stab of intense dislike.

'It's the only way I'm assured of a sensible conversation in this village, Turner. Where else could I find a creature with at least some wit?'

The other man scowled and stepped out of the sunlight into the shade of the forge, his doughy face flushed red with heat and bad temper.

'Always so quick with that tongue. It'll land you in trouble one of these days and I won't be sorry to see it.'

Fell wiped his grimy hands on the front of his apron, attempting to stem the rise of his irritation. Samuel Turner was somebody he wouldn't wish to see at the best of times, and even less so while roused by the thought of Lady Thruxton's cruelty and Sophia's distress. He had dogged Fell's stride since they were boys, always ready with some dull-witted jibe about bastards and travellers. Even as a grown man the paunchy farmer still tried to needle Fell whenever he could and it was with a growing difficulty that Fell kept his composure.

'What is it you want? I assume this isn't a social call.'

'You assume correctly. I wouldn't set foot here unless I had good reason.'

At Fell's flat stare the farmer's frown deepened. 'The shoes I commissioned from you Friday last. I need to take them today.'

'They aren't ready yet. We agreed on next week—come back then.'

Fell turned back to his anvil and took up the hammer again, ignoring Turner's angry curse. He couldn't suppress a glint of satisfaction in denying the other man's demand, even if it was the truth: there were few people in Woodford as determinedly insufferable as Turner, an overgrown playground bully with an equally overgrown sense of his own importance.

'You don't seem to understand. I need them *today. Today.* Do I need to spell it out further, so simply even a half-bred gypsy bastard like you can grasp it?'

Still with his back to his unwanted guest Fell hesitated. His blood was beginning to run hotter and surge within him with dangerous force, tempting him to answer Turner's hostility with some of his own. Already piqued from his thoughts of Sophia's suffering at the hands of her mother Fell's temper felt frayed, raw at the edges and easily provoked, but he forced himself to take a deep, steadying breath.

Remember what Ma said. They're just words... Words I'm sick of hearing.

Fell drew in another breath and moved round to look Turner full in the face, seeing he'd stepped closer and was now almost alongside

Fell at the fire. The farmer was shorter than him by at least six inches and far less powerfully built, a low-slung belly contrasting sharply with Fell's work-honed muscles. If Fell abandoned his usual self-control and they were to come to blows, there was no question who would win, a fact that didn't seem to have occurred to the man who glowered up at Fell with piggy eyes. No doubt he thought himself safe—Fell had never risen to any bait and there must seem little danger now in taunting him despite the strength in his arms.

'Well?'

'Well nothing. They'll be ready next week as agreed.'

Out of the corner of his eye Fell saw Lash move closer with the strange, stiff-legged creep of a hunting beast. Turner must have seen it, too, for he backed away a step and cast an angry glare over both dog and master.

'Too distracted by your gypsy woman to complete your work on time? Perhaps I ought to warn the rest of Woodford you can't be relied on any longer, now you doubtless have other… *activities* to occupy you.'

The sensation of being doused in icy water washed over Fell to make him halt in whatever he'd intended to reply. He knew exactly what the other man was implying and it made every sinew in him tense with anger, casting aspersions on Sophia's honour that were grossly untrue. Turner simply wanted a reaction, frustrated at not being able to get his way—but he didn't know how close to the wind he was sailing, his slight against Sophia suddenly bringing Fell's blood to the boil.

'Don't say that.'

'Why not? Isn't a pretty Roma distraction precisely what she is? The same as your mother for whoever your father was?'

Fell smiled, the curve of his lips brittle and his eyes bright and cold. His heart had begun to beat more quickly, almost as savagely as he had hammered the iron laid across his anvil. 'Don't speak like that about my mother or my wife. I'm not in a good humour today and I should hate for you to bear the brunt of it.'

Turner puffed out his chest like a cockerel. 'Do you threaten me, Barden?'

'Do you insult my family, Turner?'

The farmer's face twisted unpleasantly, but for the first time he seemed to realise how poorly matched he was against the simmering rage in Fell's eyes. When he didn't answer Fell nodded towards the door and turned his back once again with grim finality.

'I've wasted enough time on you this morning. See yourself out and find somebody else to make your shoes. I don't need your business.'

He heard Turner's wordless sound of fury, but didn't trouble himself to watch him leave, instead intent on regulating his shallow breathing. The desire to meet the man's malice with a hard blow pulsed through his veins and for a long moment Fell stood with his eyes closed as he tried to force it back.

How dare he say that about Sophia and Ma. If he only spoke ill of me I could take it, but to spit such filth about them—

Lash's loud bark of alarm sliced through his thoughts and Fell spun just in time to bring an arm up across his face, deflecting the poker Turner held in his hand. The corner of it just caught his cheek and he felt a swift sting bloom into vivid pain that dribbled down his face, but he didn't stop to think before raising his own fist and bringing it round to land squarely on Turner's nose.

The farmer reeled backwards, the poker dropping from his grasp to clatter to the ground. He staggered for a step or two, one hand clutched to his face and the other held out in front of him as if it could possibly keep Fell away.

'You've broken it!'

Fell lurched towards him, his fingers itching to grab hold of Turner's lapel and haul him off the ground.

'You would attack a man with his back to you? Knowing he was unarmed and unprepared?'

Turner glared at him above his cupped hand. When he moved it away Fell saw his nose bent at a strange angle and blood dripped from it, more like a scene from a butcher's shop than a blacksmith's.

'Gentlemen's rules don't apply to the likes of you, Barden!'

The edges of Fell's vision seemed to be blurring, clouding over with hopeless rage. His jaw was taut and his pulse leaping, begging him to raise his fists and show Turner exactly what the likes of him could do—just as the other man balled up his own hands, both only hesitating when a shadow cut across the sunlight still streaming through the open forge door.

Sophia's wide eyes flitted from the stranger's face to Fell's, taking in what lay before her. Both men were flecked with blood, she saw with an instinctive twist of her insides, and each stood like a boxer about to aim a heavy blow. The reflexive urge to flee from their fury seized her with cold fingers, recalling the way Mother's features would set into a rigid mask of rage, but the sight of the fresh wound on Fell's cheek stopped her in her tracks.

'Stop this!' She looked again from one to the other, two crimson-streaked faces turning her stomach once again. 'Stop it at once!'

Fell's brows twitched together and his fists dropped a fraction, although the other man seemed less inclined to obey. He shot a glance at Fell, assessing the momentary distraction as though he might take advantage—until Sophia limped over the threshold and stood between them as firmly as she could manage.

'This is no way to behave. If you've a disagreement, you ought to settle it like gentlemen, not savages!'

'Easier said than done when one party *is* a savage.' Turner almost spat the words, although he backed a pace away from Sophia's white face. 'He attacked me without warning!'

She heard Fell's inarticulate sound of anger, but held up her hand, the most severe look she could manage creasing her brow. Whatever fleeting glint of apprehension she'd felt on bursting into the forge was retreating now, instead anger at the stranger's actions and desire to support her husband overtaking her fear. It was the strangest thing to feel protective of a man more than capable of defending himself, but there it was, the same desire that had seized her in the grocer's when she had faced down Mrs Cairn, and now when she spoke her voice was cold.

'That is a lie. I saw you enter the forge and could clearly make out what was happening through the open door. You set upon my husband while his back was turned and if you had any honour you would leave now without another word.'

There was a long beat of silence so tense it could have been shattered with one of Fell's hammers, before the squat man curled his lip.

'Protected by a woman, Barden? You're even less of a man than I thought.'

Sophia saw how the tendons in Fell's neck flexed with the effort of keeping his restraint and laid a beseeching hand on his arm. He glanced down at it and she felt a skewer of something pierce her as a complicated look passed between them like a streak of lightning.

'Mrs Barden is more your saviour than mine. Now you heard her. Get off our property.'

Fell dismissed Turner with a contemptuous jerk of his chin and Sophia watched as the farmer stumbled to the door, affecting to leave of his own volition rather than to escape the disconcerting tic in Fell's clenched jaw.

'I've better places to be than this hovel. But you'll regret this day; I'll make sure of it.'

Lash followed him outside with a low growl and pinned-back ears, leaving Sophia alone with Fell—and too preoccupied by her racing heart and concern that Turner might come back to immediately realise her hand still rested on warm muscle, until a dry laugh brought her back to her senses.

'So that's what you meant by spirited, was it? Perhaps I shouldn't have asked to see the fire in your belly. For a moment I was almost afraid.'

She tried to smile, releasing his arm with a shadow of reluctance. Not only was the shape of his muscles delightful, but they had the added bonus of keeping her upright, something the dripping wound on Fell's cheek called into question as it made her head swim.

Blood. There would have to be blood.

He must have seen her pallor, as he kicked a stool out from beneath his bench and nodded quickly towards it.

'You should sit for a moment. Seeing that must have been unpleasant.'

Sophia eyed the stool with keen longing, but shook her head.

'It's you who should sit. You're injured.'

'Just a scratch. Turner came off worse, I'm pleased to think.'

Fell touched his fingers to his cheek and inspected the blood that stained them, Sophia gritting her teeth on her revulsion. A horrible combination of nausea and apprehension curdled her insides at the scarlet that slicked Fell's face, but she knew what she had to do.

'Come back to the cottage and I'll take care of it.'

There was a flicker of one dark eyebrow. 'I thought you didn't like blood?'

'I don't, but I find I like the sight of you bleeding even less.'

The other brow rose to join its twin, but to Sophia's relief Fell neither argued nor questioned her further, instead following her across the sodden yard and into the shady kitchen without a word.

Sophia saw how her hands shook as she poured water into a bowl and took up a clean rag. Fell sat on a low wooden stool and watched her uncertain activity in silence, his mismatched eyes giving no hint of whatever thoughts were unfolding behind them.

With unpractised fingers Sophia wetted the cloth and took a breath before applying it to

Fell's injured face. Bile rose in her throat at the sight of the blood and she hurriedly tried to distract herself from the nausea clawing at her stomach.

'Who was that man?'

Fell grunted. His forehead creased briefly at the first touch of the rag, but he submitted without complaining. 'His name's Turner. He's delighted in taunting me since we were boys and today he finally went a step too far.'

'What did he do?'

'It's of no consequence. I'd say I hope he's learned his lesson, but men like Turner don't have the brains to learn much of anything.'

There was no doubt more to it than that, but Sophia said nothing as she continued to clean the wound. It wasn't deep, but it bled freely, the water in the bowl growing steadily pinker with each soak of the cloth. Unease still stirred through Sophia's innards, but in truth another sensation had begun to hold sway, one that managed to capture her attention more than her fear of blood. Leaning over Fell with her hands on his face brought them as close as the first time she had brought her lips down on his, in the silent darkness of the forge, and now the temptation to repeat it whispered to her so loudly she feared Fell might hear its voice. His skin was warm and roughened by black stubble that grazed her fingertips with each careful stroke, the friction travelling through her to lodge behind her breastbone. Standing so near, she could catch the scent of the forge that clung to his shirt, smoke and fresh sweat mingling to make a uniquely masculine fragrance more pleasing than any other she'd ever encountered.

What would he think if I were to kiss him again?

The question crossed her mind before she could stop it.

In the darkness of our bedchamber is one thing; what about now? When there's nowhere to hide and he could see my feelings laid out in the light?

Ever since he had comforted her the day before she had wanted to do just that: press her lips to his and take whatever consequences that might bring. He'd been so kind, so quick to offer reassurance she hadn't believed she deserved… She'd thought revealing her past would drive Fell away, but instead his sweet reaction had kindled her feelings for him into brighter flames and now all she desired was to let him know how much that comfort meant. It was still uncertain whether he was right or Mother, but either way his belief in her was something beyond price.

'You're good at this. Gentle.'

Fell's voice took her by surprise, altogether too engrossed in her thoughts. She peered down at him, half-suspecting he was jesting.

'Clumsy, you mean.'

'I meant what I said. You've skill as a healer.'

Sophia blinked, her brow furrowed doubtfully. That particular compliment was the very last thing she expected to drop from his lips—lips she ought to spend less time dreaming about—but she couldn't deny the pleasant warmth it sent spilling through her.

'I didn't know I had skill at anything.'

Fell shrugged. 'Well, now you do. I'll ask Ma to teach you some of her tricks when she returns next—I've a feeling you've a gift for it.'

He closed those odd eyes for a moment, thankfully missing Sophia's rosy blush. The blood fled to her cheeks and burned there, a heated reminder of his words as she turned them over inside her mind. Never before could she recall anybody telling her she was good at anything, let alone something as useful as tending wounds. A novel feeling rose up to smile upon her like a burst of sunlight, one she struggled to name until with a start she realised what it was.

Pride.

The very idea of it was one she felt she ought

to turn away from, yet Fell's low mutter wouldn't be denied.

First hope for my sinning soul and now pride. What will this strange man conjure next?

'Oh. Why…thank you.'

'Aye, well. I should be the one doing the thanking. It took courage to stand between me and Turner, and possibly magic to make him ashamed. I don't know anyone else could have managed it. That was very well done.'

Courage? Very well done?

They were the kinds of things she'd wished Mother would say, long ago when Sophia was a child who didn't yet know any better than to waste her time longing for a day that would never come. Instead, it was Fell who spoke them, unprompted and apparently in earnest, and the glow of hesitant delight Sophia felt occupy her very being was one she had never thought she'd ever feel. A lit candle seemed to have taken up residence in the hollow of her chest, burning there with a warm light she never wanted to snuff out.

Fell's gaze found hers and she saw something in it that made all other thoughts turn to background murmurs.

'Have you given any thought to what I said yesterday?'

She stilled, the damp cloth hanging from her fingers. The worst of the blood had gone from Fell's cheek, leaving behind a clean gash like a tiny curving mouth, but it couldn't tempt her to return its smile. 'A little.'

Liar. You know you barely slept last night for thinking of it.

'And what conclusion did you reach?'

The secret candle's flame flickered a little beneath the cold wind of Sophia's doubt. She held Fell's stare for a heartbeat, but the steady look in his eyes made her glance away in confusion.

Ever since I can remember Mother told me the way things were. I never had cause to question it. Can there truly be something in what Fell says now?

The desire to believe her husband was so strong it almost took her breath away all over again and now Sophia felt her head swim in the same way it had at the sight of blood spilling down his face. It was a face more precious to her than any other, she could no longer deny, and the desire to accept his words once and for all seized her in a punishing grip.

And yet...

She shook her head, still not meeting his eye, and when she spoke she cursed herself for sounding so unsure.

'I still don't know. You were so kind to comfort me yesterday, but you must understand what it's been like for me—to think one thing for all these years and then be told another. It isn't that simple.'

With her gaze trained stubbornly on the floor it made her jump to feel a hand unexpectedly touch her downturned chin and lightly raise it up. Her eyes flew to find Fell's, mouth opening but no words starting from her lips at the explosion of sensation coursing from her chin down her neck to curl in her throat like a river of pure gold.

He watched her for a second; just one second with his fingers to her face as gently as he might cradle a newborn babe, so frank and honest it took Sophia's breath away before he slowly retracted his hand.

'I understand, although I'll say this: what you did today was something no useless person could have done, no matter what your *mother* might say.' There was an edge to his voice so startlingly close to anger it took her by surprise. 'You deserve far more than neglect and contempt. It's time you started to believe it.'

Chapter Eleven

Days blurred seamlessly into each other at the cottage, bright mornings giving way to hazy, sun-filled afternoons, followed in turn by humid nights to begin the cycle again.

As August wore on Sophia's skin became more golden, the sun chasing away the unhappy pallor left by imprisonment at Fenwick Manor and encouraging a smattering of freckles standing proud across her cheeks. The black tint had faded from her hair and once again it shone like burnished copper in the light, a flaming river that ran down Sophia's back with an abandon she'd barely thought possible.

Nobody seeing her now would think she'd been born into luxury, her formerly porcelain face tanned and the bright gown on her back—a gift from Fell she'd blushed to receive and thanked him for far more than was necessary—

more suited to a proud Roma woman than a lady. Even Mother herself might have hesitated before being able to identify her own daughter, changing as she was day by day from the unfortunate creature she had once been into something… else.

Sitting now on the front doorstep, her bare feet soaking in a puddle of sunshine, Sophia examined a callous on her palm with a curious mixture of dismay and satisfaction. The lovely white hands of which she'd once been so careful were more like those of a real maid now, a twist of fact mirroring the fiction she'd once hidden behind. The skin at the base of each finger was rougher, hardened by *actual physical work*— a house wouldn't run itself, she'd realised, and it was with an absurd burst of pride she traced what felt a little like a medal.

Pampered, idle gentlewomen didn't get anything as vulgar as calloused hands; but Sophia would never be one of those ever again, and as she felt the ruined softness it was a tangible reminder of how far she had strayed from her former existence—and how much further she could still strive, now her future might hold more than guilt and fear.

'What do you say, Lash? How many fires will I need to build before my fingers look like Fell's?'

The dog stretched out beside her on the bare earth thumped his tail without opening his eyes and Sophia absent-mindedly ran a hand through his dusty fur. Speaking of Fell reminded her how evasive he'd been about where he was going that afternoon, loping off up the lane out of Woodford with his usual long strides. In his absence Sophia had enough time to fetch more wood for the stove, sweep the kitchen and draw water from the pump—and still he hadn't returned from his mystery errand, leaving her with little else to do but sit with her face turned towards the sun and the summer breeze gently stirring the Titian locks of her hair as she lost herself in thought.

For weeks now the secret she carried had sat inside her like a stone, a weight she couldn't shift no matter how hard she tried. Her feelings for Fell remained as strong as ever, renewing themselves with each smile and touch of his hand until her arms felt as though they might snap from the strain of being so tightly prevented from reaching out and twining around his neck. Each night they spent together was as wonderful to her as the first, the perfect melding of their bodies in a rhythm they worked on with delight that couldn't be faked. More than that: the tiniest thread of hope now wound its way through her thoughts to wonder if his appreciation for her might have grown beyond the physical.

Lash huffed a tortured sigh and turned over, momentarily breaking Sophia's reverie to make her smile. Nothing could distract her for long, though, and within moments her mind was dragged back to the blacksmith who lingered in her dreams as well as her bed.

A few short weeks ago Sophia would have known without doubt she was the creator of her unhappy former life, but now she was no longer so sure. Fell's belief in her had shaken the very foundations of the woman she'd always thought she was, a direct challenge to every cruel word Mother had instilled in her since she was a child. The desire to accept there might be a crumb of truth in Fell's assertion that she wasn't to blame for Papa's death had gnawed at her ever since he had taken her cold hand and sent a flood of fire roaring beneath her skin, a recollection that even now made her shiver despite the glaring sun. Surely a man who lacked any tender feeling for her wouldn't have said those words, or looked into her eyes with such unnamed emotion… It was enough to make her wonder and that wonder took advantage of her longing to make her ache for Fell both in his presence and when he was away. It was an itch impossible to scratch, a yearning like a starving man seeing a banquet just out of reach behind a pane of glass...

The sound of hooves clipping steadily along the lane behind the cottage made Sophia's head snap round, heart immediately leaping to settle into a beat that would have shamed a hummingbird. It was nothing new for a rider to appear, wanting shoes, but each time it reminded Sophia of the nightmarish day Phillips had trotted into the yard as if he owned it and held her future on a knife edge. A wedding certificate safe in the top drawer of the sitting-room bureau had taken all Phillips's power away should he ever return, but still the idea of Mother or Septimus discovering where she had fled made her blood run cool in her veins. Probably she'd live in fear of them for ever, the scars of Mother's cruelty marking Sophia for life and nothing completely erasing the terror she might one day wake up to find herself back in the decadent prison of Fenwick Manor.

She was on her feet and halfway through the cottage door when she realised the identity of the man sitting easily astride the grey mare entering the yard, a sudden flash of heat in her chest registering his face before her brain caught up with her heart. Fell lounged in the saddle as if he'd been born to ride, one hand resting on the reins and the other laid nonchalantly on his broad thigh, and the curve of his lips at Sophia's look of confusion did nothing to slow the racing of her pulse.

'Good afternoon.'

'Good afternoon yourself.' Sophia shaded her eyes with her hand as she squinted up at her smiling husband, noting that he looked uncommonly pleased with himself. 'I see you've brought a friend home for dinner. Whose horse is this?'

'Yours now. If you want her.'

'Mine?' Surprise made Sophia's voice a little higher and Fell's grin widened.

'Yes. Well, mine, too, of course, but I imagine you'll become her favourite. Bess feels more kinship with women, I fancy.'

The mare pushed her velvet nose into Sophia's outstretched hand as if in agreement and delicately nibbled at her palm with soft lips. Her silvery flanks gleamed in the sunshine and her warm brown eyes gazed at Sophia so kindly her new mistress was taken with her at once.

'I hadn't realised you were in need of a horse.'

Seated high above her, Fell shrugged, the same old movement of muscular shoulders that always caught Sophia's eye so effortlessly. 'Not for myself, particularly. I was thinking more for you. I can walk any distance, but I'll not be the man dragging his wife and children behind him when it would make more sense to have a cart, or for you to ride at the very least.'

Sophia nodded, feeling a familiar blush climb her neck and spread across her cheeks. It was the one that crept up any time Fell mentioned their future, the prospect of them as parents to little ones they would make together in nights when she would lie breathless in his arms. She would be a better mama than Mother had ever been, she had sworn fiercely to herself more than once; no child of hers would ever be made to feel worthless or bow its head beneath the weight of guilt it might not deserve—just as she now questioned her own sins, prompted by the man who leaned down to hold out his hand.

'Up you come. See what you think of her movement.'

He beckoned her closer, ready to haul her up to sit before him on Bess's broad back. Sophia hesitated, part of her wanting to grab on while another doubtfully took in the worn tack.

'That isn't a side saddle. I couldn't possibly...' She trailed off, thinking quickly. Riding astride with her skirts hitched up to show her ankles?

Only a lady 'couldn't possibly' and I am no longer one of those. Mrs Barden can do anything and everything poor Miss Somerlock could not—and might even take pleasure in it.

Before any remnant of her prissy manners could complain Sophia thrust her feet back into her boots, grasped Fell's fingers and the next moment there she was, attempting to find a comfortable position with a leg either side of the horse and her back warmed by the heat of Fell's body pressed behind her. He sat tall and immovable and it struck Sophia as feeling like being in an armchair with such a broad chest to lean back against—but then he twitched the reins and she scrabbled to clutch the pommel for fear of falling, and Fell's hand sliding around her waist to anchor her to the saddle overcame all other thought.

'Ready?'

His voice so close to her ear lit a stack of kindling inside her to burst into flames, joining the smouldering of her spine held against the long length of Fell's body. Seated so intimately it was as though they were connected by more than just proximity; Sophia felt her breathing change to match that of the man at her back, her chest rising and falling in symphony with the firm one planted so immovably behind her.

For a fleeting moment it was hard for Sophia to tell exactly where she ended and Fell began, one moulded against the other so tightly nothing could have slipped between.

Without waiting for a reply Fell gently tapped Bess with his heels and she obligingly lengthened her stride into a brisk trot, carrying them out of the yard and down the lane that cut through Woodford like a dry river. Heads turned as they passed the squat houses and scattered shops, as always outright curiosity present in the eyes that followed the horse's progress to make Sophia wish she'd thought to put on a bonnet. She just had time to spy Turner sloping out of the tavern as they rode by, his bruises faded now but his nose still a misshapen lump that did nothing to enhance his already unfortunate face. He stared after Fell with powerful loathing that made Sophia shudder, the malice in his expression so reminiscent of Mother's contempt tiny hairs stood up on the back of her neck.

'I don't think Mr Turner has forgiven you yet.'

Even without twisting to look back at him Sophia could tell Fell's brow would be furrowed with scorn as he snorted audibly into her hair. They'd left the village behind in a few of Bess's easy footfalls, but Sophia doubted Fell would have troubled himself to look at the farmer even if he'd been standing beside him.

'Don't expect he ever will. He'll think he's the victim even though he tried to land the first blow. As far as I'm concerned I did him a favour—at least a flat nose makes his face interesting now instead of merely unpleasant.'

Sophia folded her lips into a straight line.

I wish I could disregard the man's anger as easily as Fell has. I can't help but worry he might try to repay us.

If life at Fenwick Manor had taught her anything it was to always expect an attack, the instinct to watch her back ingrained so deep it was like a brand on her soul. Fell didn't seem worried, but perhaps he ought to be, if the intense hatred on the farmer's face was any indication of the dark path of his thoughts.

Oblivious to the growing unease of his wife, Fell gently squeezed her waist, sending a thrill on a rapid course from his fingers to her sensitive nape.

'What do you think of her? Will she do for you?'

Bullying her brain into considering something other than Fell's hand against the thin material of her dress, Sophia nodded. The grey mare's gait was smooth and she responded to the slightest direction, quite content to carry her riders out into the fields that ran alongside Savernake Forest. Her head bobbed up and down with the rhythm of her hoofbeats as she cantered over sun-bleached straw and stubble left over from harvesting, ears twitching with the fragrant breeze that moved around them. The same air lifted Sophia's hair to drift about her shoulders, sunlit copper flying up for Fell to bat out of his face. He released the reins for a moment to gather the tresses in his fist and lay them to one side of Sophia's neck, exposing the fragile skin between her shoulder blades that immediately prickled at the sensation of Fell's laugh.

'I ought to insist you tie it up if we're going to ride like this. I'd rather not have a mouthful of hair for my supper.'

Unseen by the man at her back Sophia tightened her grip on the pommel, his laugh stirring what felt like feathers in her stomach in a tickle of pleasure. Out in the wide open fields, leaning back against the firm chest of her beloved with sunlight dappling her hands and a delicious scent in the air, a steady beat of happiness grew inside her like a flower coming into full bloom. There was nothing more she wanted in that moment than for it to last for ever, for Fell to be free of the sadness she so often heard in his voice and their heartbeats falling into step with each other without even trying. She could have stayed the rest of her life in that saddle with Fell's hand on her waist and her skin rejoicing at his nearness—and the decision to tell him just that made itself abruptly, Sophia's lips parting of their own volition to form the words she'd longed to speak.

Perhaps the moment is now. There might never be a better one.

It would take all her courage, but she should finally tell him her truth: that she loved him and had for longer than she could say, a steady beat deep within her as insistent and essential as her pulse. Whatever he might reply would be worth the wait; they were bound together now for the rest of their lives and how could it be wrong to tell him how happy the prospect made her, for the first time revelling in an existence that for so long had held only pain?

'Fell. There's something I wanted to tell you.' She could hardly summon up the words, so stilted they were almost lost on the breeze. 'It's been on my mind for some time...'

He didn't reply.

Too intent on something else to hear her, he brought Bess up short and Sophia twisted to follow his gaze to where an unusually patterned black and white horse stood hitched to a tree at the very edge of the forest.

'Is something the matter?'

She peered up at him, heart still hammering and trying to decipher the set of his handsome features. He didn't answer, instead saying nothing as a wry smile unfurled across his face.

'What? What is it? Where are we going?'

Without a word he turned Bess's head and spurred her into a canter once again, still not giving a satisfactory reply to Sophia's growing confusion. It was only when she tugged insistently at his hand that he leaned down to speak into her ear, each breath dancing over the delicate shell to make her want to sigh out loud.

'Into the forest, Mrs Barden. There's someone I want you to meet.'

Before she could respond they were halfway across the field, Fell's undecipherable smile still in place—and Sophia cloaked in disappointment so intense it was as though she'd been winded.

Ma's dark hair was shot through with more silver than the last time he'd seen her, but there could be no mistaking the woman kneeling with her back to Fell as he and Sophia dismounted beneath the cover of the trees. She looked over her shoulder at the sound of approaching footsteps, hands full of the wild herbs she was gathering and her face as guarded as ever like an animal ready to run, until she recognised her son and rose with a cry of delight, more like a girl in her happiness than a woman of fifty.

'My boy!'

'Hello, Ma.'

She came towards him with arms outstretched and their familiar comfort wrapped around him to hold him close. He towered above her, her head barely reaching below his chin, but for a moment he almost felt like a child—back in his mother's embrace after months of separation and simply relieved to know she was safe.

'How did you know I was here?'

'I recognised Camlo hitched at the forest edge and thought you must be somewhere close by. I'd know that piebald monster anywhere.'

Drawing back a little, she reached up to touch his stubbled cheek, inspecting his face and the mark left by Turner's poker with the close scrutiny of a mother. 'I thought I'd come to surprise you, but it seems you got there first. If I hadn't stopped to pick…'

The rest of Ma's sentence died in her mouth as a glance to the side revealed Sophia for the first time, hesitating beside a tree with hands clasped uncertainly in front of her and unwittingly showcasing her wedding ring as plain as day on her slender finger. Ma blinked at it, then at Sophia's rosy face—and then at her son, who struggled to contain his amusement at the blank shock that made her look as though she'd been struck smartly over the head.

'Ah. Yes. There have been a few changes since last we met.'

He held out a reassuring hand to Sophia, who rustled through the leaves strewn across the forest floor to take it. At once the usual flare of tamed lightning crackled the length of his arm to circle in his chest at the feeling of her skin on his, still so intense even after a month of marriage, but he set it aside to draw her closer and watch proudly as she sank into a graceful curtsy only a woman trained as a lady from birth could have managed.

'Ma, I'd like you to meet Sophia—my wife.'

Essea's dark brows drew together a fraction as she took in her daughter-in-law's elegant greeting, although she found a smile for Sophia when her head came up again with shy unease.

'Well! I can't say I saw this coming, but what a wonderful surprise! It's a pleasure to meet you.'

Her tone was friendly enough, but with an unpleasant jolt Fell saw something in his mother's black eyes that gave him pause. It wasn't dislike, instead more akin to wariness he still recognised with disappointment.

It was that ladylike curtsy. Ma knows Sophia isn't one of us.

For the first time he realised he wanted Ma to approve, a sensation he found he didn't particularly enjoy. He'd been so carried away by his own feelings for Sophia he'd lost sight of how strange she must seem to others of his kind, refined and composed with manners unlike anything they were used to. Ma had noticed the gulf between them at once—but she would have to learn to live with it, Fell decided grimly as he saw how his wife's hands shook a little with nerves he longed to chase away with kisses. Sophia had been treated so despicably by her own mother there was no way in hell he would allow her to feel unwanted by anyone else's ever again—not even his own, their relationship complicated in its own unique way.

'The pleasure is all mine, Miss... Mrs...' Sophia hesitated, that ready blush springing up as she groped for the right way to address an unmarried woman whose son stood mere feet away as proof of her delicate position.

A shadow of Ma's usual humour crept back

into her eyes and she patted Sophia's hand with straightforward ease. 'Essea. Do just call me Essea. No need to stand on ceremony with me.'

The smallest smile touched Sophia's lips to kindle warmth beneath Fell's ribs. Perhaps Ma might take to her new daughter-in-law after all, her natural kindness winning against the caution he'd seen swim through her expression like a slow-moving fish. Ma was a maternal creature through and through, and he could only hope the two Barden women *might*—with a little luck—*just* be able to foster some kind of relationship both of them would come to cherish: the unloved lady yearning for a real mother and the Roma never blessed with a daughter of her own.

'Will you come back to the cottage now? I dare say you must have some stories to tell after six months' travel.'

Fell offered an arm to both women and each slipped a hand through the crook of an elbow, one balancing out the other so opposite in every respect. The only common thread between them was the man who escorted the unlikely pair back to their horses, watching as Ma leapt up into the saddle with the practised ease of a woman half her age. She was still handsome, her sepia skin a little richer than Fell's tawny bronze, but the straight black brows and shape of the eyes the same for both, although once again—and unwanted as always—the subtle differences between them prompted thoughts of his unknown father Fell couldn't dismiss. From whom had he inherited the square line of his jaw, so unlike Ma's more rounded chin, and the hazel that glowed bright in one eye? The reminders of his uncertain identity flooded in, the niggle of tension Fell felt whenever Ma returned already beginning to creep beneath his skin.

Not this again. I've other more important things to occupy my mind, surely.

At his side Sophia cut a fleeting glance up at him and he attempted to curve his lips in reply, although they refused to stretch into anything more than a grimace. The same old feeling of inadequacy, the same old questions and doubts that had taunted him ever since he could remember reached for him again with icy fingers, attempting to pull him back below the surface of angst and wretched torment that called his name with Ma's return. It was the usual pattern that followed her sporadic appearances: happiness to see her, but a renewal of the knowledge she was everything he was not, secure in her identity as Roma and armed with an unassailable sense of self. He didn't want to walk that road yet again, wishing only to enjoy his mother's company without the discontent that accompanied it.

But how can I? How can I know that peace when she will never reveal the secrets of my lineage?

Truth was, he couldn't. The feeling of being only half-complete was something he would have to live with the rest of his life—until he and Sophia had a family of their own, a thought that helped tamp down the well of bitterness within him. With Sophia at his side perhaps this time things might be different, perhaps some light at the end of the tunnel he had travelled alone for so long.

I can only pray we might find our way together, Fell thought as he helped the wife he had come to love up on to Bess's broad back and spurred the horse for home. *For there's no way I can turn from her now.*

Fell stared unseeing at the dim ceiling of the bedchamber with both hands behind his head and a frown creasing his weathered brow. From somewhere to his right came Sophia's quiet breathing and the warmth of her sleeping body, hardly curbed by a thin nightgown and untroubled by the blankets kicked once again to the end of the bed. On the other side of the closed door Lash's gentle snores combined with the swish of trees dancing in a night breeze outside the curtained window, sounds of darkness that at one time Fell might have found soothing. But not tonight.

Why is Ma behaving so strangely?

The question repeated itself with irritating persistence, but still Fell was lost for an answer. For the whole of the afternoon and into the evening she'd watched Sophia out of the corner of her eye, quick to smile and make conversation, but always returning to that subtle scrutiny when she thought Sophia wasn't looking. There was no malice in it, more as though she was trying to puzzle something out, but still Fell didn't like it—or know for sure what it meant.

Surely she can't dislike her. There's nothing there to dislike...although I'll admit that potentially I might be biased.

Sophia shifted slightly in her sleep and Fell cast her a glance through the gloom. *She'd* given him no cause for worry, at least, brewing endless pots of tea for Ma and making up a shake-down bed in the sitting room for their guest. In all respects Sophia had been a gracious hostess, if not an experienced one, and it was touching to see her efforts to make Ma feel welcome in their home. Her good heart shone through in every action, increasing the devotion she drew from her husband more and more each day without even knowing it.

It was a truth so bare and steadfast there was no point trying to deny it even to himself and Fell allowed it to roll over him like water off a duck's back. The feelings he had tried to suppress for so long were ungovernable now, running riot inside him in a hurricane of helpless emotion, and even the lesson Charity's rejection had taught him couldn't force them back. Sophia ruled his soul as well as his home, reigning queen of both with only knowledge of the latter—although her unfeigned delight in the night-time and the gleam of the smile she showed him during the day made him wonder if, against all odds and his own good sense, the tiniest crack might be opening in the defences around the castle of her heart...

'Must you think so loudly? I can hear the cogs turning.'

The sleepy voice from his right made Fell start and he looked across to meet Sophia's bleary eye peering at him through the darkness. The moonlight struggling to fight through the curtain dimly illuminated her face, tanned in the sunshine, but by night bleached bone-white and ghostly beneath wild hair.

'Not even you can hear thoughts.'

'Perhaps not, but I can sense when something is on your mind. Such as at this very moment.'

She rolled over on to her side, nightgown bunching around her knees and drawing Fell's attention even in the gloom. She had such long, slender legs and the dim awareness of them took him straight back to the day they met when he had gently washed dry blood from her ravaged skin. There would always be a scar there now, shining silver against her white shin, and one he suddenly ached to trace with warm fingers to make Sophia's breath pause in her throat.

He cleared his own throat, never more relieved than at that moment that his wife *couldn't* read minds.

'Not much in particular. I was just thinking about Ma.'

The sound of hair against pillow showed Sophia nodded her head. 'She certainly had some interesting tales about life on the road. To think she went all the way to Stratford and back! I don't think I could have lasted a half-hour, let alone above six months of solitary travel.'

Still with his hands behind his head, Fell shrugged. 'It's the way she was raised and all she ever knew for the first eighteen years of her life. If she hadn't met my father…'

He allowed the words to peter out, abruptly losing interest in his own train of thought. That path brought only shame, unhappiness and frustration with his stubborn mother, none of them things he wanted to experience while trying to sleep, but they came anyway, stealing over him like malevolent shadows to nest like lead weights. They were the same emotions that had clawed at him in Savernake Forest earlier that afternoon and in the darkness they somehow felt all the more powerful.

When he lapsed into silence Sophia waited a while, then ventured a quiet murmur.

'Something troubles you. Please don't deny it.'

'It's nothing.'

'It doesn't seem like nothing.'

Fell sighed, cursing himself for his lapse of control. Sophia was far from the fool she believed herself to be—or had done once at least. Like an arrow shot true to its target she hit upon his feelings so accurately it was as though she had a spyhole into his thoughts.

'Only foolishness on my part. It's always a joy to see my mother, but when she returns it reminds me…'

'Reminds you of what?'

Too late did Fell realise there was no way of turning back. Caught between Sophia's gentle questioning and his own desire to bite his tongue on a confession he hesitated, unsure which path to tread. On another night he wouldn't have wavered, able to deny the vulnerability his wife suspected…but with Ma sleeping comfortably in the sitting room, the living embodiment of his struggles with himself, his usual strength deserted him.

I can't forget that Sophia was truthful with me about her own fears, either.

The memory of her wretchedly unhappy face the day she'd revealed her secret shame came back to needle him, a picture that made his jaw tighten. Despite her misgiving she had laid herself bare to his judgement so there might be no secrets between them and, in the quiet of the night, Fell knew he owed her that same respect.

I can't lie. She should know the real man she married in all his forms—insecure boy included.

With his jaw still set, he muttered as well as he could manage.

'Of everything I lack. Knowing who my father is, what it feels like to truly belong… I've always been the odd one out, never sure who I am or where I come from. I'd never tell Ma for fear of grieving her, but part of me has felt as though it was missing since the day I was born. She is whole, but I am only half—how am I to know myself when so much is in shadow?'

The muscles of his shoulders felt strained and Fell passed a hand over them, kneading the tension beneath the skin. Breaking the silence he'd imposed on himself for years might have relieved some of the stress held in the tightly knotted sinew, but as seconds passed without Sophia's reply Fell wondered if his admission had been ill advised.

Perhaps that was the wrong course. The only other person I ever told of my true feelings was Charity and look what happened there.

Thoughts of the woman he'd loved before had no place in his marriage bed and he pushed them aside with sudden despair. Sophia's wordless presence was a terrible thing, the moments spent waiting for her to speak stretching out into a bleak eternity she eventually broke with a whisper so sweet it could have broken Fell's heart had it not already been safe in her keeping.

'I think… I think perhaps you *do* belong now. Here. With me. I know it isn't the path you might have dreamed of or even chosen if given another choice, but I certainly don't think you're the odd one out and I can't imagine a husband kinder or more capable than you. You are yourself—no part in shadow, nor anything other than whole.'

Shielded by the darkness Fell lay still, one hand still locked on a shoulder, but suddenly curiously unable to feel a damn thing.

'Is that how you see me? Truly?'

If Sophia's voice had been faint before, now it was hardly there at all, the merest thread only someone listening very hard could have caught. 'Of course. Couldn't you tell? After all these weeks? I finally feel as though I have a home now and it's you I have to thank.'

The mattress dipped as Sophia slid towards him and carefully, as though fearing she might be told to stop, slipped an arm across his chest. Cautious fingers found his cheek and stroked softly, lingering where the poker had torn his skin to trace the fresh scar with a tenderness that took Fell's breath away.

'So I will say thank you, Fell. It wasn't some high-born lord who saved me or an heir with his father's name. It was you—and you are *enough*.'

It was with ardour that made her gasp that Fell took Sophia in his arms then and kissed her, neither one of them quite prepared for the intensity that followed to leave both fighting for breath and unable to break the burning connection of their bodies. Fell relished every sigh, every flutter of Sophia's lashes against his cheek as he bore down on her and felt himself overwhelmed by her softness, by her willingness to give herself to him with a passion he hadn't known she possessed. She in turn traced the ridges of his muscles to places she had never dared before, whatever restraint she had been tied by abandoned to the velvet night. Her sharp breaths in his ear spurred his movements on until all rhythm disappeared and pure instinct reigned supreme, the sweat of two bodies mingling to dampen sheets tangled beneath.

Fell held Sophia closer, feeling the curved planes of her pressed against him so tightly not even a leaf could have slipped between. Her lips were parted and her eyes shut, pale skin gleaming dimly in the moonlight ghosted by a sheen of sweat. She smiled when he moved again, eyes still closed, but breath hitching at the feeling of his hands roaming her heated skin to settle somewhere no lady should allow a blacksmith to caress—but she wasn't quite a lady any more, Fell thought with sudden blinding insight that almost—but not quite—made him pause in his exploration.

She's changed because of me. Could it be I've changed, too—and perhaps for the better?

He said nothing as the thought made a home for itself in the forefront of his mind, a niggling distraction from the delightful way Sophia arched with each pass of his hands.

Could it be the truth? And Sophia's view of me likewise?

It was a wonderful idea, surely too amazing to be real—but then Sophia took Fell's face between both hands and kissed him so deeply he growled in the back of his throat and all other thoughts were chased away by the woman who had managed to bring him entirely under her spell.

Chapter Twelve

'She's the only one left, sir, and my father says he'll drown her if I can't find someone to take her in.'

The voice coming from somewhere outside the bedchamber sounded both very young and very unhappy to Sophia as she dressed hastily, pulling on the same shabby old gown she'd worn to flee Fenwick Manor. A tentative rap at the cottage's front door had woken Fell at once and she'd only been able to watch blearily as he cursed and left the warm seclusion of their bed. Now as she drove pins haphazardly into the fiery pile of her hair she wondered who would have been brave enough to rouse Fell so early, lifting the door knocker at barely past dawn and sending him stumbling into the pale morning light.

After what happened last night, however, that

person might have done me a favour. Will I be able to look Fell in the face again, having told him in so many words the secret workings of my heart?

'That would be a real shame, but are you certain there's nobody else? I don't know your father would like your asking me.'

Fell sounded equally troubled, his voice growing louder as Sophia left their chamber and moved through the cottage. Poking her head into the hall, she saw him at the open front door, looking down at whoever stood on the outside step concealed by his towering frame.

'No, sir. Anyone else who wanted one already came forward. I just thought, with you being known in the village to love your dogs like people...'

A misplaced foot on a creaky floorboard made Fell turn, catching sight of Sophia peeping into the hall. For a moment their eyes met: one long look filled with such wordless understanding it chased away all other thought, the simple cosiness of the cottage and the sunshine streaming in through the open door fading away beneath the power of two unwavering stares. Whatever had happened in the soft darkness had meant something to Fell, too, Sophia realised with a sudden flare of heat deep inside; the words his torment had torn from him had loosened her tongue to speak the truth she couldn't conceal, her feelings surely now laid bare for him to do with as he would.

'Good morning, Sophia. May I introduce you to our visitor?'

Fell broke the taut instant between them with a self-conscious smile and Sophia came forward with a shyness she wished she could have left behind in their chamber. Standing on the step was a little girl holding a large lidded basket, who looked up at Sophia with such bright hope in her blue eyes that Fell laughed.

'This is Sarah, the thatcher's daughter. She's got a sorry tale to tell and by the looks of it I think she's decided already you're just the person to hear it. I'd wager she can sense a soft heart from a mile away.'

Sophia mustered a smile for the child, although the soft heart in question leaped at Fell's fond description and a feeling of curious warmth swept through her right down to her toes.

'Oh? What tale is this?'

She crouched to bring herself level with the little girl's earnest face. The poor mite couldn't have been more than six or seven and she looked at Sophia with the complete lack of judgement only a child could manage—the first person in all of Woodford to peer at her with anything other than curiosity or distaste.

Sarah clutched the basket tighter to her chest, whatever lay inside shifting suspiciously. 'My Duchess had her pups on May Day, miss, and all but one were taken by people wanting a good dog. Only the runt was left behind and now my father says if I don't find somebody to take her he'll drown her in the maidening tub. He says now she's weaned and not feeding from Duchess any more he doesn't want to pay to keep another dog around the house.'

'Drown her—?' Sophia glanced up at Fell in horror, who confirmed her fears with a grim nod. 'Surely not!'

'He will, miss. He said he'll do it and I know he will.'

Little Sarah's china-blue eyes filled with tears and without thinking Sophia reached to stroke her hair, moving instinctively to offer comfort in a way nobody had bothered do for her at the same tender age. She smoothed the russet curls, sensing Fell's gaze on her downturned head, but not daring to look to see what expression danced in his mismatched eyes.

'Well? What do you think?'

From the way he asked the question Sophia knew he had already guessed her answer, but still it gave her quiet pleasure to gently wipe the girl's eyes with her apron and deliver her unsurprising verdict.

'I think you already took in one stray in need of a home. Why not another, given the alternative?'

'Why not indeed?' He sounded pleased and a swift cut of green eyes towards black-hazel showed approval that made her flush to see. 'There's your answer, then, Sarah. You can hand her over and be done with it.'

The girl's face lit up and she all but pushed the basket into Sophia's arms, watching with delight as the lid was lifted and Sophia saw for the first time what changeling she had agreed to take into her home.

'Oh!'

The sandy puppy barely filled both hands as Sophia lifted her out, a tiny wriggling shape covered in downy fur and made up mostly of paws and a flapping pink tongue. One leg looked slightly stunted and she was a deal smaller than most pups Sophia had seen, but the little dog evidently had the heart of a lion as she strained up to lick Sophia's glowing face.

'She's beautiful!'

'I think so, too, miss, but nobody else wanted her. Because she was the runt and had a twisted leg.'

Sarah patted the squirming creature's head with a gentle finger and picked up her basket to leave. 'You'll take good care of her, won't you? I would have kept her if I could...'

Sophia straightened up, catching the wistful tilt of the child's head. 'Of course. And you're free to come to visit her whenever you wish. Would you like that?'

Beside her she thought she heard Fell murmur a quiet word, but other than the tingle that skittered down her spine at the sensation of his breath on her neck she paid him no mind as Sarah's smile returned and she nodded, skipping away down the path and out through the gate like a lamb in a hand-me-down shawl.

Left alone with her husband, Sophia kept her gaze fixed on the dog cradled against her chest. Now there was nobody to act as a buffer between them her uncertainty came back with a vengeance, a steady pulse of heat spreading under her skin she knew must have reached her cheeks. Would he say something about what had passed between them in the warmth of the night? She hardly knew if she *wanted* him to acknowledge her honesty or to turn a blind eye to the outpouring of her soul, not quite saying the three words she longed to, but surely obvious to anyone with a particle of sense.

I love you. That's what I've wanted to say for so long and still do now—if I could only summon up the courage I found the day Ma returned.

He had opened up to her in telling her of his private thoughts, the innermost working of his mind, and why would he have done that if he didn't esteem her in some real way? It might not be love for him, but it was a start, and only the faint memory of Mother intruding at a moment she was least wanted stopped Sophia from throwing caution to the wind entirely and sinking into Fell's well-muscled arms.

'Why would a man like that want you?'

'Stupid, useless girl!'

'How you're my daughter I've never understood. What did I do to deserve you as punishment?'

The picture of that scornful face, so twisted with malice it obscured all hint of the beauty for which Lady Thruxton was famous, came to halt Sophia's wild desire in its tracks. The same old flurry of shame and doubt threatened to wash over her again, trying to steal the tentative hope Fell's night-time confession had stirred in her soul.

Stupid...useless...a waste of precious time... No.

She gritted her teeth on the spiteful whispers, driving them back with sudden force.

Fell himself said I'm none of those things. He thought it was Mother who was in the wrong, who spoke out of turn, not me—if I hope to earn his love I should do him the favour of listening when he speaks his mind, just as he did last night.

The puppy gave a sigh and without preamble relaxed against the worn bodice of Sophia's dress. The next moment she was sound asleep, worn out by the excitement of the morning and so delightful she managed momentarily to distract her new mistress from the unpleasant thoughts that worried at her with sharp teeth.

'I'm not sure the thatcher will like the idea of his daughter coming here to visit.'

Fell had stepped out into the sunny yard and now he stretched languidly, long arms straining above his head and the movement lifting the hem of his old shirt. It rose an inch or two above the waist of his breeches, revealing the same tantalising glimpse of his toned abdomen that always made Sophia want to stare despite the churning in her stomach.

She shrugged, feigning indifference she didn't feel. 'I doubt she'll tell him. I wouldn't have—no doubt another sign of the disobedience Mother was always at pains to squash.'

Fell huffed a short laugh, sounding almost dog-like himself in his wry amusement. 'I believe the word you used was *spirited*. Would you have kept a dog hidden away if you'd thought you could have got away with it?'

'Quite possibly—before I was given good reason not to rebel any longer. I always wanted a pup of my own, but Mother would never allow it.'

'I remember you saying. It must feel good to be able to do all the things you wanted when you were younger, but never had the chance.'

Sophia paused in gently stroking the silky top of the puppy's head.

I never considered that before. I suppose he's right about that, too.

'Do you know, it does. I confess it will take time to get used to the feeling of being free from any mistress but myself.'

'That's the truth. Nobody will ever order you around or make you feel deliberately unhappy ever again. Please believe that I won't allow it.'

When she looked into Fell's face Sophia saw any trace of humour had faded, replaced by a seriousness she'd rarely seen there before. The sculpted lines of his brow and jaw were firm, so resolute it raised a lump in her suddenly dry throat. He was strong and kind and *hers*, somehow, by some bizarre twist of fate—on paper at least. He was her husband and she was his wife, and as they watched each other in the quiet brightness of the sunlit yard Sophia felt the urge to utter those three little words pulling at her again so irresistibly it was like a siren's song in her ear.

Say it now. Now is the time!

But then the moment was gone.

Fell's mother came into the hall, hair tumbled from sleep, and Sophia excused herself with a stiff smile to light the kitchen stove for tea. It seemed the chance always slipped through her fingers like sand, drifting away on the wind and laughing at her attempts to take hold.

I will tell him. Just...not today.

By the time Ma went in search of Fell that evening a slight chill had wended its way into the air. August had almost run its course, September teetering on the brink of starting and the first hint of autumn hanging in the breeze that raised goosebumps on Fell's skin.

He looked up from the charcoal clamp he had almost finished constructing from earth and wood, his face streaked with dirt and hands ingrained likewise. Ma's footsteps barely made a sound on the dry grass as she walked behind the cottage, coming towards him with a smile that didn't quite touch the lines at the corners of her dark eyes.

'Did you need something?'

She shook her head, but the curve of her lips still didn't light the rest of her face and Fell felt a flicker of unease. 'No, no. Sophia has been looking after me very well. I just hadn't had a chance to speak with you alone yet since I returned.'

Fell nodded, carefully laying his axe down as if he wasn't suddenly alert to the hesitation in his mother's voice. 'Was there something in particular you wanted to say that meant you couldn't speak in front of Sophia?'

There was a pause that said more to Fell than words and he sighed heavily.

I suppose I should have expected this.

Whatever had been on Ma's mind since she met Sophia was evidently too much for her to keep hidden any longer, her close study of her

startling new daughter-in-law revealing something she now wanted to discuss. 'Whatever
it is, I'd have you say it now rather than make
sheep's eyes at me the rest of the evening.'

'Sheep's eyes indeed. Insolent boy.' Ma tried
to laugh, but it fell false and flat as she gathered
her skirts around her and perched on a pile of
stacked logs next to the clamp. 'I ought to box
your ears for that.'

'A little late to curb my tongue now, I think.'

He pushed his hands into the small of his
back and felt the muscles release some of their
tension from a day spent working bent almost
double. An early night would take care of the
rest, but there was no chance of that as Ma sat
in uncharacteristic silence, looking away from
him across the darkening yard.

Fell followed the direction of her gaze to
where Sophia stood before the old outbuilding
beside the forge that had been pressed into use
as a stable. Bess and Camlo peered out over the
split door and Sophia was speaking to them, too
far away to hear her words, but easy enough to
guess. She held the puppy out to each in turn
and even from a distance the glow of her smile
as the horses carefully sniffed at the little dog
made Fell's heart turn over in his chest.

'She's named it Letty, I believe. Strange name for a dog.'

Fell nodded, although a glimmer of recognition sparked at the back of his mind.

After her friend. The only one she ever had.

The thought took him back to the day she'd revealed her shame, tears standing out in her green eyes to taunt him mercilessly, and he tried to set it aside before the urge to cross the yard and take her in his arms called too loudly. She was much happier now by the looks of her: cradling Letty in one arm while the other hand stroked the top of Lash's head, spreading her affection equally between the two with the fairness he'd come to expect from her.

Ma watched Sophia likewise, although when she spoke it was clear she didn't follow the same train of thought as her son.

'She's no farmer's daughter, is she?'

It wasn't a question. Fell heard the note of something in her tone but couldn't quite put his finger on it, knowing only that it wasn't delight.

'No.'

'So who is she? In truth?'

Essea turned to Fell and regarded him with quiet concern, black eyes fixed on him so immovably for a moment he felt like a boy again, waiting to find out if he was in trouble.

But he wasn't a boy any more. He was a man and a husband besides—and the wife he had come to accept that he loved with every fibre of his being had dropped the smallest hint she might be growing to feel the same and for that Fell owed no apology to anyone, not even Ma.

'She's the woman I chose to take as my wife. Isn't that enough for you?'

An unwavering stare was all the reply he received and with a rough sound of irritation he glanced over his shoulder. Across the yard Sophia finished whatever conversation she'd been having with the horses and turned back for the cottage and Fell waited until she was safely inside before he answered.

'Her name is—*was*—Sophia Somerlock of Fenwick Manor. You must have heard of it. She ran away and I found her injured in Savernake Forest, so brought her back here to recover. Will that satisfy you?'

He spoke more sharply than he meant to, but he could see in which direction Ma's thoughts had strayed and he didn't care for it one bit.

She doesn't like it that Sophia was born a lady. I can see it in her face.

She'd certainly paled, her lips tightening into a straight line and brows slanting down in a look so close to dismay it made Fell bridle a little. What could be her objection? They were an unlikely couple, it was true, but surely there was no need for his mother to look as though she'd heard some news she had been dreading.

'Gentry?'

'Aye. Her mother remarried to a Lord Thruxton. No love lost between them, from what I gather.'

'But why did she stay on and marry you? Why didn't she leave when her leg was better?'

Fell kept his voice as level as he could despite the unease building in his insides. 'We came to an understanding. There was an agreement between us—I married her to keep her from a forced connection she wanted to escape.'

'A bargain of sorts? That's all it was?'

'If you want to call it that.' Said out loud his marriage to Sophia sounded almost distasteful. He'd always known it wasn't a romantic tale, but the twist of Ma's mouth only underlined the fact.

'But you care for her now.' It was another statement that wasn't really a question, Essea's shoulders tense and back ramrod-straight on her uncomfortable wooden perch.

'Of course I do. She's my wife.'

'You know what I mean. You *care* for her—more than just out of mere obligation.'

He could hardly deny it. Surely even the most dull-witted of people would have seen how often his lips turned up in Sophia's presence, or how his body instinctively curved towards her seemingly without his awareness. Ma was as far from a simpleton as it was possible to be and there was no chance she hadn't noticed the new gleam of life in her only son's eye.

'What if I do?'

Ma's own eyes closed then, her head drooping as though Fell had just confirmed her worst fears. When she peered up at him through the gathering dusk it was with sorrow so deep it stung him, the terrible unhappiness of a mother in anguish.

'Guard your heart,' she muttered so softly the words were almost lost amid the evening's chill.

Fell's brow creased into a frown. 'What?'

'You heard. I like Sophia very much. She's a sweet soul and pretty with it, but...'

'But?'

'Remember Charity.'

If Ma had dropped a lit match into a heap of gunpowder, it still couldn't have blown a bigger hole in Fell's stomach. He stood completely still, only able to watch as his mother reached for his hand and held it with fingers cold with worry.

'Remember how your heart broke for her? I

would do anything to spare you that pain again, of loving a woman you cannot truly have. I can see the same thing happening now and it makes me want to weep.'

Fell shook his head mechanically. With one short sentence Ma had uncovered his most secret fear and dragged it out into the light, leaving him with nowhere to hide from her scrutiny. He wanted to cast her doubts aside and did so as best he could, his reply sounding hardly human coming from his abruptly dry mouth.

'It's different this time. We're already wed.'

'You said yourself it was a bargain, not the meeting of two hearts. I wouldn't have you risk yourself again, at the mercy of one not meant for you…'

'My own mother thinks I don't deserve her?' Anger leapt to circle in his gut, hot and determined to chase away the weakness of uncertainty. 'Is that how you feel?'

After all the years he'd suffered loneliness and rejection, never thinking to find a spare ounce of happiness, she was trying to throw cold water over the fledgling flames of his hope for the future? It was more than he could bear and he knew his face must have set into a rigid mask of ire.

But Essea Barden was made of sterner stuff

than to quail. Years spent living on the road had tempered her courage until it shone like burnished brass and she met her son's eyes with unblinking determination. 'That's not what I meant. I just couldn't bear you to know that grief again. You admitted your marriage was one of necessity, not feeling—she's another kind of creature completely, no better and no worse, but so different I don't know how there can ever be real feeling between you. You're from entirely separate worlds that do not usually combine.'

She still held Fell's hand and he withdrew it to rake stiff fingers through his hair. There was truth in her words—that couldn't be denied—but still he turned from it.

Sophia is nothing like Charity. She's given me no reason to doubt her and I won't insult her by comparing the two so different in every respect.

'Why are you so *sure* it could never work between us? What have you seen of marriage between two different worlds to think you can possibly predict that outcome?'

Ma cut her eyes fleetingly to the side, hesitant in the face of his question. Even with biting dismay running its claws through Fell's innards he found her pause suspicious, only increased by her low mutter in reply.

'More than you know.'

'What do you mean by that?'

'Nothing. Forget I spoke of it.'

'*No*, Ma.' Fell heard the edge to his voice, but couldn't hold it back, seeing the surprise that crossed Ma's face at his forcefulness. The same frustration that welled up whenever she shut her mouth like a clam overcame him again and suddenly he couldn't stand it any longer. Whatever she thought to hide wouldn't escape him—she owed him that much, some explanation for the shadow she was so determined to cast over his happiness. 'Not this time. If you've something to say, some secret you're trying to keep, this time I want to hear it. You've kept things from me for too long and I won't accept it any more. I'm not a child—whatever you have to say I am grown enough to hear.'

In her defeat Ma looked so much older that for a moment Fell felt a flicker of guilt. Perhaps he shouldn't have pushed her so far—but then the image of Sophia flitted before him and he hardened his heart on thoughts of mercy.

'You won't like it.'

'Even so. I'll hear what you're thinking all the same.'

Ma smoothed down the front of her dress, its bright red faded to dull crimson in the dusk. She had the distinct air of one trying to prolong the inevitable, but at Fell's raised brow she heaved a sigh.

'Your father, Fell. He was a gentleman far above me in station and our relationship shattered like glass. *That* is why I fear for you— I've been where you stand, loving one out of my reach, and I've seen the sorry outcome of this story with my own eyes.'

Fell stilled. Like a statue carved from ice he stood quiet, turning his mother's words over as if to force them to make sense.

Finally, some part of the truth. After all these years... But I never once suspected...

'My father was gentry?'

He almost choked on each syllable, disbelief only growing at Ma's curt nod.

'Yes. To take a farmer as my man would have been ambitious enough; a gentleman was sheer madness. I don't think I need explain the hundred reasons it didn't work, or why I fear for you following in my footsteps.'

At any other moment, on any other night, Fell knew he would have pushed for more. The tantalising hint of his father's identity was more than Ma had dropped in thirty years, a clue he might gather up in the quest to make himself whole. On this night, however, Sophia's face was all he could think of, his determination to prove his mother wrong blinding him to his powerful curiosity, and he couldn't turn from the path he had chosen until he reached the bitter end.

'I am not you and Sophia is not my father. There's nothing to say history will repeat itself with us.'

Ma's answering question was direct and unflinching.

'Have you told her you love her?'

'Not yet.'

'Then I ask you to wait until you've truly thought about what I said. Your happiness is the most precious thing in the world to me. If you're right and Sophia is the kind of woman you claim, waiting a while to confess your feelings won't make a difference. Just…please. Please think twice on what you do.' His mother's voice shook a little with valiantly suppressed feeling that cut like a knife through the cacophony of Fell's thoughts.

He looked down at her, hardly seeing her sitting on the pile of wood and surrounded by darkness growing thicker with each minute that passed. They regarded each other in silence, each aware of the pain of the other, but powerless to make it go away.

She was right. I almost wish I hadn't heard her thoughts. But I did and I can't forget them—although I trust Sophia not to take me down the same path Charity led me a merry dance on.

What of the revelation about his father? That was something he would need time to digest, coming out of nowhere to make him question things he'd never considered before. His name, his rank, his position in society…all things Fell wanted to know, but with Ma's doubts stirring the fire inside him he had no attention left to spare for anything other than defending his wife.

'Very well. I'll think about what you said. But know this: Sophia is nothing like Charity and in time I hope you'll see it.'

He turned for the cottage, leaving his mother to stare after him with heartache dulling her ebony eyes. She'd acted out of love for him, Fell knew, and yet he couldn't seem to manage to look at her as he walked away.

Chapter Thirteen

With her eyes closed Sophia exhaled slowly through parted lips, one hand pressed flat to her abdomen and the other supporting her against the rough bark of a tree. The nausea that had assailed her since she woke showed no sign of abating and she took another deep lungful of damp forest air, willing its freshness to chase away the turmoil in her innards. It had rained heavily all through the night and the hem of her skirts had grown more muddied with each step she took away from the cottage, hoping to find some relief among the stirring leaves.

Whatever can I have eaten to make me feel like this?

Another wave rose up to make Sophia clench her jaw. A consequence of her attempts to cook, no doubt, the vague feeling of sickness had plagued her for the past few mornings and she passed a hand over her face as she waited for it to fade.

Neither Fell nor his mother seem afflicted, though, although I know Fell has barely slept a wink these past two nights. He persists in waking me with his tossing and turning, but denies anything troubles him when I ask.

Now she thought about it, Fell's behaviour had been a little odd for a couple of days. There was nothing Sophia could quite put her finger on, only a vague sense of his mind being on something he didn't wish to share. Perhaps she'd ask him again when she returned to the cottage, just as soon as this cursed nausea abated enough for her to walk…

The sudden sound of snapping twigs and rustling leaves coming from somewhere close by made Sophia straighten from leaning against the gnarled trunk. At her feet Letty sprang up likewise and pounced off in search of the newcomer, who paused to see the puppy appear like a lioness protecting her cubs.

'I know that fierce creature. Does this mean your mistress is somewhere near-about?'

Essea's smoky voice drifted towards her, familiar now, but still with the unusual cadence that always caught Sophia's ear. Her pronunciation of certain words was strange but beautiful in its novelty and her tone, although deeper than that of most women, held a world of feminine mystery Sophia couldn't help but admire as its owner appeared through the trees.

'Good morning, Essea. I hadn't expected to meet anyone here.'

'Nor I, so a pleasant surprise for both of us. But are you well? You look pale this morning.'

'A little bilious in truth. Something I ate, I imagine.' Sophia attempted a smile that was more like a grimace and bent carefully to usher Letty away, trying simultaneously to both ignore her nausea and pretend she wasn't acutely aware how the other woman watched her narrowly. The darkness of Ma's eyes was unsettlingly similar to the obsidian half of Fell's, her son even sharing the new deep purple shadows now underneath.

Belatedly Sophia saw the strain in Essea's face and felt her brows briefly contract. When the Roma woman had first arrived she'd seemed perfectly easy, but now she looked as though she hadn't been sleeping well either and her features were drawn tight with worry that Sophia couldn't understand.

'Are *you* well?'

Ma tried to smile, its stiffness only increasing Sophia's concern. 'Merely tired. Nothing to alarm you.'

Sophia made as if to answer, although she regretted opening her mouth when her innards gave a lurch and she dug her fingers into the bark to stop herself from uttering a low groan. She was powerless to resist when Ma took her arm and guided her to a fallen tree, following where she was led and sinking down gratefully on to the damp wood.

'Sit there a moment. Get your breath back.'

Essea perched beside her with feet drawn up and arms around her knees, straight-backed and surveying the forest while Sophia willed her head to stop spinning. It was the most unpleasant sensation and for some minutes she sat with her chin dropped to her chest, trying to breathe slowly and deeply as the cool breeze soothed her burning cheeks.

'Do you feel better now?'

'A little. Thank you.' Sophia managed a croak, wishing for a glass of water for her dry throat. 'It seems we're all out of sorts this morning.'

'How so?'

'Fell has barely slept of late and then he's up with the lark. I must have eaten something that didn't agree with me and, if you'll forgive me, you look troubled yourself. What a trio we are today!'

Still looking down at the leaf-strewn ground,

Sophia missed whatever expression flitted across Essea's features, but her voice was wary enough to give Sophia a good idea of what she would have found there.

'Do I look troubled?'

'A little.' Sophia tried another smile, although discomfort had begun to stir inside her that had nothing to do with her roiling stomach. Essea's tense face and now equally concerning tone made her uneasy, unsure what was going on behind that still-handsome countenance.

More than likely her worries involved Fell in some way, Sophia thought, and as she racked her brain a glimmer of inspiration came. She remembered now: Letty had been so excited to meet the horses two evenings before, making Sophia laugh with her delight. A sideways glance on her way back to the cottage had showed Fell and his mother deep in conversation, so grim-faced and intent she hadn't wanted to interrupt. It had seemed odd at the time and she'd put it out of her mind, but now it resurfaced to make her pause.

Perhaps they have quarrelled. That's why she looks so worried.

Doubtless it was none of her business if they had, but the stiffness of Essea's posture stirred

Sophia's pity and she laid a hand on her mother-in-law's arm.

'Might it ease your mind to share your cares? I'd like to help if I can. I'm sure there need be no secrets among family.'

The swiftness with which Ma's head snapped in Sophia's direction left her in no doubt something was dreadfully wrong. Alarm spread through her, ringing warning bells as Essea's eyes roamed her face, suddenly more rigid than ever before. 'No secrets? Am I to understand then that Fell has spoken to you of what he told me—?'

'I don't know what you mean. What did he tell you?'

Essea shook her head, a rapid tic like a startled bird. 'Nothing. Nothing at all. I misspoke.' Her mouth snapped shut just as Sophia wanted her to continue speaking. The Roma's jaw had closed like the heavy door of a vault and to Sophia's growing dismay Ma looked as though she could have bitten out her own tongue for letting something slip.

What could she mean? What was it Fell told her that she doesn't wish me to hear?

Her heart, already quickened by Essea's uneasy words, skipped faster as she tried to order her racing thoughts into some semblance of calm. A sensation akin to drops of cold water skating down her spine crossed Sophia's skin, the damp forest air suddenly cloying.

If it was anything good she would tell me and certainly not be so troubled. Whatever Fell spoke to her about cannot be a mere trifle...

'Was it something concerning our marriage?' With a tight throat Sophia named her worst fear. It had to be, surely. What else would cause Essea to look so disturbed, important enough to rob both her and her son of sleep? 'Won't you tell me that at least?'

'Please don't ask me. I should never have spoken out of turn.'

The icy droplets at Sophia's back increased to a freezing downpour that invaded her very bones.

That means yes. It must do. And it must be something bad—if Fell had spoken well of me, why would Essea feel the need to keep it a secret? Given his behaviour the past few nights and how ill at ease he seemed this morning, it's clear now there was something on his mind... something he did not wish for me to know...

The answer came to Sophia in a flash so blinding it took her a moment to see it clearly.

Of course. How could I have been such a fool? She could date the change in Fell's behaviour to the day after she'd all but confessed her love for him in the stillness of the night. It had begun after she'd seen his intense discussion with his mother—had he been confiding in her the situation Sophia had forced on him with her heavily hinted feelings? He still smiled at her readily enough, but with an undercurrent of something else she realised with a rush of shame she'd been too stupid to truly see, and he watched her now in a way he hadn't before. At the time she'd been hopeful it was interest— now she wondered if it had been more wariness at what she might say next.

How could it be otherwise? When in my foolishness I completely misunderstood?

She gripped the gnarled bark she sat on, but hardly felt how it cut into her numb hands.

How characteristically idiotic to imagine anything different. In her desperation for acceptance she had mistaken his friendship for something more, allowing herself to be carried along by her own wistful fancies until she could no longer separate fact from fiction. The truth was plain: greedily she had tried to snatch too much, not satisfied with what was already offered and more than she deserved. Fell was too kind to reject her completely, but the strain in his face the past couple of days surely told her all she needed to know. She had embarrassed both him and herself with her veiled declaration that could never be returned; because Mother was right. Who could ever love someone as worthless as Sophia, a walking disaster unable to tell affection from mere regard?

'Sophia? Sophia, are you still unwell?'

Essea's voice seemed distant, a vague mutter Sophia barely heard above the beat of her own heart and sick thud of blood in her ears. Fell's mother sounded worried, however, that much she could tell. No wonder Ma had looked so tense, no doubt carrying her son's discomfort with her and crushed beneath the weight of his unenviable situation.

Which I put him in. How Mother would laugh to see what a mess I've made of everything— but that's hardly a surprise, is it?

With discord in her stomach and her head beginning to throb with the effort of holding back tears, all she could manage was the shakiest murmur.

'No, I'm not. You needn't sit with me any longer, truly.'

The autumnal air raised goosebumps on Sophia's arms and she rubbed at them with cold fingers. Every last thing she had dreaded concerning her love for Fell was unfolding in front of her eyes—not only was he discomfited by her affection, but his poor mother had been dragged into the mire alongside Sophia's heart to drown in the flood of her stupidity.

Essea couldn't possibly know how Sophia ached for her feelings to be returned, or the fathomless depth of her regard for the man both women loved in very different ways. How could she, when Ma was a woman of substance and wit no doubt accustomed to devotion and Sophia a poor creature hardly worth a moment of Fell's time?

All at once she wanted to be anywhere but sitting in the forest beneath Essea's contemplative gaze, feeling her innards twist with pain both physical and emotional that she longed to escape. There could be no running from it while not alone and with an effort Sophia got to her feet.

'If you don't mind, I think I'll return to the cottage now.'

'Of course.' Essea rose likewise and stood tall and alert, as at home amid the rustling leaves as Sophia would have been in a parlour. If two women had ever been more different it would be hard to imagine, although the unhappiness of both tied them together somehow as Sophia caught her mother-in-law's sleeve.

'I'd thank you not to tell Fell about this. It might grieve him to think he had caused me pain, when in truth his friendship has been the most wonderful gift I've received in all my life.'

Another secret I shouldn't have shared, she thought grimly as she saw a complex expression flit through Ma's ebony eyes.

But somehow she didn't seem to have enough energy now to care. All she wanted was to be left in peace with her heartache and to come to terms with the fact Fell was out of her reach for ever, so close and yet so far, and untouchable all the same. With her soul in tatters and her head bowed with the weight of suffering, Sophia turned blindly away—so she didn't see the confusion in Essea's face as the Roma woman watched her go.

Fell saw Sophia enter the yard through the small forge window, pausing with hammer raised and sweat glowing on his forehead. Usually he would cuff it away, but this time he had no attention to spare for anything other than the sight of his wife, her pretty blue gown and burnished hair a match made in heaven for his appreciative eyes.

Now's the moment. I resolved as much and I can't break my word even if it's only to myself.

He'd done as Ma had asked and nobody could say he hadn't. Ever since she'd come to find him at the clamp with her worries and questions Fell hadn't been able to think of anything other than the feelings for his wife he burned to tell her, considering them over and over at his mother's request. If she'd hoped he would come to a different conclusion, however, she would be disappointed—all his thinking had done was convince him the time had come to confess all to his unlikely love and pray she might reward his boldness with more than a kiss.

She knows everything about me now. There's nothing left to hide behind since I told her the inner workings of my mind and the insecurities I'd tried to outrun for so long. I can only hope she accepts me despite them all.

The intriguing hint Ma had let slip about his father shouldn't matter a jot. Whatever had happened between them was in the past and nothing that could be applied to Fell's own situation. The temptation to tell Sophia of his discovery had gnawed at him ceaselessly, but he had fought it back; talk of his father could wait until he'd had the chance to speak of his own heart. Depending on Sophia's reaction, she might even be able to help him convince Ma to give in and tell the full story once and for all.

The thought of his mother caused Fell's lips to twist as he crossed to the forge's open door and ducked beneath the low frame. Frustration at both her timing and refusal to elaborate further curled inside him like a snake, irritation he couldn't quite escape. She knew how much Sophia meant to him; why had she felt the need to intervene and so damnably vaguely it raised more questions than it answered?

Sophia had drawn closer to the cottage and Fell stood on the forge step and watched her approach with admiration. Her posture was a thing of beauty, each footstep light and quick with the grace of a dancer now her leg was entirely healed. In that moment he could have blessed providence for making her take the injury so close to his home—any other forest and he wouldn't have been the one to find her, missing out on hopes of a love returned that he cherished so close to his heart.

Courage, man. This moment has been a long time coming. Failure to speak now is not an option.

She was still too good for him. That much would never change. But surely they had found a link between them that couldn't be denied, a trust built on a solid foundation so different to the sand upon which his love for Charity had teetered. He *must* be right this time: Sophia could see past his shame and all he lacked and spy the man inside, a man who offered his soul up to her and would hear her reply.

Beneath his singed shirt his heartbeat began to increase its tempo until he could feel its thrum right down to his toes. Each pace Sophia took in his direction, her face downturned and Letty trotting at her heels, strengthened his resolve and helped him gather all his mettle to call out.

'Back from your walk, I see. Did you happen to almost fall beneath a tree again this time?'

He smiled, sure Sophia's own lips would lift at his dangerous jest. She was learning to laugh at herself now she didn't take all teasing as proof of her flaws and that laugh was one he loved above all others.

But her mouth curved the wrong way, downwards instead of up, and with a vicious pang of one skipped beat Fell saw everything had changed.

She paled at the sound of his voice and in the fleeting glance she threw towards the forge he caught something he didn't recognise dulling the green shine of her eyes, a sight that skewered him with pain that took his breath away. There was no trace of the light or humour he had come to expect in her expression—only a blank void utterly lacking in anything approaching warmth.

He couldn't help a backwards step, knocked off balance by surprise and agonising dismay. What had happened to her ready smile and the rosy flush of her cheeks? She looked drawn and unhappy and continued into the cottage without a word, for all the world as if she'd rather he hadn't seen her at all.

He continued to stare at the cottage's green front door long after it had closed behind her. Now concealed behind thick walls she was out of his grasp physically, but the power of that one long look showed that wasn't the only way in which she was untouchable.

I don't understand. What did I do?

The desire to leave the forge and stride after her squeezed him in its grip, but his legs seemed to have turned to stone. There was nothing he could do but linger in the doorway and watch as his dreams came tumbling down around him and he realised the extent to which he had been a fool for a woman—yet again.

I should have seen it before. To have let myself be so blinded by the longing for peace at long last!

Of course Sophia now regretted the sweet

words she'd whispered in the seclusion of their bed. What woman wouldn't curse herself for having humbled herself for a half-Roma blacksmith, and a bastard at that, even if her kindness had been born of pity for his sorry confession? Sophia had been more gentle than Charity, at least, but still in the end it seemed she had decided his affections were something she could do without.

Hardly seeing where he stepped, Fell stumbled back inside and braced himself on the scarred surface of his bench. It was the same one Sophia had sat at the night she'd come to the forge with a proposal he had never expected, neither one of them foreseeing the outcome of their bargain. Pain so sharp it felt like a knife in the gut pierced Fell at the memory of Sophia's moonlit face, frightened but determined and already more appealing to him than he should have allowed. She'd managed to sway him from his doubts with her kisses and had led him by the hand towards his own destruction, unaware she did so, but condemning him all the same.

And so now I love her, just as I did Charity, and just as before I have no hope of my feelings being returned.

Why had he ever thought differently? He had nothing to offer any woman and certainly not one like Sophia. She was above him in every single, solitary way and he deserved the punishment of heartbreak for getting ideas above his station. Ma had been right to warn him off and he hadn't wanted to listen; now he would pay the price and had no one to blame but himself.

He couldn't take it a moment longer. To be so close to Sophia, knowing she was inside his cottage and yet far beyond his reach was too much to bear when he could no longer touch her, a torture he couldn't endure for one more second. Even screwing his eyes shut did nothing to shield him: she was imprinted beneath his eyelids, standing with the sun on her hair and bright skirt stirring in the breeze, a laugh on her lips that made his soul sing each time he heard it. She was everywhere and nowhere all at once and in desperation Fell tore the apron from his chest.

'I need to get out. I *must* escape this torment.'

Lash stood up from his post at the door as Fell passed him, the dog falling into step with his master as he left the forge and crossed the muddy yard. Together they turned up the lane into Woodford, Fell only pausing for a moment as he saw Ma emerge from Savernake Forest with her basket slung over her arm and unease clouding her tawny face.

I've no wish to hear any more of her worries for me now. Not when it turned out she was right all along.

He threw out his chest and carried on walking. The look in her eyes was too like the one she'd worn two evenings previously, when her honesty had brought his dreams crashing down around his ears and left him unable to so much as glance at his wife now for fear she might see his weakness. All he wanted was to escape those thoughts and so he called over his shoulder without giving his mother a chance to speak.

'I'm going to the tavern. I'll be back this afternoon.'

Ma's mouth opened to call after him, but Fell was already gone, moving blindly into the village and not breaking his stride until the Red Lion hove into view and he plunged through the door as though the tavern could offer him salvation.

The landlord looked him up and down as he entered, but Fell's money was apparently as good as anyone else's and it didn't take long for a full mug of ale to slop across the bar in his direction. Fell seized it like a lifeline and made for one of the sticky benches, taking a deep pull on his drink to level the foam and wending his way past the men already on their fourth tankard of the day despite the sun not yet sitting high above the thatched roofs. One or two of them glanced at him, but for the most part nobody paid any mind to the blacksmith who dropped heavily into a corner and cradled his drink between battered hands.

Lash had followed him inside and now sat near Fell's worn boots, wearing an expression of solemn sympathy, ears twitching forward at his master's bitter laugh.

'Never have to tell you when something's the matter, do I? You can read it in my face.'

He patted the dog's warm head and took another sip, hardly tasting it with all his attention diverted elsewhere. It might take a couple of tankards to find relief, but find it he would, he swore harshly to himself—anything to help drive away the thoughts of Sophia that had chased him from the forge and pursued him into the village, still circling now despite the ale slipping smoothly down his throat. The Red Lion ought to be a sanctuary from the wife he now sought to avoid both in body and soul; even if she wished to see him—which she had made abundantly clear she did not—she would never set foot in such a low establishment, frequented as it was by the hard drinkers of Woodford whose language would make her blush. Usually he wouldn't enter either, but all of a sudden the company of men just as desolate as himself had found some curious appeal.

No sooner had he settled to the serious business of solitary suffering, however, than it was interrupted and by one of the last people would have Fell chosen to see.

Turner set his tankard down hard on Fell's bench, spilling its dregs across the grimy wood. The farmer didn't seem to notice, however, as he treated Fell to an unpleasant grin and sat down opposite without so much as a word of invitation.

'Barden. Not often we see you in here. Everything well at home?'

With his back to the small, dirty window, Turner's profile was lit proudly by the sun struggling through the panes, his recently flattened nose lending it an unusual shape Fell considered for a moment before he replied. The farmer was an irritation he could have done without while bitter agony clamped a hand around his throat; but rising to the implied sneer might mean a barring from the landlord before Fell had sunk enough ale to put Sophia from his mind and that he couldn't have. The question couldn't have come at a worse time, all Fell's hopes for the happiness of his home dashed to pieces upon the floor.

'Well enough.'

If Turner caught the warning note, he didn't show it. Instead his ugly smile widened and he leaned forward, hands dangling between his knees and watery eyes holding such gleeful malice Fell was suddenly on his guard.

'Glad to hear it. It makes me very happy to know there's no trouble between you and your lady wife. You must be fond of her, I imagine.'

He watched Fell take another mouthful, his spiteful gaze never leaving his face. For his part Fell took his time in swallowing, thinking quickly where Turner could be going with his line of enquiry. It was the most civilised conversation they'd ever had, aside from the undercurrent of malevolence, and he didn't trust it one bit.

If only you knew, Turner, you would laugh yourself into an early grave and consider it worthwhile. Besotted would be more the word— if I thought you knew what that meant. If you knew the pain inside me now, it would be like all your Christmases come at once.

'Of course.'

'Yes. Yes, I could tell you cared from the unfortunately short meeting I had with her that day in your forge. Do you recall?'

Fell inclined his head. Beside him Lash stirred restlessly, eyeing the farmer with distrust that could all too easily descend into flying teeth.

'*I* certainly do. You gave me this gift to remember it by.' Turner pointed to his nose. For a moment his grin flickered, but he hitched it back into place. 'But no hard feelings, Barden. I think eventually the best man won.'

Laying a steadying hand on Lash's neck, Fell said nothing. This was Turner as he'd never seen him before, almost cunning in a low kind of way, and it aroused his suspicions no end. Still, there was nothing the man could actually *do* for all his strangely passive nastiness, surely, and Fell tried to brush off the discomforting feeling of being baited. Perhaps Turner was merely drunk—it wouldn't be the first time Fell had seen it and would no doubt not be the last.

Turner patted at his pockets. 'I seem to have forgotten my watch. Do you have the time?'

Fell grunted. Couldn't the man just leave? The longer he stayed the more Fell could feel his temper fraying at the edges, misery and shame building within him like a storm. 'A little after eleven.'

'Is that right? I should be leaving.' Turner got to his feet, Lash tensing a little as the man swayed slightly too closely. 'I'm to meet with a cousin of mine at half-past. I can't be late.'

Fell didn't reply, only watching the farmer with growing unease that mixed with the despair already in residence. There was still something he couldn't quite put his finger on; some triumph in Turner's face that Fell didn't understand. It made no sense, yet he couldn't shake the uncanny feeling, instinctive caution making his muscles tense without his command.

Straightening his hat, Turner flashed Fell the grin again, this time compounding its hideousness with a sly wink. He put his hand into his pocket and brought out a coin, dropping it on to Fell's bench with a conspiratorial nod.

'Here, have another on me. You should sit and enjoy yourself while you can—you never know when happiness might end. I'd make the most of it if I were you.'

Chapter Fourteen

The kettle whistled shrilly on the hob, its piping voice breaking Sophia's blank stare into the hearth where yesterday's ashes lay as grey and lifeless as her heart. Nausea still gnawed at her and she closed her eyes briefly to force it back as she rose slowly from the kitchen bench and lifted the kettle from the heat. A cup of tea would do nothing to heal the ravaged hollow inside her chest, but it might help tamp down the sickness in her belly that wouldn't leave her alone, its persistence an aggravation she could have done without.

As if I needed anything else to lower my spirits. I don't know when they've ever been more laid out in the dust.

She gave the tea leaves a poke, sighing at the sudden sound of a knock at the front door. Essea would open it, hopefully. Sophia was in no mood for company or for dredging up a smile for whoever waited on the step, although she knew the guest wouldn't be calling for her. Most likely they would be wanting Fell for smithing or help with a horse, but they'd be out of luck in either case.

Ma had mentioned he'd gone out to the tavern—*in order to avoid me, no doubt*—and wouldn't return until the afternoon. It was only half past eleven now, a glance at the clock on the mantel showed, and surely her husband had no reason to hurry home again.

The telltale creak of floorboards signalled Essea had answered Sophia's plea and she turned her attention back to the kettle. Perhaps a little honey in her tea might settle her stomach, something in its sweetness cutting through the bile that crept up each time she swallowed. There was some in the larder, or had been last time she'd looked, and she was about to look again when raised voices made her pause.

'I tell you, there's nobody here by that name. You may *not* come in!'

'Stand aside, mistress, or you'll soon wish you had.'

'I will not. You can't—'

There came the sound of scuffling, then a sharp breath of something so close to pain it sent

Sophia flying to see what could be happening outside in the hall—but she only took two steps before a figure appeared in the doorway and for one agonising instant her heart ceased to beat.

'Miss Thruxton. So I've found you at last.'

Phillips's lopsided mouth curved upwards even more as he surveyed his prey with a satisfaction that lit his cold eyes. Sophia's own stretched wide in mute horror, her lips parting in a silent gasp and all words deserting her as her worst nightmare stood before her and held out a rough hand.

'Your lady mother bids you come home. I'm to ensure you arrive there as quickly as possible. You must come with me now.'

Pure, crystal-sharp ice flooded Sophia's veins and she staggered, unable to comprehend what was happening.

What is this? Can I be dreaming?

Only moments ago she'd been thinking of honey and Fell, and now Phillips was in her kitchen and Mother knew where she lived, and the new life Sophia had scratched up for herself had been torn neatly in two by the sinister apparition in front of her. It was every worry made flesh, each dread given form, and from the depths of her soul Sophia dragged up a strangled hiss that tore at her dry throat.

'My name is Mrs Barden and *I won't go.* Leave this house at once!'

Phillips's face hardened, both surprised and displeased by the defiance everyone had thought so beaten out of his mistress's quiet, compliant daughter. Sophia saw the flicker of anger and might have flinched from it had terror not fixed her to the spot.

She seized the edge of the kitchen table, leaning against it for support as her mind reeled and stars flickered brightly before her eyes. It couldn't be happening, it just *couldn't*—yet there he was, the man she'd hidden from all those weeks before, finally having found her and now reaching to take hold of one fragile wrist.

'Come along now, miss. Don't make this more difficult than it need be. I've got my orders and I've never let Lady Thruxton down yet.'

Sophia stumbled backwards, but the hand had already closed over her suddenly icy skin. She tried to pull away, but the strong fingers bit down to make her cry out in pain and fear so intense anyone else might have let go, yet Phillips merely hauled her closer, capturing her other wrist and half-guiding, half-dragging her from the kitchen into the hall.

'Stop! Stop it! You're hurting me!'

Hardly able to snatch a breath, Sophia twisted from side to side, chest heaving and head spinning with terror and nausea that made her limbs feel as though they might fold beneath her. Nothing she could do made a bit of difference, however, to the man who towed her mercilessly towards the open front door.

'I'm sure I'm very sorry, Miss Thruxton, but your mother insists you return. Mr Septimus is likewise very eager to see you. Very eager indeed.'

The air fled Sophia's burning lungs at his words and she threw herself backwards harder than ever, planting her feet and scrabbling for purchase on the wooden floor. Out of the corner of her eye she saw a shape sprawled not far from her boots, a figure gasping on the ground as though winded from a heavy blow and black hair pooling against the bare boards—

'Essea!'

Ma tried to reach for Sophia's skirts, determination flaring in her black eyes even as she fought to regain the breath knocked from her. She threw out a shaking arm, fingers closing scant inches away from Sophia's flailing legs as Phillips set his jaw and hefted her on to his shoulder with a grunt of impatience.

'I'd hoped to avoid this. I'll have to ask your

mother's forgiveness for handling you so in-delicately.'

Sophia jerked in his hold, eyes never leaving Ma's desperate face. Her heart slammed against her breastbone time and time again, dizziness beginning to steal over her and the edges of her vision growing dim.

'What have you done to her? Put me down! Put me down this instant! I must make sure—'

It was as though she hadn't spoken at all. Without even a moment's hesitation or a swift glance to check on the woman he had knocked to the ground, Phillips stepped out into the yard, carrying Sophia on his shoulder as if she was a sack of grain and paying no mind to how much she struggled to free herself.

Another man stood beside the door, leaning against the jamb and watching proceedings with interest. Phillips nodded to him as he emerged, reaching into his coat to withdraw a purse bulg-ing with promise.

'It's her right enough. Thank you for the in-formation, Cousin. Your reward, as discussed.'

Eyes stinging with furious tears, Sophia lifted her head to look at her betrayer. Who-ever it was had sold her for a purse, it seemed, just as she'd always feared, and when she saw his identity it was without the smallest glimmer of surprise.

Turner took the purse at once and weighed it lovingly in his hand. His lips shrank back from his teeth in what she realised was his attempt at smiling and he gave a mockery of a bow.

'A pleasure. As was meeting you, ma'am. I *thought* you were a good deal too fine for the likes of Barden and, when I remembered my cousin Phillips's mistress had a daughter gone missing, a lady fitting your description, I couldn't rest until I'd made sure you were rescued.'

Sophia clenched her jaw shut as hard as she could, restrained hands balling into fists she longed to let fly at Turner's smirking face. If Fell hadn't already flattened his nose to a cowpat, she might have done so herself, rage and fear and grief combining to push the tears past her lashes and run down her face.

Damn you. Damn you, damn you—why couldn't you have let well enough alone?

Oblivious to her dismay or perhaps just unmoved by it, Phillips settled his burden more comfortably on his shoulder. 'Where's the man who calls himself her husband?'

'Up at the tavern, drinking away his sorrows.

He'll have more than he started with when he returns to find her gone.'

Phillips's dark chuckle only made Sophia hate him all the more.

'Aye. He's in for a shock and no mistake—not that he deserves any better, Roma bastard that he is. We'll leave before he returns. My lady is keen to have her daughter home as soon as possible and what my lady wants she gets.'

Turner's grin widened and Sophia turned her face away, unable to bear his triumph.

Would Fell really be saddened to discover she'd been carried off? Surely there was a chance he'd welcome her absence. It might turn out that Phillips had done him a favour, a thought that made Sophia's stomach twist all the more violently. It pained her to imagine it, but could that be right? For all his desire for a family Fell still had to tolerate his wife, and her presence must be more distasteful to him now than ever before. Might he decide to cut his losses and abandon her to her fate, their marriage tossed on the scrapheap alongside Sophia's love for the man who held her future in his hand?

She heard the farmer turn to leave, boots squelching in the puddles left by last night's rain. It might very well be the last time she ever

saw the yard, the cottage or the forge, she realised with fresh misery—how wretched that
her final memory of the place she'd come to
call home would be tainted by Turner and his
poisonous greed for vengeance.

'If you're keen to be off, I'll say good day to
the both of you and send my compliments to
your mistress. I feel we've done each other a
good turn this day, my dear Cousin.'

Fell drained the dregs from his mug and
wiped his mouth with the back of a hand. In
truth, he had no taste for the landlord's bitter
ale, but each sip took him another step closer to
sweet oblivion, where he might find a moment
of solace from thoughts of Sophia that didn't
know when they'd worn out their welcome.

He closed his eyes and pressed two fingers
against the lids. As yet he'd found no relief.
Even the serving girl reminded him of the wife
he'd left behind in the cottage, her profile un-
cannily similar although not—*obviously*—quite
as fine. Hidden among the smell of tobacco and
stale beer he should have been able to forget her
for at least a half-hour, damn it, but apparently
not if every woman in sight somehow recalled
Sophia to the forefront of his mind.

Stretched across Fell's feet, Lash suddenly

raised his head, ears pricked as Fell became aware of a presence at his shoulder. Turning slightly, he saw young Winters from Down Farm hesitating there and felt his heart sink even further into his boots.

More unwanted company. A nice enough lad, but I'd sooner drink alone today.

'Barden. I'm glad to run into you here. May I speak with you?'

At Fell's uninterested glance the younger man took the bench opposite, Turner's vacated seat, and leaned forward so earnestly that even in the depths of his misery Fell couldn't suppress a flicker of unease. First Turner, then Winters. The two didn't usually socialise beyond a friendly enough nod—why had he sought him out now, looking so uncomfortable, but determined to have his say?

'Is something amiss?'

'Possibly. In either case I thought you'd want to know.'

Winters leaned towards him even more and now Fell was certain there was something wrong. He pushed his tankard to the side.

'What is it?'

'It may well be nothing, but I'll tell you all the same. I went to call in at the forge before I came here and found Mr Turner and a gentleman I'd never seen before waiting outside your house. Turner said you weren't at home and that he was there to call on your wife, but I knew there was no friendship between you and his manner seemed…off, somehow. Nothing I could put my finger on, but I didn't like his friend, either. A great scar across his face and eyes so cold it were like he looked straight through me.'

Winters sat back a little, passing the brim of his hat back and forth through nervous fingers. 'I'm not making accusations. I just thought you ought to know. You saved that gelding's life and I never forgot you were the only one to help me.'

For a moment Fell didn't know what to say. A man with hard eyes and a scarred face, shown towards his house by Turner when he knew Fell wasn't home…

A lump of the coldest ice crystallised in his stomach and Fell lurched to his feet, Lash springing up likewise in mirrored alarm.

Phillips. It has to be. Turner gave Sophia away to punish me for humiliating him—the most perfect revenge he ever could have taken.

Winters looked a little startled at Fell's heavy clap to his shoulder, but there was no time to waste on anything other than reaching the cottage. At that very moment Sophia might be in danger and the thought drove Fell on like a crazed bull, flinging the tavern door open so forcefully it banged against the wall behind and sent more than one drinker spluttering into his tankard.

He was an unstoppable force as he tore from the village in the direction of his forge, Lash loping at his side as if he understood what was at stake. With every step Fell's apprehension increased until he could scarcely focus on anything else, villagers fairly skipping out of his way and his face set in an expression he didn't realise bordered on murderous. Reaching the yard, Fell didn't even pause to open the pretty wrought-iron gate, instead jumping the wall like it was no more substantial than a line of pebbles.

'Sophia? Ma?'

The door to the cottage lay open and for a painful second Fell's heart stood still. There was no sign of Phillips or Turner…but neither did Sophia emerge. When Ma stumbled out, Fell seized her by the shoulders and looked into her face.

'Where is she? Did she manage to hide?'

'He took her. I tried to stop him, but he forced his way inside…'

Belatedly Fell saw how Ma's hair was wilder than usual and one side of her face was slightly swollen as if she'd been struck. The sight released him from his animalistic rage for a moment and he stared at her in horror, hardly able to believe both his ears and his eyes.

He came to my home, attacked my mother and stole Sophia away?

His heart began to jump all the more quickly, picking up speed as he shuffled the facts into order. Part of him could hardly credit it, but the mark on Ma's cheek didn't lie, the blotchy skin stirring embers in his innards that burst into flame.

'He hurt you? He laid hands on you as well as taking Sophia?' The nerve of the man took his breath away, rendering his senses accursedly dull and making clear thought impossible. The red mist that was descending only blurred his mind further, throwing him into a fog of confusion as he groped towards the light.

He tried to take her cheek in his hand, but Ma impatiently waved him aside. 'It's nothing. I've had far worse. But Sophia—what will you do? Do you mean to fetch her back again?'

Fell was moving again before he even realised it. Still rational thought abandoned him, acting only on impulse roaring up from the most primitive part of him that now burned with fury he hadn't known he could feel. Sophia must be terrified, back in the hands of her hunters, and the picture of her blanched with fear combined with Ma's wounded face sent him striding towards his makeshift stable as if marching to war, careless of anything but avenging the two women he loved. Fetching Sophia back to Woodford was *exactly* his plan and no man on earth would prevent Fell from doing that while he had a breath left in his body.

Take my wife? Strike my mother?

He bit down savagely on a growl, feeling the blood course through his veins with new vitality that fed his determination. Sophia was his very reason for living, he had long since accepted, but it wasn't just his love for her that drove him onwards so powerfully. It was the idea of her being held against her will, forced to act against her inclinations that breathed fire into his lungs and twisted his lips in something close to a snarl. She'd finally found a place she thought was safe from those with no interest in her happiness and to have it torn from her now was more than he could stand. She deserved everything that was good and even if she didn't return his feelings she belonged among those who valued her for herself and not for what she was worth.

'Wait. Wait!'

Ma hurried a few steps behind as he flung open the stable door, Bess and Camlo moving restlessly inside as if sensing his agitation. Lash paced likewise and even little Letty seemed to know something was amiss as Fell began to saddle Bess with unthinking speed.

He glanced up as his mother seized his arm, her face tight with strain. She looked every bit as appalled as he felt, but she shook her head and didn't let go of his sleeve.

'Wait a moment. Think. If you turn up at Fenwick Manor, they'll call the constable at once and who would believe a Roma black-smith over the landed gentry? You'll end up in gaol and there will be no chance of saving Sophia then.'

Fell shrugged. A faint whooshing sound had started up in his ears, the noise of his own blood thrumming with fury and urgency he could hardly comprehend. Every second he delayed was a second Sophia spent terrified and alone, and the idea raked at him ferociously. 'It's a chance I'll have to take. What other choice do I have?'

'It's not a question of a choice that *you* have. It's mine.'

'What?'

His mother's fingers clenched harder in the

fabric of his shirt, a reflexive twitch that even in the depths of his torment Fell recognised as fear.

'I think it's time…' She hesitated for a moment; but just a moment. The next second her head came up and she raised her chin, looking her son dead in the eye with the courage he'd always admired. 'I've held this day off for far too long. It's time I truly told you who your father is; it might be your only hope.'

The sights and smells of the stable dimmed for an instant as Fell took in Ma's words, hardly able to conceive he'd heard her rightly. His heart still raced and Sophia's petrified countenance still loomed as large as ever, but for one beat he couldn't move, only able to summon up two words to answer the dynamite his mother had just thrown into his chest.

'Here? Now?'

'Yes. It could be the one chance you have of getting your wife back.'

Astounded, Fell gestured wildly about the stable. 'Before you would only tell me he was high-born. Is this *really* the moment you choose to unveil his name? After thirty years of asking?'

She let go of his arm and twined her hands together so tightly Fell saw her knuckles shine white, but he found he could only stare as she took a breath like one about to leap from a cliff.

'Not just his name—it's his *title* that will count. It might be the only thing to save you.' Ma hesitated again—but then the words spilled out in a breathless rush of desperate confession. 'Fell...your father is St John de Broughton, Earl of Atworth. I was, and still am, his legal wife—and you are Fell de Broughton, Viscount Stockley, his only legitimate son and heir.'

Fell didn't move as much as a muscle.

One hand lay perfectly still on Bess's reins and in an odd, disconnected part of his mind Fell was pleased to note it didn't shake as with two short sentences Ma destroyed his comprehension of himself and everything he thought he'd known for the past thirty-one years. It was a terrible, otherworldly calm, chilling and disarming at the same time—and robbing him so completely of speech Ma could continue, desperately and without interruption.

'Please. *Please*, my love. Allow me to explain. I chanced upon your father when I was all but a girl and he a handsome man some years my senior with no relatives to curb his wild fancies of marrying so far beneath him. My own family were afraid and tried to warn me, but I believed myself in love... By the time I realised what kind of man he truly was it was too late—we were already wed and I was entirely in his power—'

She broke off, dark brows drawn together as if in great pain. Fell watched her through what felt like a clouded mirror, listening intently and yet with the uncanny sensation he was trapped in a dream. It couldn't be real, the tale he was hearing, but there was raw truth in the way his mother forced herself to carry on with her voice low and haunted.

'His love for me was twisted and dark. It was as though he would own me like a prize, sculpt me into the kind of woman he wanted, and when I resisted he resorted to the only way of controlling me he knew: with his fists. For the first few months I was black and blue until I learned how best to please him and crept around his great house like a whipped dog, a pitiful thing with a forced smile and my heart always filled with fear. I was too ashamed to return to my family, so opposed had they been to such an unequal match, and besides, I felt I had to honour my wedding vows. I'd made my bed and I had to lie in it…until I realised I was with child.'

'Me?'

It was more a sound than a word, a guttural rasp from Fell's dry lips and throat filled with broken glass. Sick dread flared in his gut as the reality of Ma's past unfurled before him, her suffering and unhappiness that made him want to reach out and take her cold hand in his. A hundred questions reared up, battling for superiority over his concern for Sophia and his mother who looked as though she plumbed the very depths of her worst memories to bring them into the light.

Ma nodded, her features cloaked in emotion so intense it pierced Fell's soul. 'The moment I felt you move for the first time was when I knew I had to escape. I loved you before you were even born and the thought of how your father might insist on raising you turned my blood to ice. I could stand his temper when it was just me who took the brunt of it, but the idea of him turning it on you was more than I could stand.'

Fell swallowed painfully, a forced convulsion that hurt his throat.

I can hardly credit this. Can this truly be so?

'Did he know that you carried me when you ran?'

'Yes. He was delighted at the prospect of an heir to shape in his own image—the very thing I wanted least in the world to befall you. I would have been allowed no input in how you were raised; by that time my low birth was an irritation to him and the differences between us too vast to ever be governed. I was terrified for what your fate might be with him as your guide.'

'But he never knew where you'd fled? Or what became of us afterwards?'

'I wrote to him. Only once, a few months after you were born. Rector Frost had to help me as I had no learning, but I swore him to secrecy and, bless him, he took my sorry tale to the grave. I told your father he had a son, a fine healthy boy with the best parts of both of us and beautiful, mismatched eyes the likes of which I'd never seen before—and by which he would recognise his legitimate heir, should the baby ever grow into a man who came seeking his inheritance. But I never told him where we were, for fear he would try to take you from me and infect your life with cruelty as he had done mine.'

Fell held his head in his hands, fingers raking through tousled black hair. If there had been a chair in the stable, he might have sunk into it, so dizzyingly did his thoughts chase one after the other until his head spun and bewilderment swallowed him whole. Confusion and disbelief swirled inside him, jangling his nerves and tossing him amid a heaving sea. It was too bizarre to countenance: Ma, a countess? Himself, the heir to an earldom and who knew what fortune? Scant moments ago he'd been a Roma bastard and nothing more—now he was in line for a peerage that would elevate him higher than even Sophia's own family?

'Why didn't you tell me before? I lived my whole life thinking I was one thing, when all along I was something else entirely! And this is the moment you choose to enlighten me, with my wife carried off and your poor face bruised by her captor? Your timing is impeccable!'

A lesser woman might have taken a step backwards at the wildness of Fell's tone, but instead Ma seized his arm again, speaking so passionately her voice cut through the clamour of his turmoil.

'I know I should have told you. I've wanted to for years. But heaven forgive me, I was afraid of what you might think of me, of how you might react. I took you from a place of luxury into a tiny village miles from your birthplace and thrust you into a world so unkind I saw how it affected you each day—can you understand why I couldn't bring myself to admit to you that I was the reason for your suffering? I was terrified of losing your love and frightened half to death you might return to your father and become the kind of man I wanted to save you from being.'

Her desperate gaze sliced Fell down to the bone, a meeting of three black eyes and one hazel interloper whose origin was so shockingly revealed. Fell looked down at the woman who had been both mother and father to him for thirty-one years and felt himself still, the flames leaping inside him flickering lower as he took in the real fear she wore like a mask.

'Will you ever be able to forgive me? After all the pain I caused you?'

Some shadow of that pain echoed now as Fell considered her pleading face, turned up towards him so beseechingly it stung. Her secrecy had been at the root of all his feelings of inadequacy, his entire existence now something that didn't make any sense. If only she'd told him sooner, had trusted him not to follow in his father's brutal footsteps...

But didn't she act out of love? From some misguided attempt to protect me?

That couldn't be denied and, despite the discord churning in his innards, Fell knew it was a truth worth clinging to.

He took her hand and gently disengaged it from his arm, feeling the ice in each fingertip. 'I can't pretend I'm not hurt you kept this

from me. For thirty years... *Thirty years, Ma!*
A whole lifetime of concealment and secrecy
that could have been avoided if only you had
trusted me with the truth. I can't say that doesn't
grieve me. But you need never fear losing my
love—not then and certainly not now, despite
all that's passed between us. That will never be.'

Ma's jaw tightened so hard tendons flexed
in her neck and she nodded just once, blinking
to chase away the tears that had gathered at the
corners of her eyes.

'I'm glad of that. In turn, I want you to know
this: if you chose to seek him out I wouldn't
stand in your way. He was a poor husband, but
the choice is yours now as to whether you wish
to try him as a father.'

'This isn't the time to think about that.' Fell
squeezed Ma's hand with rough affection, finely
tuned throughout the years to say far more than
words. There were more questions to be asked,
more secrets to be unravelled, but with Sophia
trapped in her worst nightmare there wasn't a
moment to lose. He and Ma had so much to discuss; but not while his beloved lived in fear, and
the ghosts of Ma's past—and his own future—
would have to wait. 'We can discuss *that* later.
For now, I must go.'

He swung himself up on to Bess's back and

gathered the reins in his fist, ready to ride out when Ma laid her hand on the horse's grey neck.

'One final thing…'

'There's more? Am I to find out I'm actually a prince now?'

His mother smiled, thinly, worry for her daughter-in-law and concern for her son still clouding her expression, but a definite curve of her lips all the same. 'I owe you another apology. I allowed my own experience of marrying a high-born to sway my judgement of your situation and to think the worst, but I can see now what I didn't before: Sophia loves you, unless I'm very much mistaken. I should never have suggested otherwise.'

Fell stiffened, wonder and agitation stirred by the disclosure of his father's identity falling away to leave behind only stunned blankness that must have shown on his face.

What? What was that?

'What do you mean? Why do you say that?'

His heart shivered in its rhythm, falling over itself in its haste to know what Ma could possibly mean. It wasn't true, surely—he'd misheard, or misunderstood, left so rattled by the morning's events he was half-mad and thinking things that couldn't for a moment be true.

Ma shook her head pityingly, her smile growing in strength as she took her hand from Bess's neck and moved to one side. Nothing now stood between Fell and the open stable door, somewhere beyond which the wife who might or might not love him must be beside herself with fear.

'I have my suspicions, but I think it's up to you to find out for certain. What are you waiting for? Go and ask her yourself!'

Chapter Fifteen

Sophia sat quite still, hands clasped carefully in her lap and shoulders pulled back with perfect deportment. Anybody chancing upon her arranged demurely in Fenwick Manor's best parlour would have thought her very elegant indeed, not suspecting for a moment concentrating on her posture helped Sophia suppress the desire to scream.

If I start, I might never stop. I could lose my wits sitting here waiting and then I'd be no different from Septimus's first wife after all.

She looked about her at the lavishly decorated room, trying to tamp down the nausea she could feel rising in her throat. It was a luxurious prison and yet a prison none the less, the key grating in the lock at Phillips's retreating back and the windows shut tight against the approach of autumn. There was nothing she could do but wait, watching the minutes tick by on the face of a gilded clock and pray for the deliverance she knew would not come.

How could it?

Even if Fell came after her—and there was no guarantee that he would, given what she had gleaned from Essea as to his feelings— what could he do? They wouldn't let him in the house and Mother would send a servant running for the law before he had time to blink. The only chance she had of escape was to insist on the validity of her marriage, a legal state even Mother's tantrums could do nothing to alter. She would need to summon all her courage and face the oncoming storm, Lady Thruxton's wrath certain to shake the walls and make chandeliers ring with her fury.

It was as though Mother could sense Sophia's fear. From the other side of the locked door came the sound of light footsteps, followed by the turning of a key—and then she stepped into the room, a graceful dark-haired woman of middle age who looked at Sophia with such triumphant coldness it made her daughter shudder.

'Well, now. Home at last!'

Lady Thruxton moved so smoothly it was as though she was on wheels, coming towards Sophia with her hands outstretched. A smile played about her full lips, but her eyes were hard and chill as two chips of flint and Sophia recoiled from the reaching fingers.

'Sophia!' Mother chided her, pressing a hand against her chest as if mortally wounded by her daughter's retreat and yet relishing the power to unnerve. 'Don't you want to embrace your poor mother who has been in agonies these past months? I grieved so, not knowing where you were. You ought to thank me for taking the time to find you and apologise for all the trouble you caused. Such a terrible, disappointing mess. If I were you, I'd be quite ashamed.'

She paused expectantly, the age-old rhythm of their relationship so familiar it was second nature to follow. They both knew their parts in this dance: Mother injured by Sophia's many failings and Sophia asking forgiveness for her flaws, begging to be absolved. That forgiveness might be offered after a while, but not until Mother had said her piece, usually at a volume the whole manor could hear and most gratifying when accompanied by the sight of Sophia's regretful tears. A handful of months might have passed since their last encounter, but what was that balanced against the habit of a lifetime— Lady Thruxton in charge and Sophia pleading to be let out from beneath her boot?

But the delightful imploring didn't come.

'Hello, Mother.'

Sophia slowly lifted her chin to meet her mother's eyes, seeing the flit of confusion and then anger there and bracing herself for impact. Once upon a time she would have thrown herself into the role set out for her, but with sudden surprise she realised something had changed— nothing she could put her finger on, but there all the same as she watched Lady Thruxton's temper rise.

'Don't "hello, Mother" me, girl.' The cruel smile had slipped and the words were hissed with real venom that stung Sophia's heart into a rapid beat. 'You should be counting your blessings to be back in this house and showering me with gratitude for bothering to retrieve you! And the state of you…hair quite wild and a disgrace of a gown—don't you know what a slattern you look?' She stopped again, leaving another space for Sophia to fill with the pleasing shame and remorse she owed for her actions.

Sophia swallowed, tasting the sour bile that turned in her stomach. Fear still gripped her, but curiously less tightly than when Phillips had dumped her in the parlour, and certainly less than when he had snatched her from the forge. She'd expected to be beside herself to see

Mother, but now the woman in question stood there with building rage flushing her cheeks she seemed a less daunting prospect than before, alarming but not quite the all-encompassing monster Sophia remembered.

It's because of Fell. It has to be.

The words he'd murmured in the kitchen all those weeks ago echoed in her head, repeating themselves until she had no choice but to listen. She'd doubted them of late, it was true, but they must have taken root regardless of her caution and delved deeper inside her than she realised. They'd made her question all she thought to be fact and now she couldn't help but wonder, timidly at first but more strongly by the second, if her husband had been right all along.

'*You deserve far more than neglect and contempt. It's time you started to believe it.*'

Mother's face had darkened to a dusky rose at Sophia's silence, the lack of contrition fanning the flames of her ire. Sophia wasn't playing the game for the first time in her life and for one glorious second it seemed her mother was caught off balance, a sight so wonderful she couldn't help but marvel. In that moment Lady Thruxton seemed so much smaller than the woman of Sophia's memory, diminished somehow by the healing power of Fell's words.

He might never know what comfort she found in them, drawing the strength from his kindness not to crumble beneath her mother's spiteful glare.

But then a malicious gleam grew in Mother's eye and with the smile hitched back into place she spoke silkily as she sat down beside her daughter on the richly embroidered sofa.

'Lord Thruxton and Septimus have been hunting in the park, but I believe they are due to return any time now. Imagine their delight when they find you safely home! Dear Septimus in particular will be most gratified to have his intended back where she belongs.'

This time her words had the desired effect. Sophia stiffened, her already galloping pulse charging ever faster as the panic she'd forced back railed against her defences, testing the walls for weak spots it might break through.

'I'm not his intended. I'm a married woman.'

The image of Septimus's handsome, merciless face swam before her to make the nausea roiling inside her bubble all the more. He could do nothing to her now, she reminded herself fiercely, and yet the naked terror she'd felt on the night she ran from Fenwick Manor reached for her again with icy fingers.

He can't touch me. He can't touch me.

Can he?

'Don't you dare argue with me.' Mother's tongue was a razor flashing out to cut Sophia to the quick. 'Your pitiful imitation of a marriage counts for nothing. Your so-called husband will give you up at my asking and the rest is easy enough to undo. It will be as though you were never wed at all.'

Sophia's skin tingled with cold fear, the fire curling in the parlour grate doing nothing to lessen the chill that crept upon her like mist. Mother *couldn't* dissolve the marriage, surely— yet the idea burrowed into Sophia's chest to snatch her breath.

Fell would never bow to her demands. He might not love me, but he would never be so weak as to abandon his honour on Mother's say so, even if he regrets taking me as his wife. He's a better man than that—better than she'd ever understand.

Mother watched her closely, a grim kind of enjoyment flickering in her expression. It reminded Sophia of a cat toying with a mouse, the little creature fighting to escape while its captor sharpened its claws.

'You *will* do this, Sophia. You owe me your obedience after all the harm you've caused both now and to your poor dear father.'

Looking down at her clenched hands, Sophia hesitated. It was the same old song Mother had sung for almost twenty years, vicious and designed to keep her daughter in line. For every one of those twenty years Sophia had believed it—until a lowly blacksmith had come along to finally make her question it.

'*Nonsense.*'

She raised her head, throat tight with apprehension, but the truth no longer willing to be denied. Those months with Fell had shown her a world beyond that of guilt and grief and despair, and she wouldn't be pulled away from it without a fight. Fell might not return her love, but his teaching was priceless in a different way, a gift he'd given with no idea of its value.

'That wasn't my fault.'

Mother's face tightened, the skin around her eyes hardening into a porcelain mask of disbelief.

'I beg your pardon?'

'Papa's death. It wasn't my fault.'

Lady Thruxton stared as though she couldn't understand what she was hearing. Sophia could hardly credit it either: two decades of shame falling away in a matter of moments as effortlessly as taking off a coat. If anybody had told her how brave she would become when faced with Mother's wrath she wouldn't have believed them, even now scarcely able to comprehend where she found the courage to defend herself. It was wonderful and terrifying at the same time, Fell's words ringing in her ears to spur her on further than she'd known she could.

There was little time to celebrate, however. Mother surged to her feet and stood over Sophia like a mountain, or perhaps more like a volcano for all the molten malice that spewed from her snarling lips.

'Stupid, useless girl! Of *course* it was your fault!'

Sophia flinched away, pressing herself further into the sofa's luxurious cushions. Mother's rages were nothing new, but there was something uncanny about this rant—her eyes flashed and her fingers curved into talons as though she would rake her daughter with sharp nails. 'Every misfortune to ever befall me has been your fault! If you'd been less vacant, less of a burden around my neck—'

She broke off, head snapping towards the parlour door. Both women watched as the handle began to turn, Sophia with fresh dread and Lady Thruxton with wild triumph that made her look all the more unhinged.

'That will be Septimus now. We'll see what he thinks of your excuse for a marriage!'

She flew across the room and seized hold of the handle, flinging the door open to reveal the man outlined in sunlight on the threshold. He stepped forward into the room—and Mother fell back as though struck by lightning.

'Who are—how did you gain entrance? Where is Phillips?'

Fell smiled—the most perfect, roguish, beloved smile Sophia had ever seen—and it catapulted her heart straight through the parlour ceiling and into the autumn sky.

'With respect, madam, one man is no obstacle when the objective is my wife. To reclaim her I would best a hundred—and it was a pleasure to start with him.'

If he hadn't already been so entirely, hopelessly in love with her, Fell could have lost himself all over again to the sweet relief on Sophia's face, the welcome of her answering smile a reward more precious than gold. His knuckles smarted from the generous blow he'd bestowed on the deserving Phillips when he'd tried to bar the front door, leaving the man with a mark the twin of the one blooming on Ma's cheek, but the pain ebbed away as he took in his wife's dearly familiar countenance. There might as well have been nobody else in the room for all the notice he could spare, Sophia holding his focus and driving all other thought far away.

She's here and she's safe. Thank heaven for that.

He hardly knew what he'd been fearing, but she looked well, a little paler than he would have liked, but unharmed by Phillips's manhandling and her mother's fury. The urge to catch her up and hold her in the powerful circle of his arms called to him and he moved towards her— or would have done if Lady Thruxton hadn't barred his way.

'So you're the man who fancies himself my daughter's husband, are you? I fear you must prepare yourself for a disappointment: for she's going nowhere!'

He glanced at the older woman standing with arms wide as if she had any real hope of stopping him. Her face was the same shape as Sophia's and could have been handsome if it hadn't been suffused by a mix of indignation and self-satisfaction.

And you're the woman who almost destroyed Sophia's spirit. I wonder which of us dislikes the other more?

'The only person facing such misfortune is

you. My wife and I will be leaving presently and I'm afraid you can do nothing but watch us go.'

Out of the corner of his eye he saw Sophia rise to her feet, a little unsteadily, but with a determination that kindled fierce pride beneath his ribs. At long last she was standing up for herself, refusing to be cowed by cruelty she didn't deserve, and his admiration for her flared hotter as she took the first step towards him and final escape from her old life.

But her mother hadn't finished.

'You dare show me such disrespect? Such impudence?' Lady Thruxton's voice rose impressively. Its pitch and volume soared upwards, giving Fell an unwelcome view of the performance Sophia had been made to endure more times than she could count. 'You, who are nothing and so base-born you're unworthy of a single glance from me?'

Fell could have smiled.

Does she think to wound me with her words?

Her poison was no worse than the insults he'd borne ever since he could understand their sting, powerless to hurt him in a way he hadn't been injured already. She could rave and scream and curse him as much as she wished, she had no hold over him. The only person with any influence now was the silently watching wraith with copper hair he wanted nothing more than to bury his face in.

'I've no wish for even that much. Sophia and I will take our leave now and then you need never trouble yourself to look at either of us ever again.' With immense pleasure he turned his back on the harpy before him and held out his hand to his wife. 'Will you come with me?'

Sophia hesitated. For half a breath she looked from his hand to her mother's furious face and back again, seeming to consider the instinct ingrained in her since she was a child—and then she slipped her little hand into his palm and a thousand fireworks exploded into a shower of stars in the pit of Fell's stomach at the blessed feel of her warm skin on his once again.

He brought her closer, gathering her against him and slipping an arm around the narrow span of her waist. In part it was to reassure her, but also himself that nobody could part them now, not her mother or any henchmen she might send their way. For Sophia he would lay down his life, he knew without the barest shadow of a doubt, and as he looked down into the flawless jade of her eyes the moment to tell her seemed to have come.

Should I ask her if she feels the same? Ma

seemed so sure and yet the idea of being so fortunate is more than I dare to hope.

All the months of uncertainty and secret longing might come to a head with a handful of sweet words, his desires confirmed or dashed to the ground. He wanted to give himself to her, put his whole being into her keeping and trust his heart to the protection of her delicate hands—so soft, yet with the power to harbour or crush the fragile soul within them. There was nothing else to do now but speak, to unleash his yearning and pray it would find a safe haven with the woman he loved…

'Stop. Stop right where you are! You will not leave! I will not allow it!'

Lady Thruxton's shrill rage cut through the air, never less welcome, but insisting on joining the festivities. With valiantly suppressed irritation Fell tore himself away from the entrancing sight of Sophia's upturned face and threw her mother a shrug.

'It isn't in your power to allow or disallow. As a married woman Sophia has no need of anybody's permission but mine—and I wouldn't even *attempt* to impose such controls on an independent woman with a mind far sharper than my own.'

At his side he felt Sophia stir and he tightened

the comforting arm. Was it surprise that made her catch a sharp breath, or pleasure at his deference to her? Either way his praise did nothing to placate her mother, whose face turned an alarming shade of puce.

'*That* is no impediment. Do you understand? To annul a marriage to a penniless gypsy is as easy to me as breathing!'

Fell smiled, as pleasantly as if Lady Thruxton had said something agreeable at a genteel card party—and produced the trump card from his sleeve.

'But can the same be said of a marriage to a future earl?'

He *felt* the rapid turn of cogs inside Sophia's mind as she tried to understand his meaning and gritted his teeth on a laugh.

Take your time on that puzzle, my love. I can still hardly believe it myself.

'An earl? You talk nonsense!'

'Indeed, madam, I do not. You have the pleasure to be addressing Viscount Stockley, son of the Earl of Atworth and future bearer of that very title.'

A hush fell over the room. Lady Thruxton's lips twitched as though she would say something, but no words escaped, momentary uncertainty and mistrust crossing her twisted features. Fell barely noticed her, however, entirely captured by the dawning wonder on Sophia's lovely face.

'Fell…what can you mean? What are you saying?'

'I'll admit to being as surprised by the revelation as you are, but I can assure you of its truth. Ma—who is fine and well despite your man's cowardly attack, thank you, Lady Thruxton—told me this very afternoon of her unlikely marriage to my father, which took place many years ago. They are still wed to this day, making me his heir and, if I'm not mistaken, your mother's social superior.'

That was too much provocation for Lady Thruxton to endure. She raised herself to her full height and turned a glare on Fell so filled with white-hot rage a lesser man might have quailed.

'You *lie*. You're the illegitimate whelp of a Roma maid and don't try to deny it. The man who revealed Sophia's whereabouts told us of your parentage in all its revolting detail. This is a gross falsehood and I will not be taken in by it!'

Sophia flinched beneath his arm at the blistering venom spat in their direction, but Fell held firm. She would never be afraid of her mother again if he had anything to do with it, never again made to feel the way she had for more than twenty unhappy years.

'You're welcome to check my claim yourself. A letter to my father will confirm it, I'm sure, although I can't imagine he would be pleased by your attempt to deprive his only trueborn son of his legal wife and mother to those next in line.' Fell raised a challenging brow.

Getting on the wrong side of an earl? She'd rather eat her own parasol, I've no doubt.

'Now, if you'll excuse us, I shall take Sophia home.'

Lady Thruxton blinked. For the first time a thread of worry snaked through her expression and she appeared lost for words as Fell redoubled his grip on Sophia and led her to the door.

They were almost through it, Sophia drifting along beside him as though in a dream, when her mother's voice came chasing after them.

'Sophia Thruxton!'

Both Fell and Sophia stopped, looking behind at the older woman suddenly haggard with resentment and disbelief.

'Are you truly going to abandon me? After everything I've done for you?'

Fell bent to murmur a warning in Sophia's ear, but she gently brushed him aside, the sweet sadness of her smile a lance through his bursting heart. She gazed at her mother with such sorrow and understanding it was painful to see and doubtless an agony of sorts for her to feel as she made her choice.

'I think you mean *to* me, Mother. I can see now what I received from you was not fair. Fell has taught me that.' Sophia spoke softly, her words feather-light and yet somehow definitive—the most tender of brutal goodbyes. 'And Thruxton was never my name. I was Miss Somerlock, and then Mrs Barden, and now Viscountess Stockley—and none of those women wishes to lay eyes on you ever again.'

Fell's arm was still locked tight around Sophia's waist as he guided her to where Bess was tethered on the imposing drive, which was just as well—without it she might have stumbled, so bewilderingly did her emotions hurl themselves around her head. The revelation of his parentage, his newly discovered title, her own bravery in turning away from Mother with breathtaking finality... Too many voices clamoured for her attention, but the one that shouted loudest was the one that gave her the most cautious hope.

He came for me after all.

When all was said and done that was the truth. Fell had ridden out to rescue her despite her fears of his indifference and as the delicious warmth of his strong arm soaked through her gown she wondered how she ever could have doubted him.

Can it mean something more? Was it mere duty that dragged him here, or could it be his feelings for me are deeper than I ever dared dream?

She hardly wanted to examine that question any closer for fear of what the answer might be. For all her growing hope and the cautious light that had begun to creep beneath the shutters fastened tightly around her heart, she couldn't know for sure—and to ask outright would be to walk the line between unimaginable pleasure and crushing pain that could turn her fragile soul to dust.

'Thank you for coming. I confess I wasn't sure at first that you would.'

Fell stopped for a moment, boots ceasing to crunch on polished gravel. With Fenwick Manor looming at his back, glaring after them with windows like unfriendly eyes, for a moment he looked slightly alarming—before his face softened so fondly Sophia felt her own grow hot.

'And to think I praised your intellect to your mother. Don't make me doubt myself so soon afterwards!'

He snorted at her surprise and shook his head, sunlight casting on the black sheen of his hair. 'Did you truly think I'd leave you? After all we've been through together? My one and only wife?'

A short distance away Bess raised her grey head and watched, waiting patiently for them to reach her. Part of Sophia wanted to run to her, leap on to her back and leave Fenwick Manor far behind, but the largest share couldn't seem to move from the spot she stood frozen to. A curious tickle had begun to grow beneath the bodice of her gown, spreading outwards until her whole chest flamed as she peered upwards into Fell's open face.

My one and only wife? Even with a whole new world now lying at his feet?

She moistened dry lips with the tip of her tongue, noticing with a start of *something* how Fell followed the movement almost hungrily. The arm around her waist was unshakeable, as solid and firm as a mighty oak, and within the safety of its embrace Sophia found the courage to name her fear.

'You still wish to remain married to me? Even though now, as the son of an earl, you could have any woman you desired?'

Whatever response Sophia had been expecting, it wasn't the one she received. Fell's brows cinched together and he lifted a hand—and placed it so carefully on her cheek she couldn't help but gasp out loud.

'I don't wish to think about my father now. All I know for certain is this: there's just one woman I desire and she stands in front of me, speaking such nonsense I fear I may have to kiss her to stem the flow.'

He bent his head to hers so slowly she was hardly aware he had moved, yet their mouths met and, true to his word, Fell stole every syllable from Sophia's unresisting lips. They surrendered to his and yielded completely, even her breath snatched away by the clever thief who drew her closer against his chest.

Sophia's thoughts scattered to the four winds, every hesitation and fearful doubt fleeing from the intensity of Fell's kiss. Both arms came around her and held her fast, their unbreakable protection blocking out the rest of the world and shrinking her entire existence to focus on the play of their mouths. The wild staccato rhythm of her pulse accompanied the weakening of her limbs, legs turning to water as Sophia's hands tangled in the fabric of Fell's shirt and clung with a grip so tight her knuckles gleamed white under the skin.

Nothing and nobody could part them now. Fell's hand traced her spine and she reached on tiptoes to rise further into his embrace, wanting nothing more than to stay for ever in the paradise of his arms. When the very tip of his tongue sought hers she sighed, the tiny sound prompting Fell's dark chuckle—and he pulled away a fraction, looking down into her heavy-lidded eyes that had clouded with heady sensation.

Carefully, so gently it made Sophia's bones ache with joy, he flattened one hand over where hers nestled among the folds of his shirt. Under its scant cover she felt the thrum of his heart, rapid pulsing beneath hard muscle she suddenly longed to touch with fingertips made clumsy by want.

'Every beat is for you. It will never know another.'

Green eyes met a mismatched pair with wordless wonder growing in their mossy depths. *Can that be so?*

Sophia stared upwards, the features she'd come to love so well creased into a smile—with the smallest glimmer of doubt underlying the perfection of that curve. If she didn't know better, she might imagine he worried for her reply, as if it would be anything other than a return of his feelings so frank it left little room for dignity.

Never had Sophia dared dream of something so sweet. It was as if Fell saw every part of her with those uncanny eyes, the good and the bad and the parts of which she was ashamed, and fitted them together to make a woman worthy of being loved. The scars Mother left might never truly heal, but they would wane in time, Fell's tenderness already soothing the pain until her wounds faded from vivid scarlet to silver and barely there at all.

'Your heart beats for me? The poor disappointment of a daughter never expected to amount to anything more?'

One dark eyebrow flickered upwards as if it disagreed with her description, but Fell nodded none the less and it was Sophia's turn to allow her lips to hitch. With one hand still guarding her husband's heart, she stretched to cup the back of his neck, feeling the soft curls there and admiring them immensely before drawing his face back down to hers.

'Well then—I shall give you mine. I trust you'll treasure it, for it has been in your keeping longer than you know.'

She felt the shape of his smile beneath her lips for only a moment before he snatched her from the ground. As effortlessly as he might lift little Letty, Fell swept Sophia from her feet, one hand at her back and the other behind her knees as if she weighed nothing at all.

With a startled squeak she clung to his neck, surprised but revelling in the delight of being pressed so tenderly against his chest. 'What's this? What are you doing now?'

Fell's grin was radiant, its pure unfiltered elation sending the clock reeling backwards over the years to recall the younger man he'd once been before heartache had cast a shade over his soul. 'I'm taking you away from this place so we can begin our happiness in earnest. I'll bring you back to where you belong: with me in the sunlight, out from beneath the shadow this house has cast on you for longer than I care to imagine.' He stopped to look down at her, the new life in his features making her want to touch them, which she did, and then giggled when he kissed her fingers. 'May I take you home now? Or, more accurately, may Bess?'

Sophia pretended to consider, although no power on earth could help her keep a straight face. The warmth of bliss flowed in every vein, filling them with flowers whose perfume overcame the stale air Mother's cruelty had left behind.

*I have a husband who loves me. Me, just as
I am—and I will give thanks for that every day
of my life.*

'She may, but can you try to ride as smoothly
as possible? I felt so bilious this morning and although it's faded a little now I fear it will return.
It certainly has most mornings for over a week.'

Fell began to bear her towards the waiting
horse, still holding her so closely to his chest
she felt the heartbeat skip in time with her own.

'Most mornings?'

'Yes. I can't think what the matter could be.'

He paused, stilling in his work of settling her
into the saddle. 'Can you not?'

'Why, no. Something I ate, perhaps.'

Sophia couldn't see his face as he ducked
down to tighten the girth, but his voice sounded
suddenly strange, cautious yet with a note of
suppressed excitement that made her wonder.
'Did your mother never teach you…?'

'Teach me what? Unless it was how to think
myself a failure, the answer is no.'

Fell reappeared and stood looking up at her
seated high above him on Bess's broad back.
Such pride and tenderness kindled in his face
it warmed Sophia right down to her toes and,
when he hefted himself up into the saddle behind her and wrapped her in his arms, she knew

life would never be as wonderful as at that very moment…

…or so she thought.

'I think you ought to speak with Ma, tell her the nature of your symptoms. I believe you might hear some news that will make us very happy indeed.'

'Whatever can you mean?'

'You'll see. Out of interest, what title is given to a viscount's heir?'

* * * * *

COMING SOON!

We really hope you enjoyed reading this book.
If you're looking for more romance, be sure to
head to the shops when new books are
available on

Thursday 28th
May

To see which titles are coming soon, please visit

millsandboon.co.uk/nextmonth

MILLS & BOON

Coming next month

FROM CINDERELLA TO COUNTESS
Annie Burrows

All of a sudden, a solution came to him.

A solution so dazzlingly brilliant he didn't know why it hadn't occurred to him before. He'd always known he *ought* to marry, for the sake of the succession. The prospect had hung over him like a black cloud ever since he'd learned that his primary function in life was to sire the next generation. But the prospect of marrying a "suitable" girl, for dynastic reasons, had always seemed cold and cheerless. The alternative, marrying for love, had been equally repellent. And so he'd declared, loudly and often, that he would never marry.

But what if marriage was not based on either of those two alternatives? What if he could find a middle way? What if he married a girl he liked? A girl like Miss Mitcham? A sensible, decent girl who would see all the advantages of marrying for practical reasons. A girl who wouldn't make outrageous demands upon him.

And then another aspect of things sprang to mind.

"Why not make Lady Bradbury's worst fears come to pass?" That would teach her to think she could interfere in his private life.

"In, er, what way?"

"Don't be stupid." She wasn't usually this slow on the uptake. She must know what he meant. "By marrying me, of course."

"What?" Eleanor's heart squeezed at hearing her first proposal of marriage coupled with an insult to her intelligence. Besides, from the wicked gleam in his eye, it looked as though he was joking. "That isn't funny."

"It isn't? Oh, I think it is an excellent jest, as well as being one in the eye for Lady Bradbury," he said, stepping closer and taking hold of her upper arms. Not tightly, the way he'd done before, but gently. Almost as though he was handling fragile porcelain which he didn't want to damage. "Wouldn't you like to take some revenge upon my great-aunt," he said, caressingly. Running his thumbs up and down her arms in an equally caressing manner.

"I don't think revenge is a good reason for getting married," she said. Although her heart was pounding as fast as if she'd been running. Because he was tugging her closer to his body. Until she could feel the heat blazing from him.

Continue reading
FROM CINDERELLA TO COUNTESS
Annie Burrows

Available next month
www.millsandboon.co.uk

LET'S TALK
Romance

For exclusive extracts, competitions
and special offers, find us online: